MW00588152

A DAY
TO
Remember

A DAY
TO
Remember

Nancy E. Haack

gatekeeper press™
Columbus, Ohio

This book is a work of fiction. The names, characters and events in this book are the products of the author's imagination or are used fictitiously. Any similarity to real persons living or dead is coincidental and not intended by the author.

The views and opinions expressed in this book are solely those of the author and do not reflect the views or opinions of Gatekeeper Press. Gatekeeper Press is not to be held responsible for and expressly disclaims responsibility of the content herein.

A Day To Remember

Published by Gatekeeper Press
2167 Stringtown Rd, Suite 109
Columbus, OH 43123-2989
www.GatekeeperPress.com

Copyright © 2021 by Nancy E Haack
All rights reserved. Neither this book, nor any parts within it may be sold or reproduced in any form or by any electronic or mechanical means, including information storage and retrieval systems, without permission in writing from the author. The only exception is by a reviewer, who may quote short excerpts in a review.

The editorial work for this book is entirely the product of the author. Gatekeeper Press did not participate in and is not responsible for any aspect of this element.

Copyright for the images: iStockphoto.com/Julia Kuznetsova (Irish lace), Povareshka (autumn leaves), Garrett Aitken (Gold Pendant Locket Necklace)

ISBN (hardcover): 9781662922800

A Day To Remember is dedicated to my grandmother, Julia.
And while this is not her story, and she probably wouldn't
even recognize many of the characters in it, she is its inspiration.
I have always treasured the memories she shared of
her life growing up on a farm in New Hampshire and
its sweet simplicity.

But they that wait upon the Lord shall renew their strength;
They shall mount up with wings as eagles;
They shall run, and not be weary;
And they shall walk, and not faint.
Isaiah 40:31

1

She stared hard into the mirror, examining each detail. She had tried to tame her wild curls and finally gave up. She thought her nose a bit too long, and her lips full. But she was more than satisfied with her large eyes and long lashes. They were the one feature that favored her Scottish father: changing from brown to green when the weather turned gray. More than one suitor had found himself lost in those eyes. She adjusted her veil. It was a lovely Irish lace-slightly yellowed with age-but in this case, sentiment had won out over vanity. As she fingered the edges, she wondered how her mother felt when she wore it. Did she have these feelings of uncertainty?

She allowed herself to drift back, her mind recalling her simple life growing up on a farm in the New Hampshire mountains. She remembered waking in the dark of early morning. Unconsciously, she gave a slight shudder as if feeling the mountain's air send a chill through her thin satin gown.

"Julia, Julia! It's time you raised your lazy head and got moving."

Julia let out a soft groan. It would do no good to beg for more time. As she slipped her feet into her boots and pushed off the last of her covers, her foggy head began to clear. Every morning it was the same and every morning her body slowly awakened as she began her routine.

She tugged on her coat, and pulled a cap over her head. No small feat considering the mass of auburn curls that donned her head. It was so much easier when she took the time to rebraid her hair before bed. But most nights it was all she could do to brush it out before collapsing into bed. Once there, nestled among the downy softness and layers of quilts she was soon fast asleep.

As she headed out the door, Julia grabbed a lantern. It was waiting, already lit. It was one of the things her Mum did for her each morning. It was a small gesture, but it reassured her she was loved.

Julia felt the stiff grass crunching beneath her boots as she trudged to the cow barn. She could already smell the almost sweet scent of manure. She set down the bucket and lantern and with both hands, tugged open the heavy barn door. She was only twelve, but had been doing the chores of a boy for as long as she could remember. She was not the oldest. There had been a baby boy before her. He hadn't lasted through his first year. Sometimes Julia would visit his grave on the edge of the North pasture. William Roger Kelly. She'd trace her finger over the rough stone and wonder how different things would be if he'd survived.

"Daydreaming again?" Her Dad's voice interrupted her musings.

"Only a little" she replied with an embarrassed grin. She always felt so silly when Dad caught her with her mind wandering. And it seemed like he always did.

She started toward Gert. The cow's udder was full and ready for milking. Julia pulled up her stool and sat. Carefully placing the bucket beneath, she grasped a teat in each hand and began the methodical task of milking.

Julia loved this time of day. It was the only time she had Dad all to herself. Her family owned one of the largest farms in the county, so there was always some chore to be done or piece of equipment that needed repair. It wasn't as if she and her Dad had long heart to heart conversations. She was definitely getting too old to have her father as a confidant. But being close to him and knowing she didn't have to share him with anyone else, that's what made it special.

It wasn't long before Julia and her Dad were done. All the buckets had been emptied into milk cans and would soon be driven into town.

"How about I get the team ready while you collect the eggs?" Dad asked.

"Ok, but I'll get done first" Julia answered, as she dashed out of the barn and ran toward the coops. The egg basket was hanging on the hook outside the door, and with practiced ease Julia grabbed it while ducking inside. The biddies were just beginning to stir in their roosts. She almost felt bad for jostling them roughly as she gathered their eggs. With a full basket, she ran to the house determined to beat her Dad.

"Whoa, slow down" Mum scolded with a grin. She knew the game they were playing and she knew Julia would win. Will always let her.

"Got the eggs, Mum, be back soon" she tossed over her shoulder as she dropped the basket on the counter and headed back out the door.

She was so intent on beating her Dad, she barely heard her Mum say "love you!"

Flying around the corner of the barn, there stood Dad placing the last can of milk in the back of the wagon. "Looks like a tie" he said with a wide grin, eyes twinkling.

"Oh no, I got here before you finished."

"Ok" Dad said, "but you might think about going easy on me, just once."

With a look of triumph, she shook her head, climbed into the wagon and with a snap of the reins slowly drove towards town.

∽

"Hey, don't leave without me!" Julia called out as she emerged from the doorway of a small brown building.

From down the road, a small group of girls looked back in unison. They stopped walking and waited patiently for Julia to catch up.

As a rule, the rural communities were tightly knit. All the farmers knew their chances of survival increased immeasurably when they worked together supporting their neighbors. And within the walls of the county schoolhouse, friendships were forged from an early age between their children. Friendships that carried long into adulthood and even into marriage.

Out of breath by the time she caught up to them, Julia smiled, panting and red faced.

"Where were you this time?" joked Rachel, clearly the loudest and tallest of the group. She was the daughter of Andrew and Lois Merrill, best friends of Julia's parents. It was good the girls got along so well since their parents enjoyed each others company and would often share a Sunday dinner that would last long into the evening.

"I think you spend far too much time in your imagination," chimed in a small timid voice belonging to Sara, a plain blond child who took life far too seriously. Which was understandable considering that she had been orphaned as a baby and it was her maternal grandparents that were raising her.

"I know, I know," defended Julia, "but I just can't help it."

"Well, you better be careful," Bonnie interjected slyly, "One of these days we might just leave you. In there. All night. All alone."

The girls laughed. They knew Bonnie could be a prankster but they also knew her identical twin sister, Bettie, would never let her go too far.

"Come on," encouraged Bettie, "Julia's with us now and if we hurry there's still time to go pick apples before we need to get home."

Without hesitation, the five friends broke into a run leaving only a brown cloud of dust in their wake.

Darkness came fast in the mountains. Julia shut the barn door then tipped her milk bucket on a post to dry. She ran to the front of the house, knowing there were only a few minutes of daylight left.

She gazed out over the hills and watched the evening shadows crawl across the pastures. The horizon had turned deep blue and in the distance she could see silhouettes of the mountains she loved so much.

The last streaks of color disappeared. She stood for a moment while her eyes adjusted to the darkness. Around her there were small flashes as fireflies began their dance, and in her ears was the nightly serenade from the peepers in the nearby pond. Tilting her head back, she gazed into the expanse of stars.

Julia didn't know all their names, but she knew wherever she went, they would follow.

Julia let out a contented sigh and headed into the house.

Letting the door slam behind her, she plopped down on the rug at the foot of Mum's rocker. The lantern's flicker sent shadows dancing across the parlor room walls.

"Mum?"

"Yes, love"

"Can you tell me a true story?"

From across the room came her Dad's soft chuckle. He knew the story she wanted to hear before she asked.

"Oh, well" said Mum, "what story do you want me to tell?"

Playfully, Julia put her finger to her chin and thoughtfully began to tap.

"Well, you could tell me about the best day you ever had."

"Oh," Mum said, "that's too hard! I've had so many best days, how can I choose?"

With an expectant smile, Julia said "You can tell me about the day I was born."

Mum wrapped the loose yarn around her needles and set her knitting aside. Her eyes smiled as she began.

"Well, I knew the day you were born was going to be special right from the start."

"How did you know?" interrupted Julia.

"I knew because it began with a beautiful spring day. For a week it had been raining. But that day, I woke up and my room was bright. And when I peeked out the window, the grass and trees were still damp and sparkled in the sunlight."

"What about the birds, Mum?"

"Oh, on that morning the birds were chirping and singing."

Julia sat quietly, listening to Mum's story, a look of contentment resting on her face. Mum recounted the entire day, describing its wonder and beauty, until finally it culminated with the birth of her precious baby girl.

When the story closed, Julia's eyes were thick with sleep. Slowly, she pulled herself to standing and shuffled up to her room. Her bed welcomed her and she tugged at the thick covers. She pulled back an opening just big enough to slide in and with a sigh, she laid her head down.

Mum came to her bedside and stroked her hair. She leaned down and laid a soft kiss on Julia's forehead.

"I love you, precious girl."

"I love you, too, Mum."

2

Julia gazed at her reflection again. The old mirror was smoky with age. She supposed it was natural to feel sentimental. After all, it was her wedding day. Her fingers slid down the chain around her neck until they found an oval locket. She didn't need to open it to see the pictures inside. Her parent's faces were etched in her mind. Slowly she closed her eyes and she was back on the farm.

Julia left her friends cries far behind, never slowing down. Not even long enough to shout her reassurance that tomorrow she would meet up with them, ready to spill every detail.

She had run all the way home from school and almost collided with the back screen door as she skidded to a stop. Hurriedly, she grabbed the handle and felt it squeak open. The inside oak door was ajar, but that was no surprise considering the warm spring day.

Julia could hardly contain her excitement. Early that morning her Mum's labor pains had started. Her family was thrilled at the thought of a new baby. Julia was old enough now that she didn't feel any pangs of jealousy. If anything, she was relieved. Her Mum had been pregnant before, but each time had ended in a miscarriage. But this time was different. Her Mum said this was the easiest pregnancy yet.

Julia looked around the kitchen. Its neatness was disturbing. She thought there should be coffee, hot on the stove and food set out on the sturdy kitchen table. As she put her books down and paused at the bottom of the stairs, she realized that something was out of place. The house was so still, too quiet for a woman in labor. And where were her Dad and May, the midwife? She ran to the back door and looked out at the driveway. Her Dad's car wasn't there.

Panic seized her and Julia ran upstairs. Her parent's bedroom door was ajar, and as she pushed it fully open, she saw the bloodied bed sheets. Something had gone wrong. May always cleaned up the bedding after a birth.

Julia felt weak and dropped to her knees. Instinctively, she began to do the only thing she could. She started to silently pray for her Mum and the baby. She mouthed the words, until her pleas found her voice, and she continued to ask for God's help.

The afternoon wore on. When Julia became aware of the deepening shadows, she pulled herself together and began her chores.

As she was finishing in the barn, she heard the car tires on the gravelly driveway. Not knowing what to expect, Julia steeled herself and walked out into the cool air of early evening.

Her Dad looked tired. Actually, it was more than that-he looked beaten.

"Dad?"

Her father lifted his chin slightly, his eyes were moist and his hand trembled as he pulled at his back pocket, searching for his kerchief. He swiped at his eyes and said "It's a boy."

"A boy, that's great, Dad" the words barely escaping her lips in a hoarse whisper. Somehow, Julia knew there was more.

Her Dad coughed and said "Your Mum's not good."

One week later, Julia was standing in the North pasture. The sunny day was filled with warm breezes that seemed to mock her pain. The headstone was small and simple bearing her name, Elizabeth Agatha Kelly, with a delicate arch of Forget Me Nots carved into the granite.

Her Dad stood next to her, silent. After a few minutes, he held out his hand. She looked and saw a flash as the sunlight hit metal. He slowly rolled the object from the palm of his hand into hers. It was then she recognized the locket her mother had always worn. It was a gold oval on a long chain. Engraved on the cover was a bouquet of flowers that opened to reveal a double frame. Mum had told her that when she was just a little older than Julia, her parents sent her to America. As she prepared to board, they gave her the locket. Her parent's pictures were inside until she was married. That's when Mum placed her and Dad's on top.

Looking down at it now, Julia realized this was all she had left of her.

When the last of their neighbors had paid their respects, and final hugs from friends had been given, Julia headed upstairs to change out of her good clothes. Each step felt like she was walking in a fog. For that matter, that was how her entire day felt. At the top of the stairs, she decided to peek in on Alfred. Despite a difficult labor, they had been able to save the baby.

She walked into his room on the tips of her toes, hoping she wouldn't cause him to waken.

"You silly goose" she cooed.

Alfred was contentedly lying in his cradle. It was as though he knew what his entrance into the world had cost and was determined to be no trouble.

Julia couldn't resist. She lifted the baby out of his crib and for the next hour, she and Alfred sat in the rocker enjoying one another's company.

3

Slowly, Julia walked across the room. Her dress rustled softly as she moved. The satin fabric felt cool against her skin and her breasts strained against the stiff bodice. She admired its hand stitched embroidery and graceful lines. Indulgently, she allowed herself a quick turn and felt the waves of fabric twirl around her legs. Remembering the first time she saw this dress brought her back to the arrival of Blanche. After her mother's death, Dad hired a nurse to help care for Alfred. Blanche was 24 years old and considered a spinster. She had grown up on a farm a few towns over, but, instead of marrying young, she had chosen to study in Boston. Her time in the city had given her an air of sophistication that belied her country upbringing.

Julia drifted back to the day Blanche moved in. She could still picture the young woman as she entered their home, her brown tweed traveling suit hanging sharp and neat on her tall frame. It wasn't until later when she changed into a light frock that Julia noticed how slim and shapely she was. It had already been decided that Blanche would have the room next to Alfred's. As she unpacked, Julia noticed her lovely gowns and dresses. She hugged the wall just inside the door, watching with curious eyes as Blanche carefully hung each garment in the closet. One gown in particular caught Julia's eye. It was pale, pale green with tiny ivory flowers stitched across the bodice. Julia had an irresistible urge to touch it. Without realizing it, she raised her hand and slowly moved toward the gown. Suddenly, Blanche turned.

"Don't think of putting those filthy hands on my things. I could never get the smell of manure out."

Julia cringed. Rarely had Mum raised her voice and she had never been harsh with her. Blanche must have noticed the hurt on Julia's face. With a slightly softer tone she said "Maybe tonight after your bath I'll show them to you."

That evening, Julia hesitated outside Blanche's bedroom. Her hair was still damp and her flannel gown clung to her freshly scrubbed skin. She raised her hand to knock when the door opened. Julia tried to speak, but nothing came out. She lifted her face and was relieved to see the gentleness in Blanche's dark brown eyes. Her lips were soft and full, with a hint of a smile at the corners.

"Did you want to come in?" Blanche asked.

"I'm all cleaned up" said Julia, in a soft voice.

"So you are."

Blanche stepped aside allowing Julia to enter. Julia couldn't believe the transformation. She had never seen so many different fabrics and patterns. The windows were draped in burgundy damask with a layer of ivory lace on top. Blanche had laid a thick wool rug on the floor and for a moment Julia was lost following the pattern of vines intertwining with soft pink and beige roses. As her eyes made their way to the old wrought iron bed, she let out an audible gasp. The bed skirt was made from the same fabric as the window drapes. On top, Blanche had dressed the bed with crisp white sheets, a soft gold and beige bedspread, and a coverlet patterned in deep maroon and mauve roses. On the bedside table, there was a pitcher and bowl set in a circle of lace. It was covered in hand painted green and yellow flowers that made the set in Julia's room seem plain and functional. Spread out on the dresser was a lace runner with tiny red embroidered flowers. Set on top was a dark walnut music box, a small mint green alarm clock, and a silver brush, comb, and hand mirror: polished and gleaming.

Julia was stunned. After looking around, she saw Blanche standing by the open closet door. With a quiet voice, Blanche asked, "Which would you like to see first?'

That was the first of many visits when Julia would pad up to Blanche's bedroom door and wait for her to finish putting Alfred down for the night. It was at those times that Julia began to learn of another world. She learned about art and fashion and what it was to be a lady.

Blanche would open up her closet and teach Julia about a different kind of world. She'd pull down hats in a variety of shapes and colors. One had long blue feathers taken from birds that lived on the other side of the world. Or she'd pull out a brown purse that was made from the hard scales of a beast that inhabited tropical rivers. Even her gowns held their own special stories from where and when they were worn. One especially beautiful soft gray dress with pure white rabbit fur on the collar and cuffs attended the Govenors ball and danced with J.P. Morgan, the millionaire!

Then after Blanche had been with them for a couple months, a delivery came. It was shortly after Julia arrived home from school, that a wagon pulled into the driveway. The wagon's bed was covered with a large canvas sheet. The driver had just hopped down from his seat when Blanche noticed him from out the front window. She handed Alfred to Julia and walked out to greet him.

"Hey, Miss Blanche," the driver smiled, " I've got your things."

"Thank you, John," Blanche said.

John carefully pulled back the cover and revealed a Barrister bookcase. The veneer was a deep cherry and had been polished to a glossy shine. The glass panes were clear and bright, reflecting the sun's rays. On both sides of the bookcase were boxes. They were closed up tight and tied with twine. Julia watched fidgeting with curiosity. She knew it would be impolite to ask what they contained. So when Alfred began to fuss, she reluctantly pulled herself away, Julia headed back to the kitchen to fix him a bottle. She heard the front door open and then, close. John's heavy tread stomped up the stairs as he carried boxes to Blanche's room. Again and again the trip was made until finally the wagon was empty. Blanche thanked John and sent him on his way.

Out in the kitchen, Alfred lay in Julia's arms, eyes closed, breathing heavily with a bubble of milk on his lower lip. Slowly, she rose out of her chair. She set the glass bottle in the sink and with careful steps, carried the sleeping baby up to his room. Julia quietly closed the door on Alfred then, silently made her way down the hall. She gave a sidewards glance as she passed Blanche's room and saw her sitting in the middle of the floor surrounded by boxes. Methodically she would take a book out, examine its cover and binding and then set it in a stack by her side.

Reluctantly, Julia continued down the hall when she heard "Psst". She turned around and saw Blanche waving her in. It took all her self-control but she managed to calmly retrace her steps and join Blanche on the floor.

Julia knelt down next to Blanche and for the next hour they worked together sorting the books by author and subject. Each book was placed in the bookcase, the rows neat and straight. When they were done, Blanche allowed Julia to pick out a book to read. Julia had trouble deciding and was still making her choice when Blanche left to get Alfred. Finally, she settled on "Little Women". Holding the book to her chest, Julia brought it to her room. She loved the feel of the soft leather cover and smell of its musty pages. She carefully tucked it under her pillow and gave it a protective pat. She couldn't wait to come back to it later that night.

April gave way to May and after a week of rain, there finally came a day that was warm and breezy. The sun shone brightly, determined to coax buds open and dot the fields with new blooms.

It was late morning and Julia stood on the porch with her eyes half closed. She drew in a deep breath. The scent of damp earth and wet grass filled her nostrils. She exhaled slowly and decided to visit the north pasture. It had been over a month since she'd been out there and as she headed out across the field, she began filling her arms with daisies and clover. It wasn't until she was almost there and had crested the hill that she noticed she wasn't alone. On a blanket by Mum and William's headstones, were Blanche and Alfred. Julia was suddenly annoyed. She had grown comfortable around Blanche in their home, but this was different.

Julia continued, stalking across the meadow until she came to them. The frown on her face conveyed her irritation and she asked "What are you doing here?"

Blanche looked up from the book she was reading and replied "It was such a beautiful day I thought Alfred would enjoy napping in the sun."

"But why here?" Julia asked, not masking her displeasure.

Blanche took a moment, then answered, "I wanted Alfred to be close to your Mum."

Julia was silent. She was at a loss for words. Finally, she said "Mums not here, you know."

"I realize that, Julia" Blanche said. "But somehow I feel it's important for Alfred to spend time here." Putting aside her book, Blanche continued, "Did you know I tell him about her?"

"How can you?" Julia accused. "You didn't know her."

"It's true, I never met your mother," said Blanche, "but I know she loved her children very much."

"How do you know that?" asked Julia, "And what do you tell Alfred?"

"When we come here, I always tell him his mother was strong and brave. She didn't give up until after he was born. She made sure he was safe before she let go. She made sure you had a brother, so you wouldn't be alone."

Julia was stunned. "You've come here before?"

"A few times."

Anger rose to the back of Julia's throat, preventing her from speaking. Hot tears rolled down her cheeks and she spilled her bundle when she swiped at them with her sleeve.

"You miss her," stated Blanche, softly.

Julia nodded, unable to put words to her pain.

"You know, she's still with you," said Blanche.

"She's gone," choked out Julia. "I told you, she's not here!"

"No, not in this place, but in people. I've seen her photograph in the living room, you have her smile."

Julia knew this to be true. People had told her, and even she could see it in the mirror.

"And look at Alfred, already you can tell he's got her nose" said Blanche.

Julia nodded, again. Yes, she'd seen the resemblance, as well.

Blanche put her hand on Julia's chest. "But here, this is where your Mum will always be."

Julia let out the breath she didn't know she'd been holding. She understood.

Blanche looked at the flowers laying on the ground.

"Did you bring these for her?"

"Yes, but now they're ruined!"

Carefully, Blanche began to gather them up.

They're no good," exclaimed Julia. "The stems are bent and twisted."

"Hmm," said Blanche, "maybe they can be saved."

Julia looked skeptical until she saw what Blanche had in mind. She was taking the stems and weaving them together. Slowly a chain of flowers began to emerge. Julia joined in and soon they had lovely spring garlands to crown both headstones.

That night as Julia sat by her window, she closed her eyes and put her hand to her chest. She savored the moment, remembering Mum's voice and touch. She thought about her afternoon with Blanche and she was grateful.

As she lay her head down, she felt a comfort that had been missing since Mum died.

It had happened without her realizing it, she and Blanche had become friends.

At the end of May, Julia turned fourteen. She was growing up fast and on her way to becoming a young woman. Just in the past couple months she'd noticed the buttons on her blouse tightening across her chest. She and her friends whispered about personal matters but the idea of talking to Blanche about them felt awkward. Fortunately, Blanche approached sensitive topics with her matter of fact, sensible manner that put Julia at ease. And unknown to either of them, the future would reveal a tender and caring woman beneath Blanche's efficient exterior.

⸎

When the weather changed from warm spring days to summers heat, school let out and Julia spent her days working on the farm. Along with the year round chores, there was the large garden that needed tending. Weeding was a battle fought daily.

This was also when Julia and the girls were given more freedom. By early afternoon, it was almost certain they would have their chores completed. An old abandoned shed on the far edge of the Merrill's orchard was their usual meet up. It barely had any walls left, and even the roof was in a questionable state, but for the time it sheltered them from a passing shower and blocked out the worst of the sun's heat. But most importantly, it was theirs.

Julia grabbed a handful of molasses cookies and raced out the back door. She could hear Blanche calling after her, reminding that she needed to be back in time to help with dinner. A loud, "Okay, Blanche," trailed behind as she ran on, never breaking her pace.

When she finally arrived at the shed, the amount of cookies had doubled. Inside, the other girls sat on an old wool blanket with more than a few holes. Julia carefully dumped the cookies pieces onto the center and took her place near the door. Sara had already contributed a cup of ripe blueberries and Rachel produced a jar of fresh lemonade. Bettie emptied her pockets of crunchy peapods and Bonnie promised a surprise.

After the snacks had been disposed of and the girls were settled resting, Bonnie announced with a mischevious grin, "I have something spectacular to show you!"

Now Julia and her friends had grown accustomed to Bonnie's exaggerations, so they were completely unprepared for what happened next. Bonnie slowly reached under the edge of the blanket where she was sitting and with all the bravado of a carnival magician, produced the largest brassiere the girls had ever seen.

At first they were left speechless but once the shock had worn off, a torrent of uncontrolled laughter ensued. Each cup was as large as their heads. They knew this because in their glee, each of the girls had tried it on their heads. Next came their bottoms and finally, with the help of a few handful of leaves, they each modeled the undergarment wearing it as it had been intended. When they had finally exhausted its uses, the girls paid homage by hanging the bra between two nails over the doorway, thus gracing their threshold.

"Do you think we'll ever be that big?" asked Sara, seriously.

"Not a chance," commented Rachel.

"I don't know," chimed in Bonnie, "I saw an ad in a newspaper the other day. There's a man, a real doctor, that sells tonic that can make them grow."

Julia studied Bonnie's face. There were times when she had no idea if she was being truthful or pulling their legs. But there was one thing Julia was sure of….when she looked at the huge contraption hanging above her head, she knew for certain she would never use that tonic!

The girls returned home in time to tackle their evening chores. They wouldn't know until the next day that the owner of the brassiere had made a visit to Bonnie's house. By the time the twins walked through the door, she had already left. But her absence had only served to provide their mother with enough time to find the perfect switch.

◦◦◦

That summer, the farm was also seeing some changes. On the south side of their property Dad was opening up a new field. Most days he and some hired hands would head over as soon as they finished breakfast. They would spend the day digging up stumps and clearing away scrub brush. Dad wanted it ready to till by fall so he could start planting the following spring.

Also, there were renovations to the old cottage. It sat high on the ridge over looking the new field. Years ago, Julia's grandparents had lived there but she didn't remember them because they died from Scarlett Fever before she was born. It was a simple home with only five rooms: a kitchen, pantry, living room, and two small bedrooms upstairs. Dad had another crew of men replacing any missing clapboards and he had them giving it a fresh coat of white paint.

But, despite all the changes, Julia remained only mildly aware of all the work being done around her. And more importantly, she was oblivious to a friendship that was growing. The months after Mum's death had been hard for her and at times she thought the ache in her heart would never leave. There had even been times she'd find her cheeks wet, never realizing she'd been crying. But the blessings of a daily routine and a close group of chums had given her life a new normal, and by the summers close, Julia had healed.

4

A cool breeze blew a handful of leaves through the open window. They skidded and swirled across the hardwood floor landing at Julia's feet. She knelt to brush them away from the hem of her gown and noticed the edge of paper caught between the floor boards. With the tips of her fingers, she plucked until she was able to convince a small card to slide out from its hiding place. She turned the card over and squinted her eyes to read. It was late afternoon and shadows were beginning to creep across the walls. Julia went to the window and paused, admiring the view. The mountains fiery color stood blazing against a darkening blue sky. She tugged at the window to pull it closed, but summer's humidity held its grasp and the swollen wood resisted her efforts. She gave another pull, this time harder, and with a soft groan the window slid in its tracks and inched its way down to the sill. She took a moment to gaze through the wavy glass panes, still holding the water pocked note, and recalled the autumn when her entire world changed.

Julia felt a shiver. Heading inside for her sweater, she felt the gold and crimson leaves crunch beneath her boots. She pushed open the heavy door, stepped inside and grabbed it off a hook in the front hall. She slipped the heavy cable knit over her head and tugged at the sleeves. She felt the wool's soft itch through her shirt and the farm's fresh scent filled her nose. Julia retraced her steps and reached for the doorknob to go back outside. But she heard Dad call out her name, "Julia," before she could turn it.

Julia went down the narrow hall and entered the parlor. Dad was seated on the sofa next to Blanche with Alfred scooting on the floor.

Without preamble, Dad started, "Julia, Blanche and I are getting married."

She opened her mouth to speak, but then closed it, realizing she didn't know what to say. Dad sat calmly waiting for her reaction. That was when she noticed their clasped hands. Julia met Dad's eyes and from somewhere croaked "When?"

"Sunday. After church."

Julia wanted to be mature but her head was starting to spin. Her mind began to flood with questions. She forced her eyes to look at Blanche and was stunned she hadn't seen it before. Clearly Blanche was in love with her Dad. It didn't seem possible that a young woman like Blanche could fall for him.

Julia looked down at Alfred. He was such a sweet baby and he had survived so much. For him, Blanche had become more than just his nurse, she had stepped into Mum's void and completely filled it. The fondness they felt for one another was obvious. As for herself, she felt her need for mothering was past. For a moment she could feel the anger rising in her throat and for one irrational moment wanted to scream, "You can never replace my mother!" Thankfully, she choked the words down. Logically she knew that Blanche had never tried to assume that role. Instead, she had made herself available and allowed Julia to come to her. In her own time. On her own terms. She couldn't pinpoint when it had happened, but Blanche was part of their family.

"Why was this so hard?" she questioned."Why were her emotions so confusing?" As she tried desperately to put her heart in order, Blanche's voice broke through.

"Julia," her calm tone pushed the panic away. "It will be ok. I know we surprised you. Our feelings surprised us, too."

"Yes, just a bit" Julia stammered. She wished she could be as composed as Blanche.

Blanche smiled sweetly, "In time it will feel right," she consoled. "Don't worry."

Julia shrugged, "Okay," and excused herself. She went out the front door and plopped onto the porch swing. As she began the gentle to and fro motion, she tried to understand her feelings. She loved Blanche and could easily understand why Dad had grown fond of her. Part of her wanted to feel resentful, but the other part didn't. In the midst of her mullings, Julia heard the sound of faint whistling.

In the gray of early evening, Julia scrunched up her eyes. Out on the road she could just barely make out the figure of a man. She recognized the tune he was whistling, "In the Sweet By and By".

Unconsciously, Julia began to sing. She had been told she had a beautiful voice, all she knew was that she loved singing.

The man paused, then began to walk up her driveway.

Suddenly she stopped. "I'm such a dope" she thought to herself, "Now what have I done?"

As he approached the porch and entered the circle of light, she realized the "man" was just a boy. He was obviously quite tall for his age, which she guessed to be about fourteen. He had broad shoulders and a muscular build. He'd probably done the work of a man most of his life, much like the farm boys in the area. As he stepped closer, she could make out his face. He had dark, narrow eyes framed by thick brows. His nose was long and sharp, but his wide smile and dimpled cheeks made him almost good looking. His black hair was thick and straight, a little long for the style, and at the moment, tosseled and unkept.

His deep voice broke through her thoughts: "Good evening. I heard you singing. It was real pretty."

Moving closer, he stretched out his hand, and continued. "My name's Billy. My family came to town a couple days ago."

"Oh, where'd you move from?" asked Julia, not rising from the swing.

Billy took his eyes off Julia to swat a nosy moth and answered "We came from up north, near the border."

"So what brought you here?"

"Work. My Dad got a job managing a farm somewhere around here. You ever heard of the Kelly place?"

"Kelly place?"

"Yeah, you know the farm?"

"Yup," she said, trying to make sense of this new information. "You're here."

Julia heard the screen door open behind her and Dad's stern voice asked, "Hello, there, can I help you?"

With his hand stretched out again, Billy covered the last couple of feet to the bottom of the steps and said, "Hello, sir. My name's Billy McGrath. I believe I start working for you tomorrow."

"Oh," said Dad, "You're one of Don's boys."

"Yes sir."

"Nice to meet you, Billy," Dad said with an easy air, coming down to shake Billy's hand. "Your family staying at the Mountainside?"

"Yes, sir."

"They treating you right?"

"Oh, yes, sir."

"Good, good," Dad said. Her Dad towered over Billy but it was obvious that wouldn't be for long.

Then Julia heard her name.

"What, Dad?"

Will had an amused look on his face, he didn't know where his daughter had been, but her faraway gaze told him she'd gotten lost in her thoughts again.

"I was just saying, Billy and his family should come by after breakfast. It will give me a chance to show them around. Later on they can start moving in."

Moving in? Where exactly would they be moving in to? The house was pretty well taken up. Even with Dad and Blanche getting married, and she still hadn't begun to process that yet, it would still only leave one empty bedroom.

"Julia won't mind helping you get settled into the cottage." Dad turned to Julia, "You can go over after school. I can manage your chores for one day."

"Oh. Sure, Dad. I don't mind at all."

It was finally making sense. All the renovations were for the McGraths. But knowing that just led to more questions. Why did Dad need all this extra help? Even once the new field was tilled, there were always plenty of men looking for seasonal work. And, why did he need someone to manage the farm FOR him?

Julia was suddenly very tired. In one short evening her world had been turned upside down.

By now, Dad and Billy's conversation was winding down. From inside the house Blanche could be heard playfully scolding Alfred while she got him ready for bed.

Dad looked up at Alfred's window. The lamp was lit and Blanche's form could be seen as she tucked the baby in his crib.

"Okay, Billy, I'll let you get on your way."

They shook hands again and as Billy headed back down the driveway, Julia could hear his whistling start up again.

"Coming in?" Dad asked.

"Yeah Sure. Right away." She murmured.

Julia followed Will through the front door and as she was rounding the corner, almost collided with Blanche. "Sorry," she mumbled and squeezing past continued on her way upstairs to get ready for bed.

Entering the living room, Blanche smiled at Will and asked, "Who was that you were talking to?"

"The McGrath's son, Billy. They'll start getting settled tomorrow. By the first of next week, they should be ready to begin."

Quietly, Blanche strode to the sofa where Will sat with his legs stretched out. She leaned down, allowing the front of her dress to fall open, and slowly kissed Will on the lips. His hands slid up the sides of her thighs and they gently rested on her hips. This was as far as they let things go. Only a few more days till their marriage. Slowly, they separated. Will stood, and with his arm around her waist, walked Blanche to her room.

∞

The next day was like any other until Julia arrived home from school. After changing into her farm clothes and grabbing an apple out of a bowl on the kitchen table, she made the short walk to the cottage. She hadn't given much thought to its new inhabitants until she crested the ridge. As she walked up to the door, she could feel her stomach tighten. She raised her hand and knocked. The door opened with a soft creak and before her stood a woman with chestnut brown skin and pitch black hair pulled back in a bun. The woman's face broke into a beautiful smile and she said "You must be Julia. Please come in."

She stepped aside and Julia pushed through the old screen door.

"I'm so glad your dad loaned you out for today. I keep trying to make headway, but I feel like I'm going in circles" laughed the woman.

She stuck out her hand and introduced herself. "I'm Lou, Don's wife."

Julia reciprocated and clasped Lou's hand. It was strong and firm. Julia looked up at Lou's face and was pleased to see tenderness and gaiety in her dark eyes. Immediately, she felt foolish for her previous apprehensions.

The first chore they set to was wiping out the shelves and drawers of an old sideboard that had belonged to Julia's grandparents. While she began to unpack the dishes and linens, Lou cut brown paper and lined the shelves. While they worked, Lou began to tell Julia about herself.

She had grown up on a small farm in northern Maine and was her parent's only child. She had come to them after many childless years when they had given up hope of ever having a family. They considered Lou the answer to their prayers. Her

parents weren't wealthy, but all they had was showered upon
their beloved daughter. After finishing school, Lou went on to
get her teachers certificate. She was grateful her parents saw her
accomplishment before they died. At that time jobs were scarce
and Lou felt lucky to get a position teaching in a lumber camp.
It was there she met Don.

He was young and strong and handsome. He was also
bright and eager to learn. The attraction between them was
immediate and after only three months of meeting, they were
married. They stayed on in the camp with Don felling trees and
Lou teaching: even after the birth of their two boys.

"Oh, my," said Lou, "I've chatted your ear off! I've been
around men for so long I didn't realize how much I missed
another gal's company."

Julia smiled. Already she liked Lou. She was warm and
friendly with a light sense of humor and an infectious laugh. By
the end of the afternoon, Julia noticed her cheeks were actually
sore from smiling so much.

The sideboard was almost filled, and Julia was reaching for
the last box when the door slammed. She turned to see who
it was. There in the doorway stood a good looking boy that
reminded her of Billy. He was tall and lean with straight black
hair, but his skin had only a slight tan to it.

Before she knew it, he was at her feet. Julia looked at the
empty box in her hands and then down at the floor. Strewn
about her feet were beautiful, hand painted notecards. Bending
down to help pick them up, she noticed the wild flowers that
decorated each card. The strokes were delicate and from what
she could tell, no two were the same.

"I'm so sorry!" Julia stammered as she carefully placed the cards back in their box.

"No harm done," said Lou with the same gentle smile she'd worn all afternoon.

"Yeah, no harm unless Billy sees what you did," chided the boy at her side.

"Now, D.J., stop that! She'll think you mean it," scolded Lou.

"You know it's the truth, Ma."

Lou scowled.

With a slight sigh of resignation, he said "Sorry. Ma's right. Nothing to be concerned about."

Lou turned to Julia. "I guess it's time you meet my other son. This is D.J. Our first."

Julia slid the box of cards onto a shelf in the sideboard and turned to face D.J.

"Hi, I'm Julia."

She gave him a quick once over and could see that D.J. was not quite as tall as Billy. But by his deep voice and broad shoulders, he was older by a couple of years.

"Sure, nice to meet you," he said

Their eyes met and Julia felt her stomach do a flip.

D.J. smirked, turned on his heel and threw over his shoulder, "I'm going down to the barns to help Pa."

The kitchen door creaked and then slammed leaving Julia and Lou alone again. Julia could feel the heat in her cheeks and was trying to reason where her reaction came from when Lou's voice broke through.

"Well, I think that's all we can get done for today. Thanks so much for all your help, Julia."

"Sure. My pleasure. It was a lot of fun."

For the zillionth time that afternoon, Lou smiled and said, "I think I'm going to like it here...and I think you and I will be great friends!"

Julia grinned back, nodding in agreement.

5

Julia turned away from the window and looked down at the card, still in her hand. She ran her finger across the cover, then gently blew the thin layer of dust from off its surface. Her breath caught at the sight of the softly painted daisies. She began to gently pry it open when she heard a knock on the door. Quickly, Julia tucked the note inside the bodice of her dress, and smoothed it into place.

The owner of the knock tried again.

Julia answered, "Coming," as she crossed the room. She reached out for the knob and turned it. She pulled the door open a crack and peeked outside. An auburn head of curls gave him away. Julia opened the door wider and ushered Alfred in.

His upturned face waited with anticipation, and for a moment, all Julia could think of was how much her little brother meant to her. She marveled at the six year old and how handsome he was; neat and clean in his Sunday best.

Her thoughts were broken when he stamped his foot impatiently and reproached her, "Julia! Are you gonna give it to me or not?"

Julia looked hard at Alfred, trying to determine what he was asking for.

"Dad said you have something for me."

"Ah, yes," Julia remembered. Then, taking his small hand in hers, she led Alfred to her bureau. She pulled open the center drawer and exposed her collection of hankies. Alfred turned his nose up and began to leave.

Julia touched his shoulder, "Wait," she admonished.

Pushing aside piles of lace and embroidery, she reached in and released a secret latch. She heard "snap" and then a lid popped open on top of the dresser revealing a secret compartment.

"Wow!" exclaimed a wide eyed Alfred.

Julia smiled and reached in. Carefully, she removed an old hankie, the fabric yellowed and frayed. She held out her hand and slowly pulled back the folds to reveal her gift.

Julia watched Alfred's face light up. She handed it to him and began to remember another wedding and what it brought to the farm.

Sunday finally came, and Dad and Blanche were married in a quiet ceremony. Afterwards, Julia came home with Alfred, leaving the newlyweds to a brief honeymoon at a small Inn in Vermont. Dad had made arrangements for Don and his boys to care for the stock and Lou would help Julia in the house.

When Julia walked through the kitchen door, Lou was just pulling a squash pie from the oven. Julia paused and indulged her senses in the warm smell of cinnamon and cloves. As she exhaled, she heard Lou's familiar chuckle.

"Take a good whiff, but no pie till after dinner."

With a slight scowl, Julia put the baby on the floor to play and instead grabbed a handful of freshly roasted seeds from a pan on the counter.

"Okay," said Lou, "Now that that's done, we have work to do upstairs."

Julia raised her eyebrows and Lou continued, "Come on, we've got to move Blanche's things into your Dad's room."

Julia's jaw dropped as Lou's words took meaning. Of course Dad and Blanche would be sharing a bedroom.

Scooping Alfred back into her arms, she and Lou headed upstairs. After depositing Alfred in his crib to play, Julia joined Lou in Dad's room and they began the task of giving it a good cleaning. They took down curtains and stripped the bedding as they went. Next was to empty the wardrobe. That was the hardest part. In the eight months since her mother's death, Dad had never taken the time to pack up Mum's things.

Glancing at Julia with concern, Lou asked if she needed a break. She shook her head no. Then, taking a deep breath, Julia reached for the brass handles and pulled the doors open.

Compared to Blanche, her mother's dresses were simple and plain: soft calicos and muslins. Julia reached in and pulled one out. She pressed it to her face, thinking she might find some remnant of her mother's scent. Instead, her nostrils filled with the pungent odor of moth balls. Disgusted, she tossed it on the seat of the old oak rocker. Looking inside, she allowed her fingers to play along the edges of the lacy collars and puckered sleeves. Her hand fell. She felt nothing. These dresses no longer held any meaning for her.

Julia wrapped her arms around the contents of the wardrobe, and lifting, turned and dropped the bundle, joining them to their mate on the chair. Julia paused, then fished through the pile until she found a pale brown calico. She looked it up and down for wear, and then held it up, gauging its size.

"I think these could fit you...if you like."

Lou looked up from the feather pillow she was stuffing into a case. Her eyes grew big. She checked her excitement and began to protest, but Julia stopped her.

"Lou, please take them. But, only if you want to. They don't suit me. My shoulders are too broad."

"I..I..I don't think I've ever seen so many pretty dresses. Are you sure? Really sure?"

Julia's hand went to her throat. Lovingly, she ran her fingers down the chain at her neck until they found Mum's locket.

"I'm sure."

Lou and Julia abandoned their cleaning for the rest of the afternoon, while Lou tried on each garment with Julia playing inspector. By late afternoon they had set aside any that needed minor mending or alterations, and packed up the rest for Lou to take to the cottage.

The sun was setting when Julia put away the last of the dinner dishes and swept the floor. She carried a sleepy Alfred up to his room, extinguishing lights as she went.

In her room, she paused by the window. It was almost dark except for a faint light on the far ridge and the sky full of stars.

Julia gazed into the expanse and thought on all the changes the past year had brought. Little did she know, but many more lay ahead.

Over the next few days, Lou and Julia worked hard to move Blanche's belongings into Dad's room. When they were done, Julia couldn't believe the transformation.

In Blanche's old room, there was only one piece of furniture left that needed to be moved. So on the morning of the day the newlyweds were due to arrive home, DJ and Billy came to the house.

Julia and Lou were pulling the last of Blanche's books from the shelves when they heard the boy's heavy tread on the stairs.

"I hope you cleaned off those boots before you came into this house," Lou scolded.

Two faces appeared in the doorway, Billy smiling and DJ smirking with a mischievous twinkle in his eyes.

Ignoring their mother, the boys went to the bookcase and began to carefully separate each section. Once they had it apart, they carried each piece down to the living room and then began its reassembly. At the same time, Lou and Julia were bringing books and stacking them in a corner. Up and down the trips were made until Blanche's room had been emptied of all but a few memories.

Julia stood looking around at the bare windows and floor. She'd come to look forward to her visits with Blanche and wondered if all that would end, now that Blanche and Dad were married.

She felt his eyes on the back of her head seconds before she heard him clear his throat. Looking up at the ceiling with a slight grimace, she turned to face DJ. He seemed to be smiling, without really smiling. It was as though he alone knew the joke.

"Thanks for helping," she said.

"Sure, it was easy."

Why did he just stand there, looking at her?

"There's nothing else, Lou and I got all the books"

"Yup," DJ said, still not moving.

She wanted to leave, go down to the kitchen, but there was no way with him blocking the doorway.

Then, they heard Billy yell up, "DJ, Julia, come on. Ma's got some hot cider."

She took a couple steps toward the door, thinking he'd move to let her by. But DJ continued to lean against the jam, never taking his eyes off her.

It had been weeks since he'd come to the farm, and she still didn't understand why DJ left her flustered. So, with a "huff" of annoyance, Julia brushed past him, hoping by the time she reached the kitchen, her cheeks would stop burning.

It as mid-afternoon when Dad and Blanche finally arrived home. They pulled into the driveway and with great flourish, Dad scooped Blanche into his arms and carried her into the house.

Just inside the door, Dad paused and took a moment before putting Blanche down. Slowly, they turned. They both had smiling faces. Finally they noticed Julia and Lou standing in the kitchen doorway. Blanche blushed. Dad gave her a wink, excused himself, and left to get their bags from the car.

Making a show of smoothing her skirt, Blanche looked up and said," What is that heavenly smell? I'm famished."

Julia bit her lip and looked over at Lou. They both fought back snickers and Julia answered," Lou made a pot of beef stew for dinner, and the biscuits will be out any minute."

"Oh, that sounds wonderful," said Blanche, "Let's have an early dinner and then we can tell you all about our trip." She turned and headed upstairs.

Julia and Lou's eyes met and they again had to fight back the urge to giggle.

Later that evening, Julia sat with Dad and Blanche in the living room, while Alfred scooted on the floor. It was finally time to hear about their honeymoon.

Dad and Blanche had traveled to the outskirts of Rutland, Vermont and stayed at an inn that was run by a couple of sisters, Ruby and Maude. The sisters had never married, but were great romantics and took care in making sure the couple had everything they needed. Near the town where they stayed was the Sutherland Falls granite quarry. It employed many of the men in the surrounding counties. One of the workers was a permanent resident at the inn, his name was Jasper. He had quit school when he was twelve to start working in the quarry and been there ever since. Never desiring marriage, he was happy to have a home with the two sisters and a place to come back to at the end of each day. In his spare time, Jasper carved chunks of granite into little figurines.

As Blanche was describing the various animals, Dad reached into his pocket and pulled out his kerchief. Slowly, he unwrapped the folds and revealed a rose colored stone fashioned into the shape of a squirrel holding an acorn.

Julia's eyes widened, and her fingers began to twitch.

Blanche chuckled softly. She knew what that meant. She turned to Will and gave him a nudge in the side. Will looked at her and mouthed, "What?"

"Go on," urged Blanche, tipping her head in Julia's direction.

Will extended his hand, the small squirrel perched in his palm.

"For you, Julia."

"Really?" Julia asked, as she was reaching for it.

She held it and stroked the softly polished stone. Then, looking at Dad said, "Thank you, so much!"

"It was Blanche's idea," said Dad, "she picked it out."

Julia wrapped her arms around Blanche's neck, hugging her warmly. Blanche looked at Will out of the corner of her eyes, he was smiling.

"So what else did you do?" asked Julia.

"Well," said Dad slowly, "we did a lot of talking and made some plans."

Dad patted his legs softly, and taking a breath started, "I've decided to run for state senate."

Dad paused for a moment, waiting for Julia's reaction. The room was still except for the conversation Alfred was having with a ball of yarn. Julia sat picking at a thread on her shirt cuff, not quite knowing what to say or what this meant.

Dad continued, "It's something I've always wanted to do. Go to Concord and stick up for the farmers. Make our needs known. I'm well respected here, in our community. Dad stumbled on," I know there's not much time until the election, but Blanche thinks I have a good chance of winning."

Julia knew the other farmers looked up to her dad, and she thought, "He's probably right, he could win the election. But, what about the farm?"

"I know what you're thinking," interjected Dad, "while I'm off at the capitol, what will you be doing? Blanche and I talked about that, too. You see, there's a really great school not far from here, the Kimball Academy. You can go there. Get a real education. You know, you've only got a few years before you're ready to marry."

Julia's head shot up.

"Hold on, go away to school, marriage, that is not at all what I was thinking!" she cried. "I just wanted to know who would keep the farm going."

"Oh, ah…" Dad's voice became quiet. He realized he had said too much.

Quickly, Blanche chimed in, "Don't worry, Julia, none of this is going to happen right away. We, your Dad and I, got ahead of ourselves. You know, planning and dreaming about the future."

Julia stood, her face flushed with anger. "So, this is your plan to get me out of the way. By sending me to some boarding school?" She glared at Blanche, and said, "I thought we were friends!"

Julia turned and stalked out of the room. Grabbing her sweater, she left the house and went to see Gert. It wasn't often she found herself in the barns these days. The McGrath boys had taken over her chores and she felt a pang of remorse for neglecting her old friend.

Julia pulled the barn door shut behind her. She leaned against it and closed her eyes, enjoying the sound of the noisy cows as they settled down for the night. Then she walked to Gert. Julia ran her hands over the cow's warm body and felt her silky fur slide through her fingertips. Burrowing her nose in Gert's neck, Julia breathed in the familiar smell. She felt overwhelmed. Her body began to shake as she sobbed, while still holding onto her friend. When the tears had left her, Julia loosened her hold and gave the patient cow a kiss on the cheek. Gert grunted and responded with a gentle shake of her head.

Behind her, there was shuffling in the straw. Julia turned to see DJ picking something up. He rolled it in his palm before looking at her.

"This yours?" he asked, extending his hand.

There lay the rose colored squirrel. It must have fallen from her pocket.

"That? Yeah, it's mine. But I don't want it."

"You sure? It looks special."

She was about to argue, when she looked at his face. It was then she noticed a trickle of blood running past his ear. Taking a couple steps closer, she saw a gash at his hairline, swollen and red.

Instinctively, she reached out towards his face. As he turned from her, she saw the rip in his shirt and more blood.

"What happened to you?"

"Nothing. Just nothing. And if you're smart, you'll be quiet and let it be!"

"But, DJ, you're hurt."

"Here. Take this thing," said DJ, thrusting the small figure at Julia.

Stunned, Julia took the squirrel and before she could say another word, he was gone.

That night, a dark sky hung over the farm. Julia lay in her bed trying to find comfort in the worn quilts but the events of the day kept playing in her mind. She tried but couldn't shake an uneasy feeling. Eventually she fell into a restless sleep. The day's events kept her from getting much rest.

Once Will had made the decision to run for office, the farm became a flurry of activity. Each day, people would stop by to show their support in the upcoming election. Julia had always known her dad was considered a leader in their community, but it wasn't until now that she began to realize how much influence he really had. Why, even in the school yard talk had turned to her father and how he would get the capitol to notice the needs of the farmers.

As for Julia, it had been decided that at the first of the year, she would begin at the Kimball Academy for girls. So while Dad was out visiting area farms and holding court at the Mountainside Inn, books were bought and packed and Julia was fitted for school uniforms.

When the day of the election finally came, they were greeted by a morning clear and bright, a perfect autumn day. Dad left before breakfast to greet friends and neighbors as they went in to vote. He had only begun campaigning a month ago, he hoped he had done enough.

In the kitchen, Blanche's customary composure was slipping.

Crash!

There on the floor lay proof of her distraction.

"Oh, dear! What's wrong with me today?"

"Now Blanche, a broken jar and spilt peaches isn't the end of the world," said Lou.

"No, I guess not. But perhaps I better stay out of the kitchen today."

"I think that's wise," agreed Lou, as she carefully began to clean up the mess. "You let me take care of the meals, and say, why don't you get prettied up and go into town? I'm sure Will would love to have you by his side."

Blanche thought for a moment, and then shook her head no.

"Maybe I could just help around here."

Lou frowned.

"Or maybe I should take Alfred out for some fresh air and a picnic?"

Smiling, Lou walked Blanche to the bottom of the stairs, all the while rattling off all the items she would pack in their lunch basket.

Unlike Blanche, Julia went on with her day as she did any other. It wasn't that she didn't care who won, she just had other things on her mind. Things like the Kimball Academy for girls. Blanche told her it was a well-respected prep school. But she was a little vague on exactly what it was she was preparing for. All Julia knew, was that she would be living in a dormitory during the week, and most weekends coming home.

"At least I get that," she told Gert.

Ever since that night a month ago, Julia had made a promise to come visit her old friend more often.

"I don't know why you're complaining," said a voice from the hay loft.

Julia looked up, ready to defend herself, when a handful of hay greeted her in the face. She only sputtered for a moment, and then raced up the ladder to face her assailant. DJ's back was to her, and he was leaning over the edge with another handful of hay.

"Got you!" she cried.

He spun around but it was Billy.

Surprised, Julia was too long at taking action and the hay in Billy's hand was now on her head. With a soft grunt, Julia ran at Billy and sent him tumbling into a deep pile of hay, with herself close behind. Laughing and kicking, they came up for air looking like a couple of scarecrows.

Julia smiled She couldn't remember the last time she'd felt so free.

"Now that's nice to see," remarked Billy.

"What is?" puzzled Julia.

"Your smile, it's been missing for a while now."

"Oh, you noticed."

"Yeah, we've all noticed," said Billy. "But I don't understand why you're so unhappy. Do you know what I'd give to go to that fancy school?"

"Really? You would be happy if you were sent there?"

"Sure, it's an all-girls school!" laughed Billy.

At that Julia grabbed another handful of hay and rubbed it in his face. His hands shot up and he cried, "I give up, I give up."

Laughing, Julia stopped and sank back into the hay.

"Seriously," she asked, "you would really want to go there?"

"Seriously, I would," replied Billy. "At a school like that, I could paint in a real studio, with real paints. Not the stuff I make from berries and plants."

"You make your own colors?" asked Julia, in awe.

"Yeah," he said. "My Mom showed me how. It's an Indian thing."

"Ok, but you don't have to go to one of those schools to learn how to paint."

"Maybe not…" said Billy, "but if I had the chance, well, you'd never hear me complain about it."

Julia thought for a moment. Everything Billy said made sense, but she still couldn't shake the feeling that Blanche had betrayed her.

"Hey, you two."

It was Don.

"Yeah, Dad?"

"Billy, come on down and get back to work. And Julia, Blanche is looking for you."

Julia glanced over at Billy. He and DJ looked so similar. And up until now, she had thought of Billy as the ordinary brother. Yet today, it was Billy that made her feel a little better about leaving. She only hoped he was right.

A few hours later, Julia was neat and clean and sitting with Blanche, and Alfred at the Mountainside.

The Mountainside Inn held the pulse of their farming community. At its start, it had been a trading post where hunters and trappers came to sell their pelts and stock up on supplies. It also served as a post office, restaurant and social hub. If there was any news worth knowing or gossip to be heard, it could be found at the Mountainside Trading Company. For over 200 years it sat nestled in the crook of the mountains that separated Vermont from New Hampshire, and except for a few coats of paint, and the addition of six rooms that rented by the week, it remained unchanged. Even its owners, Old Francis and his wife, Maggie, were descendants of the men who had originally built and operated the post.

In its many years of existence, the inn had witnessed courtships, brawling rivals and backroom deals. It had seen the best in people and the worst. Tonight, on the close of the election, it would see both. Will stood in the center of the restaurant, surrounded by fellow farmers that had come to offer support. The election results would soon be in, and they were all anxious to hear the outcome.

Suddenly a door slammed.

"You dog!"

All heads turned to see George Barnett standing in the doorway. He was a large man, mostly from eating and drinking too much and working too little. He'd been their state senator for as long as Julia could remember. Not because he was liked but because no one had ever run against him.

Remarkably, Will remained calm and carefully picked his way through the crowd toward George.

"Good evening, George, what's the good word?"

Barnett's face turned bright red and looked like it could explode at any minute.

Good word?" bellowed George. "There are no good words for you!" he spat. Then, slowly he turned, looking hard at each person in the room.

"And all of you, traitors! You chose this." George was now facing Dad with his meaty finger pointing accusingly. "You picked this Indian lover over me?"

Dad had moved to within a few feet of George and then stopped. In a quiet voice he said, "Hold on, George, think about what you're saying."

"Oh I don't have to think about it. I know exactly what I'm talking about. You have that squaw and her half breed rats running free on your land and taking up with our daughters."

As he said this, he made a sweeping gesture with his hands as if to include everyone in the room. Then, narrowing his eyes, he stared hard at his audience and asked, "What do you think will happen once Will is in Concord? Who will control his savages then?"

Out of the shadows Andrew Merrill stepped up and stood next to Will.

"Now, George, we know you're not happy about the friendship between Abigail and Don's boy. But, that's got nothing to do…"

"Nothing to do?" interrupted George, continuing his rant. "It shows bad judgment. And Will hiring those degenerates isn't my only concern. Look at that piece of trash he married."

Will felt Andrew's hand grip his shoulder, hard. It took all his self-control not to flick it off and lunge the last few feet between him and Barnett's throat.

"That's right, hold him back. He's yours now. Hope you're happy with your choice."

With that, George spun on his heel and slammed out of the Mountainside. The room was still for about a minute and then reality set in. It must have occurred to everyone at the same time. Will had won!

Whoops and cheers erupted. Old Francis began pulling out Mason jars from a hidden cabinet and Maggie began setting glasses on the bar. They were soon filled with a light amber liquid and distributed around the room.

Andrew, still standing at Will's side, raised his glass, "To better times!"

"To better times!" the crowd cheered.

The celebration continued into the early morning hours. Julia didn't quite remember the ride home, or how she made it to her bed. All she knew was that life on the farm was changing, and the night had left her with questions and no ready answers.

6

Julia reached down and ran her fingers through Alfred's curls before giving them a final tousle. He was still clutching the hankie that held the granite squirrel. She was so glad he liked the figurine.

"Ok, now tuck that into your jacket pocket and go find Dad," she said with affection, "and don't muss up your good clothes!" she called out as Alfred slipped through the doorway.

She was just reaching for the note she'd tucked away, when the mop of curls poked back into her room.

"Hey, Julia, there's something out here for you."

She asked what it was, but Alfred had already run off. She peeked outside, and there, propped up against the hallway baseboard was a flat square package wrapped in brown paper and tied with twine.

Curious, Julia bent down and carefully picked it up, being sure to hold it away from her dress. She quickly scooted back inside, shutting the door so no one would see her. Julia began to examine the gift, turning it over in her hands. That's when she noticed the small note scrawled in pencil in one of the corners. She'd recognize that handwriting anywhere and smiled as she mouthed the words, "To Julia, with fond memories."

The twine was strung tight and tied with a nasty knot. Julia was too impatient to pick at it, so she went to her dresser and dug out a small pair of sewing scissors. They really weren't designed for the task, but Julia would have to make do.

After minutes of clipping away, the string finally gave and snapped. It fell from off the package to the floor, now forgotten, as Julia tore at the final barrier.

When the last shred of paper slipped off, Julia looked at her reward and nearly danced with glee. She loved this painting and often had wondered where it had ended up.

She held it at arm's length, admiring the composition and colors. She remembered the young woman, perched on a swing wearing only a curtain and fresh flowers in her hair. She went back to the time she first lost herself in that famous blue sky.

Snow settled in the mountains covering the farm in a clean blanket of white. The holidays came as they always had and Julia was determined to enjoy every minute. She crowded each day with ice skating parties, and sleigh rides. She immersed herself in decorating cookies, mantles and trees. She even wove a wreath from pine bows and holly sprigs and hung it on the barn door with a bright red bow. Anything to prevent her thoughts from dwelling on her upcoming departure to the Kimball Academy for girls.

But Christmas passed, a new year was welcomed in, and finally the day arrived.

Julia looked around her bedroom one last time. There was no putting it off. Slowly she walked out her door and down the hall. She was too old to cry, and too stubborn to feign cheerfulness. So melancholy was to be her traveling companion.

Sitting by the front door was the box that contained her school books, securely tied with twine. Beside it sat a trunk filled with the uniforms required at the Kimball Academy, along with a few personal items.

Julia stood before Blanche and Dad, stiff and unmoving. She wanted to hug them both and feel the old closeness, but she couldn't let go of her anger. The conversation she'd had with Billy replayed in her mind, and she felt a twinge of excitement. But, Julia wasn't about to admit that to anyone.

Blanche looked her over and picked at a couple of invisible hairs on her traveling suit.

"You look lovely. Rather grown-up."

Julia said nothing.

Blanche and Dad had told her again and again what a great opportunity this was. She was encouraged to make the most of the next few years. Each time, Julia listened, but said nothing.

The knock on the door broke the silence. DJ entered after stomping the snow from his boots.

"Ready?" he asked, impatiently.

Julia wanted to say no. But instead, she nodded her head, leaving without so much as a backward glance.

Once inside the car, Julia settled in for the long drive. In warmer months, it would only take about an hour. But during the winter, the trip could be as long as three.

The driver's door opened and DJ jumped in. Shifting into first gear, he slid off the parking brake and turned the wheel towards the road. Off handedly, he told Julia there was a bag of Macintosh apples on the floor. She looked over and noticed a napkin on the seat between them.

"What's this?"

"Ma wrapped up a couple slices of apple bread."

"Sounds good," Julia said without feeling.

DJ said nothing, but when she gave him a side wards glance, Julia could see the familiar smirk and twinkle in his eye.

"Ugh!" she thought, as her stomach began its little dance. She closed her eyes and pretended to sleep, it would be a long drive.

The trip finally ended when they finally pulled into the circle at the front of the Kimball Academy. Julia's apprehensions were pretty much gone. She decided that was one benefit to a long and tedious ride. Julia began to reach for the door handle.

"Stay put," DJ said, as he jumped out of the car.

Julia sat waiting until he came around and opened the car door for her. She felt annoyed and confused but her questioning face only made DJ snort.

"Don't you know? You're a lady now. Time to stop acting like a farm girl."

"Oh," she murmured, surprised, not really sure what he meant.

She carefully got out, accepting DJ's hand so she wouldn't slip on the packed down snow. She began to walk inside, but he held her back. Holding her chin, DJ stepped in closer. Julia could feel her heart banging against her chest.

"You've got bread crumbs on your chin," he reproved, and quickly swiped them off with his mittened hand. "Ok, that's better."

Julia felt foolish and hoped her rosy cheeks would be attributed to the chilly winter air.

"Come on, don't just stand there," DJ admonished as he started for the entrance, "After I get back to the farm, I still have chores to do."

Julia followed him inside. They entered a large room with a high ceiling, and pristine white walls. Looking ahead was a wide staircase with highly polished steps and banisters. Her eyes followed them up to the top where she could see hallways that branched to the left and right. She wondered where they led, and who was up there.

"Young lady, young lady."

Julia's thoughts were interrupted by a plump, older woman sitting at a secretary's desk nestled in a small alcove. She had a gold nameplate that read, "Miss Stone". Miss Stone wore a white starched blouse, a dark green blazer with the Kimball crest displayed above her pocket, and a gray flannel skirt. The only part of her ensemble that seemed out of place were the heavy wool socks, stuffed into a pair of bright red, knitted booties.

Julia felt DJ's elbow in her side.

"That's you," he chided.

"Young lady, can I help you?" she asked again.

Miss Stone was looking directly at Julia, with a stern face. It seemed she was trying to appear severe, but her soft gray eyes wouldn't allow it.

"Oh, yes, sorry. My name is Julia, I'm new here."

Miss Stone waited patiently. When it became clear Julia would need prodding, she asked, "Julia what, dear?"

Julia could feel DJ smirking behind her. "What was she was doing here?" she wondered. "After all, she really was just a simple farm girl."

In a quiet voice, Julia answered, "Kelly."

Miss Stone gave a slight nod and then asked DJ to bring Julia's things in. She started to dig through a file until she finally found Julia's paperwork. She began to read it over, mouthing the words and adding exclamations as she went.

"Oh, good," she murmured, "very nice." Finally she looked up at Julia, "It says here you'll be rooming with Izzy."

"Izzy?" questioned Julia.

"Oh, yes, ha, ha…" Miss Stone rattled on. "Isadore, but we all call her Izzy. Oh, you'll see, she's a delight. Yes, yes, you'll see."

DJ returned and dropped her things with a thud. He tipped his cap by way of a good bye and was gone.

Julia stood, looking around and trying to take in the Kimball Academy. Miss Stone seemed oblivious to Julia's plight and continued her inane rambling.

Her escape finally came with the arrival of Peter, a tall, gangly boy with dark brown hair and a bridge of freckles covering his nose and cheeks. He was there to carry Julia's things and show her to her room.

"Come with me," he encouraged, while muscling an armload of boxes and heading off towards the stairs.

Julia discovered later from her roommate Izzy, who as it turned out, really was a delight, that Peter was a local. He was about the same age as the Kimball girls and worked at the Academy doing odd jobs. His mother was a widow and Peter's earnings made their survival possible.

Peter knocked twice on the thick oak door, then twisted the knob with his elbow and gave a hard push with his shoulder. The room Julia and Izzy shared was much like the rest of the school; neat and functional. The only adornments were brought in by its residents, but even those were kept to a minimum lest they be confiscated at the weekly room inspections.

It didn't take long before Julia fell into the daily routine and soon the days began to blend together. She quickly became chums with the girls on her floor and spent her evenings with them trying out new hairstyles, imagining dates and dances with handsome escorts, and singing songs to the ukulele.

While the original plan had been for her to come home on weekends, an unusually harsh winter had prevented that from happening. At first, this added to Julia's sense of abandonment. But, as her friendships grew, her desire to go home diminished. So when summer break finally came, Julia reluctantly packed her trunk.

The morning of her departure found Julia sitting outside Kimball hall on a cool stone bench, her eyes closed, waiting. She had already said her good byes. And she and Izzy had vowed to write each other every week. The sun's warmth gave her face a soft glow and light breezes played with the curls in her hair. From behind she heard,

"You looking forward to going home?"

Julia knew who it was without looking.

"Hi, Peter. I guess."

"Yeah, it's gonna be quiet here with all you girls gone."

Julia felt bad for him. Peter's home life was so sad. She knew working at the school could be hard and tedious, but it also gave him friendship and a sense of belonging. All the girls doted on Peter. After all, he was the only eligible male within reach. But, both he and every girl knew they were only practicing their flirtations on him. They had been raised knowing their true destiny lay with a different class of young men.

Julia heard the sound of tires on gravel and knew her ride had come. Peter was quickly forgotten as the familiar flutter in her stomach returned as she anticipated her time alone with DJ.

She stayed seated on the bench trying not to look too interested as the driver's side door opened. But when Billy popped out, Julia quickly turned and said "good-by" to Peter, giving her face a moment to erase the look of disappointment.

"All set?" he asked, grabbing her trunk and stowing it in the back of the car.

"Yes, she nodded, and waited on the passenger side. Billy opened her door and once she was seated, gave it a firm push shut.

After they were on their way, Billy looked her over.

"You're no worse for wear. So, tell me…was it as bad as you thought?"

A smile broke on Julia's face and she began to share stories of her first months at Kimball. She took great relish in describing her floor mates. She told him about the late night kitchen raids, when the girls would hunt for sweets hidden away by their suspicious cook. She continued with tales of skating parties, and snowball fights. But it was Julia's animated depiction of Izzy that made her eyes brighten. As it turned out, Izzy was the daughter of a wealthy banker from New York City. Her parents sent her to Kimball in an effort to make her presentable and ready to debut into society. Thus far, it wasn't working.

Whenever there was salt in the sugar bowl, panties on the flag pole or a kitten in the cupboard, Izzy was to blame. Mischief seemed to run in her blood, and the other girls could either join in the fun or try to avoid the fall out.

Just as Julia was coming to the end of her tales, she glanced out the window and saw familiar surroundings. When she realized how much talking she'd done, she began to apologize.

"Billy, I'm so sorry. I can't believe I monopolized the conversation!"

Billy grinned. "Don't apologize. I like hearing your stories. And I'm glad you're happy."

She was happy. Julia was shocked and almost ashamed to admit it, but she liked being at Kimball.

Quietly, she confessed, "You were right, Billy, it is a great opportunity. I can't believe I acted so childish; so ungrateful."

"My, my," said Billy, with mock sarcasm. "You have been growing up!"

Julia smacked his shoulder playfully, knowing there was a lot of truth in what he said.

"Hey, we've got some time before dark. Can I take you someplace special?"

"Okay," she said, with hesitation. "Where are we going?"

"I think I'll let it be a surprise. But just so you know, I listened to what you said, too."

"What do you mean?" Julia couldn't imagine what she could have said that would make any difference to Billy.

"You'll see," he replied excitedly.

A few miles down the road, they made a sharp turn and were soon entering the hamlet of Cornish. Somewhere Julia had heard about this area, but couldn't recall any of the details.

After passing a few small farms, Billy turned down a narrow driveway on the right. He followed as it curved slightly to the left and came to a stop in front of an odd out building.

"Welcome to the Oaks," Billy said with flourish.

Julia looked skeptical, what could be so special here?

Billy saw the crease in her brow and held up a finger, "Just wait!"

He hopped out of the car and ran to her side. After opening her door, he took her hand, and helped her out. Not giving Julia time to scope out her surroundings, he pulled her along and up to the entrance. Billy knocked sharply, and then pushed it open.

"Hey, Max," he yelled out, all the while dragging Julia into a large, open room.

From behind an easel came a thin, disheveled man with paint smearing his face, as well as his clothing. Off to the side, a young woman slid into a bathrobe and disappeared behind a screen.

Max's face lit up as he beckoned, "Billy, come in, come in. Who do you have with you?"

Max was apon them in a matter of steps and after wiping his hands on his apron, hugged Billy quickly and welcomed them. Billy stepped aside, nudging Julia forward.

"Julia, this is Max, Max Parrish. And Max, my friend, Julia."

With mock gallantry, Max bowed and planted a light kiss on the hand he snatched from Julia's side.

"Nice to meet you," Julia said doubtfully, trying hard to remember any conversation where she'd told Billy to find a hidden barn with an eccentric.

"Max is a graphic illustrator," enthused Billy, "his paintings have been printed on magazine covers."

"Oh, my...wow!" said Julia, beginning to make sense of the scene before her.

"Max lets me paint here, I'm learning so much!"

"He exaggerates, I let him sit in the corner," said Max, with a wink.

Billy took her hand and pulled her along until she was standing in front of an easel. The painting was unlike anything she'd seen before. She recognized the delicate flowers and twisting vines, but the stately columns and lightly colored birds were different. So was the painting of a young woman covered with only a piece of drapery.

Julia's hand came to her mouth. She was surprised, but not offended. She stared at the canvas, looking past its subject. She admired the graceful lines and subtle blending of hues. His handling of the girl's form was soft, and yet somehow, he had given her an ethereal quality.

"She's lovely."

"You really like her? Like it?" Billy asked.

"Oh, yes! Who is she?"

"Alice, she lives on a farm down the road."

Before Julia could take back the words, she mused quietly, "I wish I could be painted like that."

From behind, Julia heard Max's voice, "You can. You really should!"

"Oh, no, I was just thinking out loud," stammered Julia.

"It's ok, Julia," said Billy, moving them towards the door. "Come on, I need to get you home."

Julia took another quick look around the studio, and then at Max. She blushed when she thanked him for the visit and promised to come again. She couldn't imagine modeling for him, but she was intrigued.

"Maybe someday," she mused for a moment, then quickly put the thought out of her mind.

Back on the road, Julia turned to Billy.

"You're very talented. Have you ever thought of doing what Max does?"

"Thought of it? It's all I dream about."

"So you should," asserted Julia."You should do it."

The car became quiet. The easy conversation gone. Julia felt confused. She didn't understand Billy's reluctance or what she'd said wrong.

They continued in silence down the road until they crested a hill not far from the farm. The sky was darkening, but just over the next rise, lights were glowing.

"Where is that?" questioned Julia.

"Oh," said Billy, "I forgot to tell you. There have been a lot of changes while you've been gone."

"Changes?" questioned Julia.

"You'll see," replied Billy, cryptically.

It didn't take long for her to discover what he meant. After cresting the last hill, Billy turned the car into the well-worn driveway and pulled up to her house, all ablaze. During the ride, Julia had been so immersed in their conversation, she hadn't noticed the poles now lining her road. In a daze, she pulled on the door handle and let herself out of the car. She took slow, dream-like steps towards the house, not believing her eyes.

Billy quickly caught up, lugging her trunk and chiding, "Get a move on. Blanche has a special dinner waiting."

She took the porch steps slowly, one at a time, all the while looking up and around at the glow of electricity.

The screen door opened with its familiar creak and there stood Lou and Blanche wiping their hands on their aprons, preparing to give hugs.

"When did this happen?" asked Julia with a severe tone.

"At the first of spring," replied Blanche, stumped by Julia's terseness, "once the mud dried up."

Quickly, Lou stepped forward enveloping Julia in a hug. She whispered harshly in her ear, "You be kind to Blanche. She's spent the past two weeks getting things ready for you."

When Lou released her, Julia forced a smile and remarked, "It sure is bright!"

Blanche relaxed a little, and laughed uneasily. "I wanted to surprise you. Maybe I shouldn't have turned them all on."

Julia allowed a sarcastic laugh and walked inside. She headed toward the stairs, throwing over her shoulder, "I'm just going to change and get washed up before dinner."

Blanche's voice followed, "Um, Julia, you should know. There have been other changes."

Julia stopped and without looking back, waited.

"We changed your room into a water closet. All your things got moved down the hall. Next to Alfred. My old room."

Julia headed upstairs, stomping and fuming as she went.

"How could this happen?" she thought. "My bedroom is now the bathroom? What's wrong with the outhouse? And if they did want inside plumbing, why not use Blanche's room?"

At the top of the stairs, she pushed open the door. There it was. The porcelain slap to her face.

Julia continued down the hall until she got to her new room. She held the knob for a moment and remembered when she looked forward to coming here. Back when she thought Blanche was her friend. But that was a long time ago.

Julia opened the door. The scene that greeted her was not what she expected. Her eyes scanned the room searching for her things, anything familiar. She felt anger rising in her throat. Hot tears sprang from her eyes when she tried to choke it down.

Where was her bed with the beautiful worn quilt that Mum made? What happened to her dresser?

A sudden panic swept over Julia. Her dresser had one drawer where she kept her secret treasures.

Julia spun on her heel and ran down the stairs and into the kitchen. Blanche and Lou turned when they heard her footsteps, but remained silent when they saw her anger.

"Where are all my things?" choked out Julia.

In a quiet, steady voice, Blanche answered, "In the shed. Everything can get changed back tomorrow."

Without another word, Julia slammed out of the house. She wanted to go to the barn and see Gert. She wanted something, even if it was just one thing, that had stayed the same.

Julia relaxed slightly when she pulled on the barn door. She felt its weight and a slight shudder as it opened. She inhaled deeply, taking in the scent of fresh hay and manure. Then, she exhaled, relieved. There was Gert, right where she'd always been.

As Julia was moving towards the cow, she heard voices outside. She turned to look when suddenly the doorway was filled by DJ and three other boys. She recognized the boys from school, but because they were older by a couple of years, she didn't really know them. The tallest and leanest was Jimmy Kimball. By his side was his younger brother, Davy, who was the exact opposite of Jimmy, short and stout. The third boy was Bobby Sullivan. Bobby was close in size to DJ but looked to be solid muscle and from all Julia had seen and heard around school, he was a boy no one messed with. They were all wearing

T-shirts and dungarees, still hot and sweaty after a day's worth of farm work.

Julie looked down and realized she was still wearing her school uniform. It was wrinkled and messy from the long ride home and she could feel the stains on her face after her not so happy return.

Perfect.

DJ interrupted her thoughts, "Hey, aren't you suppose to be at the house? I heard my Ma talking about some big dinner for your first night home."

"Not hungry," stated Julia, flatly.

In the background Davy was jabbing Jimmy in the ribs and whispering loudly, "Why don't we take her with us?" Unknown to Julia, Davy had always been a little sweet on her.

"I don't know, Dav, girls can be a lot of trouble. And they don't know how to keep their mouths shut!"

Davy persisted realizing this might be his only chance to gain Julia's favor.

"What's all the noise about?" demanded DJ, who was obviously the group's leader.

"Ah, Davy here wants Julia to come along," teased Jimmy, "he thinks after one night in his company she'll fall for him."

Davy's face turned scarlet and he was clearly hurt by his brother's betrayal.

"Sure, why not," decided DJ as he turned to leave, "Come on, Julia, if you want some real fun. Or," he threw over his shoulder, sarcastically," you can stay with your cow."

Without thinking, Julia began to follow. At the door she almost bumped into Bobby Sullivan, who as yet hadn't moved or spoken.

Bobby looked hard at Julia, trying to determine if this was a good idea and if not, could he risk defying DJ.

With a slight nod, Bobby moved aside and let Julia pass. He then took up the rear, closing the barn door behind them.

Silently, the boys moved into the early evening shadows. They cut through a small overgrown field and then circled around the frog pond to the opposite side. Then, one by one they disappeared from sight. Julia hadn't been to this side of their property since she was a young girl. She and Mum would come on warm spring days to catch pollywogs. They would bring two empty pickle jars and try to see who could catch the most. At the end of the afternoon, they would pour them back into the pond, laughing as the slippery creatures splashed into the murky water and sped away.

The boys were already pushing ahead through scrubby bushes and low hanging branches when Julia took one last glance at the sky. It was a dark night with no stars to be seen. There was only a sliver of moon dancing between the clouds.

"Come on," hissed DJ, "we can't wait on you forever!"

Julia squinted into the dark woods and resumed trailing the boys. The trees turned dense and she just barely sidestepped a thin branch snapping towards her face.

She felt Davy's hand on her elbow, "Stay close to me," he advised, "it gets confusing in here. I'll make sure you don't get lost."

Was he kidding? These were Julia's woods and she knew them like the back of her hand.

Julia tried to nonchalantly take her elbow back, but Davy wasn't about to let go. He had admired Julia for many years, so he held tight and firmly steered her ahead. Thankfully they didn't have far to go before they could duck through an opening in the trees and enter a small clearing.

Julia pulled her arm free and stepped away from Davy, then she looked around in unbelief. Filling the space was a shelter fashioned from a few large sheets of corrugated tin that had been overlapped to prevent cracks. This makeshift roof was mounted and nailed to four large posts that were set in the ground and had cross beams for stability. In the middle of it all was a conglomeration of tubes, coils, and a vat with a spigot. Off to one side, Julia saw turned over crates and some empty mason jars.

DJ walked over and lifted one of the crates. He took out an old lantern. After pumping the button on the side a few times, he reached into his pocket and pulled out a match. Flicking it with his thumbnail, the tip burst into flame and DJ slid it through a small hole at the base of the chimney to light the wick. He made some adjustments and soon the clearing was bathed in its soft glow.

Meanwhile, Jimmy had gone outside the circle to a pile of brush. He lifted the top layer, reached in and extracted a full Mason jar. The pale, almost clear liquid, sloshed inside its housing as Jimmy made his way back to the group. Davy took this opportunity to plod over to the stack of crates. He grabbed one and set it on its side. Then with a sweep of his pudgy hand, he gestured for Julia to sit. Slightly hesitant, she walked over and joined the other boys who were already settled. When Davy tried to park his ample bottom next to Julia she started to fall off the crate, but quickly caught herself. A side wards glance at Davy and she knew he was there to stay so reluctantly she decided to be content perched on the edge of the seat they were now sharing.

The boys looked on with anticipation as Jimmy snapped up the wire that locked a glass lid in place. He carefully removed it and with a slight tilt said, "Cheers!" and took the first sip.

Bobby's hand was already outstretched and reaching for the jar before Jimmy had even swallowed. The boys took turns until Julia felt the cool glass being placed in her hands.

"Go ahead, try it," encouraged Davy, "it's our best batch yet."

Julia wasn't sure she wanted to, but as soon as she saw DJ's face and a slight roll of his eyes, she made up her mind.

Without further hesitation, she put the glass lip to her mouth and swallowed a big gulp. The moonshine smelled like rubbing alcohol and she guessed this was probably what it tasted like. As it burned its way down her throat and hit her empty stomach, Julia gave a hoarse cough and tried not to sputter.

Disgusted, DJ admonished, "You sip, not chug. You'll make yourself sick."

Slowly lifting the jar in her hands, Julia tried again, this time taking only a couple small sips. Immediately a warmth began to envelope her mind. She suddenly felt relaxed and more than a little tipsy. When Julia started to sway from her perch on the wooden crate, DJ reached over to remove the jar still clenched in her hands. "That's enough for now," he reproved.

Davy placed a chubby mitt on DJ's wrist stopping him from taking the jar.

"Let her have some fun," he encouraged.

DJ slapped away Davy's hand and grabbed the jar from Julia. He looked hard in Davy's eyes and threatened, "This isn't the way, Davy. Let her be!"

Davy jumped up off his seat, flipping the box and dropping Julia to the hard ground.

Davy glared at DJ and snarled, "I don't know why you're acting so high and mighty. It's not like it's never happened before."

For the first time that night Bobby's voice was heard, "Shut your damn mouth, Davy! Julia's not like the other girls and you know it!"

Julia wanted to know what Bobby was talking about but her lips were too numb to form a question. So she continued sitting on the ground trying not to pass out.

Apparently her efforts failed. A while later she awoke to the sound of the boy's drunken laughter. She lifted her head off a bunched up grain sack and wondered how it got there.

When Julia tried to sit upright a searing bolt of pain shot through her head.

"Ow!" she groaned and held her temples with both hands. Her stomach began to roll and rebel against the hot poison she'd poured into it. She felt the burning determination of the liquid to return from where it had come. She quickly turned her head to the side and with one great heave, emptied her stomach. Then she let out a slight gasp, and slowly began to wipe her mouth on the sleeve of her once perfectly starched white blouse, the Kimball crest clearly displayed over the pocket.

Looking around the circle still awash in the lantern's glow, Julia saw mild concern on three of the boy's faces. The fourth face, DJ, was smirking.

"Did you have a nice nap?" he mocked.

Julia scowled and pulled herself upright. Thankfully her head had settled to a dull ache now that the moonshine had been expelled from her body. She looked over at the now empty

Mason jar and wondered how they could drink so much. She also wondered how often they came here.

She didn't have long to consider these thoughts. The boys all stood in unison and without a word, began to stack the crates and re-cover their stash with practiced efficiency.

Bobby, Jimmy, and Davy soundlessly walked off into the woods, retracing their steps along an almost imperceptible path.

DJ extinguished the light and put his hand on Julia's back, gently guiding her way. The others were far ahead when DJ stopped. Julia turned to face him. The alcohol hung heavy on his breath but almost all traces of intoxication were gone.

"You ok?" he asked, "Really ok?"

"Yeah, a little headache but I'll be fine," she replied.

"Look, Julia, I'm sorry about you getting sick. It's just," DJ shifted uncomfortably, "well, back at the barn, you looked like you needed to get away".

Julia thought for a second before answering. "I did. Thanks for letting me come along." Again, Julia paused before asking, "Oh, and what was going on with Davy?"

"Davy's a pig," DJ remarked hotly, "Just stay away from him!"

"Ok," said Julia without argument, surprised at DJ's concern. Maybe tomorrow her head would be in better shape. Then she could contemplate the things Davy had said and done.

When they reached the edge of the woods DJ gave Julia a sideways glance. He could see she was fine. "You can join us again," he offered, "if you need to."

Julia was surprised and began to thank him, but DJ had already disappeared into the dark. She squinted her eyes and could barely make out his shadowy figure moving swiftly to catch up to the distant shapes on the other side of the pond.

Julia began to pick her way home. She had no idea how long they'd been out there, but looking at the sky she knew it had to be well past midnight.

Julia skirted the water's edge and began to climb the gentle slope leading to the barn. She followed the well-worn path to the front yard which was still brightly lit.

Julia felt her stomach sink and it was not residual effects from her earlier indulgence. She crept across the yard and tried to quietly sneak in through the kitchen. She was too tired to face Blanche. All she wanted was to climb into bed, even if it wasn't the one she longed for.

Julia closed the back door with a soft push. She tip toed through the dark kitchen and entered the main hallway. The only light on was a small glass lamp on a side table in the living room. Blanche was sitting in the rocker nearby, strain etched across her face. Sensing movement, she turned her head slightly in Julia's direction. Quietly, Blanche beckoned.

"Julia, please sit with me."

Julia approached. She felt self-conscious. She didn't have to look down to know that her shirt was no longer pristine white. Dirt and pine needles clung to her skirt betraying her activities. She only hoped she could remain standing in the doorway. Maybe then her breath would escape detection.

Blanche didn't push. "I'm relieved you came home. I was worried about you."

Julia wanted to answer cruelly, but she saw a thin tear streak down Blanche's cheek. Blanche quickly brushed it aside and continued in a level voice, "Your Dad's not here. He's been away a lot. And when he's gone he depends on me to keep things in running order. I would appreciate it if you'd be to meals on time. I also expect you to make your whereabouts known." Blanche took a quick breath. Her voice wavered slightly as she continued, "I can't allow you to run off and not know where you're going."

Julia stiffened. She felt the familiar anger rising in her chest. But only wanting the day to end, she asked tersely, "Is that all?"

"Yes, for now," Blanche replied wearily. "We'll talk more in the morning."

Before Blanche could finish her sentence, Julia was out of the room and half-way up the stairs. She passed her old room and continued down the hall. She stood in front of the door to what was now her room. Julia let out a heavy sigh and pushed it open. A soft glow surrounded a bedside lamp that illuminated her new ivory white wrought iron bed. Spread on top was Mum's quilt; Julia's hand went to her mouth. She went to the bedside and lovingly ran her fingers across the soft squares of familiar fabric.

Julia allowed her eyes to wander around the room. The first thing she noticed were the windows; graced with Irish lace curtains that flowed to the tops of the baseboards. Spread out across the floor was an oval shaped rug woven in an intricate pattern of flowers and vines. Julia slipped off her shoes and ran her feet through the plush pile. Turning, she walked over to the new bureau pushed against the opposite wall. Like the bed, it was bright, ivory white. Julia ran her fingers across the top. It was perfectly smooth, not a single chip or dent. The oval mirror attached at the back framed Julia's face. She was shocked to see the rag-tag girl that looked back at her. Glancing down at her filthy hands and clothes, Julia knew that without a good scrubbing she could never climb into her new bed with its crisp, clean sheets.

A light breeze blew through the open window stirring the lace curtains. Julia felt a presence standing in the doorway. Julia turned and saw Blanche. At the same time they both cried, "I'm so sorry!"

Blanche's composure crumbled and tears of relief began to flow freely. She had always seemed so strong and in control that Julia stared in amazement.

Julia took a tentative step forward but Blanche held up her hand. "If you want...go ahead and get cleaned up. You'll feel better."

Julia nodded, "Ok, thanks." She slipped past Blanche and padded down the hall.

This time when Julia got to the door, she gave it a gentle push and entered the bathroom. Taking a good look she marveled at its beauty. The floor was tiled in black and white squares that felt cool on the bottoms of her feet. And the claw foot tub was painted pale blue with white porcelain knobs marked with crisp black lettering, HOT and COLD. Julia reached over and firmly turned them on. The pipes groaned and shook slightly until water burst from the faucet and the tub began to fill. As the water ran, Julia searched for towels. There was a large cupboard with a granite countertop and sink. The granite was gray with white speckles and had a deep well carved into the center that was adorned with another set of faucets identical to those on the tub. Off to the side sat a fancy pink tin covered with a flowery design and French writing.

Julia scrunched up her nose as she tried to make out the words. She had just begun her French studies so most of it was a mystery. But there was one thing she understood and that was the illustration of a lady soaked in bubbles. Julia pried off the lid. Her nose was greeted with the scent of mint and lavender. She took the tin to the now almost filled tub and started to pour. She wasn't sure how much to add, but felt sure she'd "just know" when it was enough. Quickly, bubbles began to form and soon the bath was ready.

Julia turned the knobs and with a mournful sigh, the water stopped. She peeled her clothes off and discarded them on the floor next to the tub. Slowly, she eased into the bath and slide down into the dense layers of foam. She closed her eyes and inhaled deeply, allowing the strain of the day to disappear. There she languished until the water became unbearably cold. Julia looked down at the gray pool she was sitting in, now void of bubbles, and pulled the plug. She carefully stepped out onto the cool tile and found a thick towel in one of the cupboard drawers. After drying off, she wrapped it around her slim figure and hurried down the hall to her room, leaving damp footprints behind.

Shutting her bedroom door behind her, Julia went to get ready for sleep. That was when she discovered a nightgown laid out on the bed. She lifted it by the straps and gazed at its beauty. It was soft cotton with tiny purple rosebuds and eyelet lace trim. She allowed her towel to fall to the floor and slipped it on. Then she went to the oval mirror to admire herself. She was about to start searching for a brush when she noticed a note from Blanche on top of the dresser:

Julia,

This bureau has a special feature. Open the center drawer and feel inside. There is a small latch. Push it aside.

Blanche

"Ok," thought Julia, not really believing there could be anything all that special.

The center drawer slid open easily and Julia reached in. She moved her fingers along its underside until she felt a small bump. Taking her index finger, she gently pushed until she felt it move. She heard a soft "pop" and simultaneously a lid in the top flew open revealing a hidden compartment. Julia smiled with delight. She looked in and saw there was a treasure already stashed inside. Carefully, Julia lifted out a velvet box. She cracked the lid open and on a bed of silk was a silver hair comb encrusted with blue stones and very stylish. Julia set the box down on the dresser top and gathered up her hair to try it out. It was a stunning piece of jewelry and Julia had fun assessing its beauty from every vantage point. Finally, she placed it back in its box. The lid squeaked as it snapped shut and she returned it to its hiding place. Once her "treasure" was safely tucked away, Julia gently pressed the on top of the dresser panel until she heard a soft "click". It was amazing! She couldn't detect even the slightest irregularity on the bureau's surface. There was nothing to betray the compartments existence.

By now Julia was exhausted. Her busy day had caught up to her, so she shuffled over to her bed and pulling back the covers, climbed in. Then, she reached over to turn down the lamp. As she did, she took one last look out the window. The clouds from earlier on remained and stubbornly darkened the now early morning sky. Julia frowned slightly, turned on her side and fell asleep.

The next morning, Julia woke to the sound of rain beating on the tin roof. She lay in bed for a few moments listening to its steady rhythm, giving her mind time to clear. She peeked her head out from under the covers and remembered she was home. Looking around, she became reacquainted with her new room. Slowly, she pushed off her covers and sat on the edge of the bed. The dull ache in her head had stayed with her through the night and was now accompanied by a thick, fuzzy taste in her mouth. She tried swallowing a couple times but still it remained.

Slowly, Julia stood and shuffled to the wardrobe. She tugged on the door handles, but the doors didn't stick like her old one and she nearly fell backward and onto the floor when they flew open with ease. Regaining her balance, she peered inside and considered her choices. She finally settled on a pale yellow frock. Once she was dressed, Julia sat at the vanity and carefully plaited her hair. Even tugging the strands into place made her head throb . Her final act was to wrap the braid in a circle at the nape of her neck and secure it with pins.

Then, Julia headed downstairs thankful for the gray, dreary day. Her eyes felt especially sensitive to the light. When Julia reached the bottom of the stairs, the smell of sizzling bacon hung in the air. That was when she noticed the persistent ache in her belly. She had no idea how late in the day it was, but she hoped breakfast would still be available.

Julia turned the corner and entered the kitchen. The sight of Lou placing a heaping spoonful of scrambled eggs on a plate already occupied by thick slices of toast and bacon made Julia smile. She sat at the heavy table where a napkin, fork, knife and a glass of tomato juice waited. Lou set the steaming plate in front of Julia and warned, "Don't gulp it down, eat slowly so your stomach stays settled!"

Julia picked up her fork and fought the urge to cram a huge bite of food into her mouth. It tasted so good! Then she began to wash it down with a gulp of tomato juice.

"Ugh, what is this, Lou?" questioned Julia.

"Like it?" chuckled Lou, "it's an old family recipe to cure a hang- over."

"Hang-over? What's that?"

"What you've got," answered Lou. "How's your head feeling this morning?"

"A little thick and hurts," replied Julia, sheepishly.

"Ah," said Lou, "and your mouth? Is that a little fuzzy? And dry, too?"

"Maybe a little."

"Congratulations, my girl," said Lou, "you've got your first hang-over."

Julia thought Lou was far more amused at her malady than was appropriate. So ignoring Lou's continued chuckles, Julia took another swig of her juice. It had a hot, spicy taste she didn't recognize and she wasn't about to ask why it seemed so slimy. The good thing, was that her stomach seemed to be responding well to whatever it was and the heaviness in her head was lifting. By the time Julia folded her napkin and placed it on the table she felt much better.

Julia pushed back her chair and walked to the counter. As she was placing her dirty dishes in the kitchen sink she heard the back door squeak open.

"Hey, Ma," DJ hollered toward the open pantry door where Lou was wiping down shelves. "Pa needs me and Billy to go into town and get some things at the feed store. You need anything?"

"Hold on," Lou yelled back.

A few seconds later Lou appeared with a damp rag in her hand and a ball of dust on her head. Julia tried to stifle a laugh, but DJ didn't hold back.

"Is that the latest fashion?" he mocked.

"What," asked Lou, as she looked herself over. The ball of fluff fell to the floor when she looked down at her skirt. "Oh, you," she scolded and taking the damp rag, swatted at DJ's arm.

DJ feigned pain and pretended to hold his arm protectively.

"Ok, ok," reproved Lou, "what is it you came for?"

"Just came to see if you need anything in town."

"I do, as a matter of fact. Wait here while I go get Blanche's list."

When Lou left, the room became uncomfortably quiet. Julia pretended to fuss with the dishes, unsure what to say, if anything.

Meanwhile, DJ went to a silver tin in the pantry and came out with a large oatmeal cookie. Taking a bite he asked, "Just get up?"

"A little bit ago."

"How're you feeling?"

"Fine now. Lou gave me some awful tomato juice concoction – said it was a family recipe."

DJ groaned and wiped the cookie crumbs from his mouth with the edge of his sleeve.

"Yeah, awful stuff," he replied, "but it works."

"What's in it anyways?" asked Julia.

"You don't want to know. It will make you sick!"

She had a feeling he was right and didn't press on.

"Got it," came Lou's voice from the hall, followed by her footsteps. She bustled through the doorway and passing DJ's waiting hand, gave the list to Julia.

"Now Julia," Lou began, "take this to the Mountainside and while Maggie's filling it I want you to stop over to Peg's place. She just finished up some mending for Blanche."

"Ok, Lou," said Julia, "Is that all?"

"That should do it."

Julia turned and looked at the spot where DJ had been standing.

"Better hurry up or those boys will leave without you."

Without hesitation, Julia ran outside to where the truck was parked. She got there just as DJ was slipping into first gear. Grabbing for the handle, Julia tugged the door open and jumped in next to Billy. The truck began to move as she was pulling it shut.

"Hey, you made it," said Billy, "DJ bet me you'd still be in the kitchen talking while we drove off."

"Thanks for waiting," Julia responded sarcastically.

It was an uneventful drive to town. The boy's conversation centered around which car they'd most like to own, and where they'd go if they actually had one.

Meanwhile, Julia laid back her head, closed her eyes and listened to the steady drumming of the rain and rhythmic creak of the wiper blade. The drive was familiar and even though she wasn't looking, Julia could tell where they were just from the bumps in the road and rounded curves. She finally looked up when she felt the truck come to an abrupt stop. DJ was parked in front of the Mountainside, which was only one block down from the feed store.

Billy groaned, then mumbled something under his breath. "Don't worry," admonished DJ, "I can handle those jerks!"

Julia looked in the direction of the feed store and saw what she suspected was the cause of Billy's discomfort. Standing on the raised porch outside its double doors were Wally, Frank Jr. and Phil. The three boys were about the same age as DJ and had built a reputation for being trouble makers.

Wally Barnett was nephew to George Barnett. While his surly nature could easily have made him George's son, he was taxed with the burden of being born to Hank, George's younger brother. Hank was a quiet man of modest ambitions. He had chosen to stay in his hometown and marry his childhood sweetheart shortly after completing high school. Together they were raising their three sons while running the supply store. Wally was the youngest of the three boys and a brute. He'd spent his youth trying to keep pace with his older brothers, loading and unloading pallets on his father's dock. It was at this time that his body had developed into a solid mass of muscle. It was also at this time that he honed his skills as a deceiver. You see, Wally was a gifted liar. As a boy he discovered his ability to weave falsehoods with truth. It was later when he realized people's willingness to believe him. The result was a dangerous combination of brawn and arrogance.

On the other hand, Frank's family was new to the area. They settled in the farm community because of a promotion his father received from the railroad. When the line was extended up through the mountains of Vermont and New Hampshire, an engineer's position was offered to Frank Sr. Knowing it could lead to better things, he took it. His wife, four daughters and only son moved from Boston's suburbs to the small rural town nestled in the mountains far away from high society. Frank Jr.'s mother, Clara, thought the town and its people were beneath her, and all of her children had learned to feel the same. But, at the urging of her husband, Clara reluctantly sought to ingratiate herself to any family of means in the area. She made a few visits to the Kelly farm shortly after their arrival. But once Clara realized the political and social connections the Barnetts had in Concord, she deemed her time better spent establishing a friendship with George and his wife, Olivia.

Now Clara was not a woman who trusted good fortune to fall in her lap. And so it was, that even while the children were still in grade school, Clara had an idea. She decided that someday Frank Jr. and Abigail Barnett should marry. It had started as a daydream, the idle musings of an overindulged woman with grand aspirations and too much time on her hands. Little by little her dream became an obsession. Clara was convinced that Frank Jr. and Abigail's betrothal was meant to be. Clara's delusion was so convincing that Frank's sisters believed it and relentlessly pursued a friendship with Abigail. They were sure the girl's future was tied to their brother. Then they would have introductions into the social circles they so desperately longed for. As for Frank Jr., it took very little to convince him that only one young lady was worthy of his affections. Furthermore, he felt justified using any means necessary to dissuade the attentions of any other suitor.

The third crony was Phil. Phil was the only son of John and Sara Keaton. Both his parents were quite young and immature when they married. While still newlyweds, Sara discovered she was pregnant. The pregnancy was an annoyance, especially since she had already lost interest in her marriage. To add insult to a situation already destined for failure, Sara was overcome with nine months of morning sickness. When her small scrawny baby entered the world, no one was surprised to find that Sara did not have the temperament for motherhood. And to make matters worse, her baby boy suffered from colic. So one day in a fit of sleep deprived desperation, Sara shook the infant until he stopped crying. Satisfied she had done her best, and looking down at her now quiet son, Sara placed him in his cradle, packed her few belongings, and walked out the door without a single regret. She headed down the road to the south and it wasn't long before she hopped a ride to the next county. And from there, she just kept going.

Later that evening, John arrived home to peace and quiet. He closed the door behind him and called out to Sara, ready to receive her daily list of grievances. But there was only stillness. John knew immediately that she was gone. Sara's disappointment in him and their life was no secret.

John ran to the bedroom. His only concern now was for his son. When he saw the small baby resting safely in his cradle, John let out a sigh of relief. But when he picked Phil up, he knew something was terribly wrong. The baby was listless, and his eyes were dull and unseeing. John bundled the babe and rushed to Doc Warner's house. After a complete examination, Doc had the sad task of informing John that his son had suffered a head trauma. What this meant was that Phil's body would grow normally. Physically he would be able to keep up with the other children. But his mental capabilities had been altered and academically he would be slow. He would always fall short of his peers.

John was not a man of means, but he was a hard worker and made enough to rent his little house in town. It wasn't long before he attracted the attention of Peggy Sullivan. She was a sweet girl. Out of her prime but handy with a needle. With no other prospects in sight, Peggy agreed to move in with John and care for Phil. A couple years later, when Phil was a toddler and only knew Peggy to be his mother, they received news about Sara. She had made her way to New Orleans and had been supporting herself pleasuring men at a seedy brothel off Bourbon St. One night a patron caught her rifling through his pockets when she thought he was asleep. The man reached down the side of the bed and into his boot. He pulled out a knife and threw just as Sara was turning toward him. The last thing Sara saw was the hilt of his knife sticking out of her belly and blood beginning to flow down her front and onto the floor.

The news of Sara's death set John free, and allowed him to marry Peg. While theirs was not a passionate relationship, it satisfied their needs. For a while. In his past, John had been known to take a drink. But now disappointed in a life gone wrong, his quiet indulgence began to give way to excess. Alcohol fanned the flames of self-pity, and that soon gave way to anger. Now, both Peg and Phil were subjected to John's nightly beatings. Peg became withdrawn and even quieter. She had no friends and her only contact with the local ladies was when she took in their mending and alterations.

As for Phil, he lived in a state of confusion. He lacked the mental capacity to understand his father's actions and longed for the only mother he'd ever known to protect him. So, by the time he was entering High School, he had begun to follow in his father's footsteps. Phil was big and strong and destructive. He was the perfect dupe for Frank Jr. and Wally to mold and use.

∞

Julia felt an elbow in her side. "What?" she cried, and looked at Billy.

He shook his head slightly, sighed and repeated, "We'll meet you back here when you're done."

"Ok," she answered and reached for the door handle. She almost had her fingers wrapped around it when it was pulled from her grasp. The door swung open.

"Hi, Julia, let me help you."

Julia scowled. There was Davy. He was standing outside the truck looking like a puppy caught in the rain. His hand hung in mid-air as he waited to assist her.

Julia willed herself not to make eye contact. She swung her legs to the side and with a little hop, managed to avoid the large puddle Davy was standing in. Without a word, she purposefully headed up the stairs to the Mountainside leaving Davy to shut the truck door.

When Julia walked inside the Inn, the scent of damp wood filled her nostrils. It was quickly followed by the aroma of sugary pastry. Julia exhaled and went to the display case to admire Maggie's pies. They were baked fresh every couple of days and each bite justified their blue ribbon legacy. Her gaze lingered over each perfectly browned crust and she silently thanked God for blueberry season. Julia became aware of a soft drumming. She glanced up and saw Maggie's frown.

"Julia, I haven't got all day." Maggie's patience had given out. "What will you be needing?"

Handing over Blanche's list, Julia wondered to the bolts of fabric. Her eyes were drawn to a deep emerald velvet. She ran her hand over the surface, watching it change from light to dark green.

"I can tell Blanche you like it," said Maggie while she began to pull items from the shelves behind her, "She was in the other day pulling swatches for your coming out."

"My coming where?" questioned Julia. She could feel her body tense and she waited for an explanation. She was fairly certain she wasn't going to like it.

"Oh, sweetie," soothed Maggie, "Didn't Blanche tell you? It's probably the most exciting and important spring of your life. For girls like you," she continued, "it's when you'll be introduced into society. You'll have a chance to meet other young ladies and gentlemen from similar backgrounds." Maggie's face took on a dreamy look, "There will be parties, and dances. All the girls will be in beautiful gowns and the boys in tuxedos."

"Ok," thought Julia, to herself, "That doesn't sound too bad."

"Of course," Maggie rattled on, "You'll spend the fall preparing."

"Preparing?" queried Julia.

"Yes, sweetie, preparing," Maggie paused a moment, waiting for some sign that Julia knew what she was referring to. The blank stare on Julia's face said it all.

Maggie explained, "You'll have lessons, sweetie. Dance lessons, and etiquette. You'll learn how to walk and sit and talk."

"Please stop, Maggie," said Julia, "I already know how to do those things."

A wide grin spread across Maggie's round face. "Of course you do, sweetie!" But you're not going to a barn dance, and these aren't the sons and daughters of country farmers." Maggie's tone became very serious, "Julia, you're going to be introduced to very wealthy families. These people aren't like all of us," she said with a sweeping motion, as if to include the small town and all the surrounding countryside. "You'll be meeting the children of bank presidents, politicians and financiers."

Maggie's words hung heavy in the air. Their meaning becoming clear. The girls at Kimball had talked about the big spring season. She could even vaguely remember Izzy saying something concerning boys and opportunities. But most of it went unnoticed since Julia never connected it to herself.

"Oh, my," uttered Julia. The material fell from her fingers. Quietly, she lifted her box of dry goods from off the counter and headed to the door. She nudged the door open with her hip and passed Davy who was waiting on the porch.

Julia headed to the back of the truck and was only jolted out of her thoughts when she heard yelling from down the street. She turned and looked to where the commotion was coming from. In front the feed store she could just make out two boys fighting.

Davy came up behind her and stated, "It's just DJ and Wally going at it again."

DJ and Wally. Julia heard the words but the only thing that registered was DJ was in a fight. Hurriedly, she tossed the box in the back of the truck and began running to where a small group was beginning to gather. As she neared, she saw Billy off to the side lying in the mud. Frank Jr. stood over him. Watching.

Julia joined the on-lookers. In the center of the now formed circle, Wally was taking swings at DJ and trying to dodge blows. Despite the obvious advantage Wally held in size and guile, DJ was clearly a more skilled fighter.

Suddenly, Hank stormed through the supply store's double doors with a wooden broom in his hands. The crowd parted and he began to hit the fighters on their backs while yelling, "Move it along! Break it up!"

The throng of spectators became uneasy and started to slowly shuffle off. It was as if they couldn't quite pull themselves away until the final blow had been delivered.

Hank continued to stand in the middle of the street yelling and swinging his broom at the crowd in a sweeping motion, pushing them away in all directions.

Finally, the two boys parted. Wally had a black eye, bloody lip, and was holding his side. DJ backed away, never taking his eyes off Wally. His knuckles were bleeding and a knot was slowly beginning to sprout on his forehead.

Meanwhile, Frank Jr. stood sneering over Billy. He gave him a final kick in the side before moving off, taking Phil in tow. As the walked past Wally, he spit blood at DJ's feet. Then, he turned and fell in with the other two. As Julia watched them walk off, she saw Phil casually toss a block of wood behind a barrel on the side of the feed store.

She turned her attention back to DJ and Billy, and rushing over asked, "Are you ok? What was that all about?"

DJ ignored her questions and went to the dock. The new buckets along with some bags of feed were waiting. With a soft grunt, DJ threw a bag over his shoulder. He started to the truck. Julia turned to Billy. He was on his feet with Davy at his side. With obvious pain, he went to the dock and began helping DJ load the truck.

Julia looked at Davy questioningly. Glad for an opportunity to impress her, Davy began. "Don't worry, Julia, these guys are always at it." Davy could see he had her full attention and went on, "It's always the same story. Frank Jr. gets jealous. Doesn't want any other fellas getting close to Abigail. Especially a red-skin."

Shock registered on Julia's face. He continued, "He doesn't care that he's only half, you know, half Indian. As far as Frank's concerned, half or whole it's all the same thing. Personally," he said with an air of authority, "I think it's an excuse. He wants everyone to think she'd go for him, even if he didn't have competition."

Julia felt a pit in her stomach. Everyone knew Frank Jr. considered Abigail to be his girl. It had just never occurred to her that Abigail might have feelings for someone else. Someone like DJ. And now it was clear that he had feelings for her, also.

The gray day had taken its toll and Julia was ready to go home. The boys were on their last trip, so she headed to the truck.

"Hey, Julia," Davy called after her, "there's a barn dance coming up. Maybe you'd want to go with me?"

Julia paused and looked over her shoulder, "I don't think so," she said wearily.

"That's ok, I'll just see you there."

Julia nodded, not really knowing if she intended to go.

"Hey, save me a dance," Davy called out, hopefully.

Julia nodded mechanically. She felt tired and just wanted to be home.

The ride back was quiet and filled with tension. At one point Billy began to complain. Something about Phil getting the drop on them, but DJ shut him up.

By the time they reached the farm, the knot on DJ's head was the size of a half-dollar and dark purple. Billy was pale. He was slow getting out of the truck and pain etched his face.

"Go to the cottage," commanded DJ, "I'll send Ma to wrap you up."

Billy didn't argue. Julia just stood watching as he began his slow and labored trek up the ridge.

Julia entered the kitchen as DJ was headed back out. Lou was at the kitchen sink drying her hands. Her forehead was creased with a frown. She threw down the towel and paused before heading out the door. "There's no reason to mention any of this to your folks."

"Ok, Lou."

"Ok." Lou hurried out, letting the back door slam behind her.

Julia stared at the box on the table. She was trying to decide if she should put everything away now or after a steamy bath. She looked down at her mud splattered clothes and ran her fingers through her wet, matted hair. There was one thing the previous night had taught her. A hot soak could wash away a world of tension. Her decision was made. The box remained untouched. Her footsteps echoed on the stairs. She would try to put the afternoon behind her.

7

A few weeks passed and Julia had quickly adopted an easy routine. She was no longer needed for work in the barns or for any of the farm chores. Don had DJ and Billy for that. He had also hired farm hands at the start of spring. A nice crew of men would arrive at dawn and leave at dusk. They had agreed to stay on until the fall harvest was brought in.

Instead, Julia helped Blanche and Lou around the house. There was always light dusting and cleaning to be done. But her favorite "chore" was spending time with Alfred. It was hard for her to believe he was already one and a half years old. Their time together was pure joy and seeing the world through a toddler's eyes made the farm new and wondrous. One of their favorite mornings would begin with a visit to Gert. Julia would watch while the patient cow endured Alfred's tugs, pokes and wet kisses. Then, when it was time to part, both he and Gert would wear sad eyes that begged for more time. Unmoved by their theatrics, Julia would swing her little brother onto her shoulders and together they would head up to the North pasture. When they got near Mum's headstone, Julia would set Alfred down amidst tall grasses and wild flowers. Alfred would play in the grass grabbing anything he could wrap his small fists around. Meanwhile, Julia would pick a pretty bouquet. With deft fingers, she would weave wreaths for Mum and baby Will.

Part of her afternoons were spent at the piano. Julia was expected to practice for an hour each day. She was a gifted musician and thoroughly enjoyed each exercise. Alfred would sit by her side and try to catch her fingers as they danced across the keys. When their time was up Blanche would take Alfred upstairs for his nap.

Julia was also required to sit and read quietly. Blanche had compiled a stack of books for her. She said they were titles every well-rounded young lady should be familiar with. At present she was trying to make her way through Melville's, "Moby Dick". Julia thought it a dry read. Each afternoon she tried to make her mind track and care just a little about Ahab's plight but instead she found herself easily distracted. She would sit by the window and hear the men outside talking. Or the truck pulling into the driveway. Each time she strained her ear in hopes of hearing DJ's voice. She knew it was foolish. Why should she care what her was up to? Or what he was doing? Why did it matter to her? He cared for Abigail. Enough so that he was willing to fight Frank Jr. for her. And though she had promised herself to never drink moonshine again, there was a part of her that hoped one evening she'd be invited to go along. But so far, she'd only caught glimpses of him during the day. And he was never looking her way.

Julia sat at the piano listening to the steady patter of a light summer rain. It had begun early that morning and its monotonous rhythm was making her stir crazy. She was trying to play loud and drown out its beat when a rap on the door came to her rescue. She jumped to answer it, almost knocking over the bench as she ran. Sheet music was left fluttering across the floor.

The front door was slightly ajar with only a sliver of face peeking through.

"Hey, Julia," greeted Billy, "Just the person I wanted to see."

"What do you need?" she asked.

"I'm heading over to Max's. You want to come along?"

Julia gave a quick look over her shoulder. Seeing no one to stop her, she pushed through the doorway and made her escape.

The drive to Max's studio didn't take long and before she knew it, they were pulling into the narrow driveway that led to the Oakes. Billy came often enough now that he no longer needed to ring the bell. So after a quick run from the truck, they found themselves standing just inside the entrance.

Julia felt wet drops running down her cheeks and hanging from her lashes. She gave her head a quick shake and sprayed Billy with water.

"Hey," he cried, wiping his face.

"Sorry," she laughed, "I didn't put my hair up today."

"That's ok," he said, "I like it better down." Billy grabbed her hand, "Come on," and he led Julia to an empty chair. "Sit here while I get set up."

Obediently, Julia sat. It was actually more like perching since the chair only had a small round back and seat.

A few minutes later, Billy returned. He had a piece of deep gold fabric thrown over his shoulder, a large pad of paper, and a few sticks of charcoal. He set the pad on a stool opposite Julia. Then, taking the fabric, he began to drape it over her shoulder and pull it across her chest. For a moment she felt self-conscious.

But Billy was so busy fussing and pushing folds into place, she might as well have been a dinette receiving a tablecloth.

Once satisfied, he instructed, "Don't move."

Billy picked up his pad and a stick of charcoal, positioned himself on the stool and began to draw.

For the longest time his face was scrunched up in deep concentration. And every once in a while he would let out a quiet sigh of satisfaction.

At first, he worked quickly, drawing in big, sweeping strokes and fast movements. He'd pause, flip the page and start again. And again. Finally, everything slowed down. His lines became more deliberate. The crease between his brows deepened and he worked on one page for close to an hour.

Julia felt tiny cramps beginning to form in her shoulders and neck. Not to mention the numbness that was setting into her buttocks.

"Done!" cried Billy, with satisfaction.

Julia didn't move. She wasn't sure if she was supposed to or if her body would even allow it.

"Come over, come see it and tell me what you think."

First, Julia gave her feet a little shake. When that didn't restore feeling, she banged them on the floor a couple times. They still felt tingly but at least she was able to slide off the chair and walk over to where Billy was sitting. She circled behind him and looked over his shoulder at the drawing. Julia's mouth fell open, but words wouldn't come out.

"Oh, come on, Julia. What do you think? It's not that bad… Right?" Billy pushed.

"Billy, I don't know what to say," exclaimed Julia, admiringly. "This is beautiful!"

Billy looked doubtful and a little anxious.

"Really, I mean it," she assured, "I've never known anyone who can draw like this."

"Thanks!" he said, obviously relieved and flattered.

"Can I see the others?"

"Oh, sure," Billy replied, "but they're just gestures – quick sketches to get me warmed up."

He opened the pad and flipped through page by page. At first the drawings were unorganized with thick lines and wild movements. But as they progressed, each stroke became more controlled and purposeful, until the final sketch.

"Now I'm ready to paint you," he announced.

"What?"

"Not today. There's no time, but definitely next time it rains."

"Absolutely!" rang a voice from the back of the studio.

They turned their heads in unison to see Max bounding toward them.

"You came back!" he cried, "I knew she would," was his conspiratorial comment in a loud aside to Billy, "Ok, let me see it."

Billy held the picture up for Max to view. Max's finger rested under his chin while his eyes moved across the paper.

"Nice work, you're improving."

Max paused before the sketch one moment more, then took his finger and pointed to Julia's hair.

"Right here … you see it? This line. This is where you lost it. If you curve it back into her body, the line will keep your eye in the picture. As it is, it leads the viewer out. They're gone … you see?" Max prodded.

"Yes," said Billy, "I'll fix that when I paint her."

"Good," approved Max, "very good."

While they were studying Billy's drawing, a quiet young woman entered the studio through the same back door Max had used. She set down a tray filled with deep purple grapes and fat, juicy strawberries alongside a pale yellow block of cheese and a small loaf of bread. Next to the tray was a tall, thin bottle with a slender neck and four glasses. She carefully pulled a stubborn cork out of the bottle's opening and began to pour a dark red liquid into each glass. When she was done, she muscled the cork back into place, took one of the glasses and left.

"Come, come," entreated Max, taking Julia's hand.

Billy carefully closed his pad and set it against the stool. Then he followed the pair over to the table. Max was already popping grapes into his mouth while beginning to slice off chunks of cheese. He handed them each a glass of wine, nodded in approval, and began to drink.

Julia watched Billy take a small gulp from his glass. It was clear he'd had it before. He and Max continued to dig into the snacks while Julia raised her glass and sniffed. It had an almost fruity smell. It reminded her of elderberries, but fermented. Hesitantly, she took a little sip. The dry, slightly bitter flavor made her nose scrunch. She had expected it to be sweet. Max and Billy were engrossed in their conversation. They were discussing how to best carry out his painting of her. Julia tried another taste. This time she rather liked it, now that she knew what to expect.

Billy paused mid-sentence, grabbed a chunk of bread and wedge of cheese. "Here, Julia, eat these," he commanded.

Julia reached out and took the food. It looked quite nice, but why was Billy so emphatic? Why MUST she eat the bread and cheese?

Billy could see her annoyance and explained. "You need to have some food in your stomach if you're going to drink alcohol."

"Alcohol, this is alcohol?"

"Don't worry, dear Julia," Max soothed. "I have cases of Elderberry wine hidden in my cellar. Prohibition doesn't understand an artist's need. Wine is the lubrication for inspiration!"

"Look," said Billy, "I can't bring you back home drunk. Ma really gave it to DJ last time. This is wine, you nibble and you sip. Understand?"

"Yes," replied Julia, meekly.

So she stood, snacking on cheese and fruit while dutifully sipping her wine. All the while she wondered how much Billy knew of her excursion into the woods.

By afternoon's end, the tray had only a few crumbs and stems and the bottle of wine was empty. The three were relaxed and Max was discussing how Billy could bring out the gold flecks in Julia's eyes. At the back of the room a creak and flutter of movement caught their attention. The young woman was back and softly gliding to Max's side. In a hushed tone she spoke in his ear and then left as quietly as she had come.

"Sorry, folks, but I have to break this up," related Max. "I was just reminded of an evening engagement and I must get ready."

Max stood to leave. He turned to Julia and in one swift motion, took her hand, kissed it and returned it to her side.

"When you come back, he stated, "I would still like to paint you."

Turning slightly towards Billy, he encouraged, "Keep working. You're coming along beautifully."

And then Max was gone.

Julia giggled. She liked Max, but didn't know what to make of him. She'd never met anyone like him before.

The ride back to the farm was quiet. Billy wore a mask of concentration and Julia was shaking off the lingering effects of the wine. When they arrived, Billy left her to go start chores in the barn and Julia went inside to help Lou get dinner on the table.

That evening after their meal was finished, Julia sat on the porch swing. She listened as the night came alive. The rain had tapered off and the sky was beginning to clear. Off in the distance the horizon was an orange blaze, wearing a cap of gray. Bright rays reached up, clearing the path for night's dark expanse. A light breeze began to stir. Julia sighed contentedly and watched the hills darken. She turned her ear to the chorus from the pond. Its serenade was accompanied by the splatter of fat drops, finally released from leaves pregnant with the day's rain. The gentle motion of the porch swing felt like a song. A familiar rhythm waiting for lyrics.

"Look at all those stars."

She hadn't even heard him drive up. Julia lifted her eyes. Above the final remnants of wispy gray clouds, was a sky dotted with light.

She closed her eyes and leaned in for a kiss. Just a soft peck on her forehead.

"Hi, Dad," said Julia, with a smile.

Wordlessly, Will sank into the space next to Julia. He leaned back and allowed his body to relax in the safety of home.

They sat, silently rocking.

It was a while later when Blanche joined them. The kitchen had been tidied up and Alfred was asleep in his crib.

When Blanche saw Will, her eyes softened. He'd been gone for a few weeks and she'd missed him terribly. Will stood slowly. In two steps the distance between them evaporated. His arms enveloped her. When Blanche tilted her face to receive his kiss, an involuntary gasp escaped her lips. Will's mouth pressed harder, his pent-up desire set free. His fingertips dug at the back of her dress, pressing through the thin fabric in search of flesh.

They suspended the moment in time, then reluctantly, parted. The porch light betrayed the blush in Blanche's cheeks.

Will took a moment to catch his breath. "We'll be going in now, Julia." His voice was low and husky, "You'll close up and turn off the lights?"

"Sure," said Julia, happy to have Dad home.

She continued rocking and gazing at the stars. She knew wherever she went, the constellations would be the same. But here, on the farm, they felt familiar.

These would always be hers!

The next morning, Blanche came down to breakfast bursting with energy. Julia was sitting at the table. She stuffed the last bite of toast into her mouth and washed it down with a gulp of fresh milk.

Blanche frowned at the display and announced, "Today you and I are going to see Peg."

Julia swallowed hard. "Why do we need to see Peg?"

"It's time to start planning. You'll be needing gowns, lawn dresses, capes, gloves and hats. Oh, and slippers! You'll have to have slippers," stated Blanche. "Next spring is very important. Not just for you, but for your Dad. You'll be representing the family."

"I know," replied Julia, flatly, "Maggie already told me. I'll be coming out."

"You'll be introduced to society," Blanche corrected. "This is the season that tells the world you are now a young woman. A lady."

Julia wrinkled her nose. "If I'm living on the farm, why do I have to do all this stuff?"

Blanche explained calmly, "Because you may not always be living on this farm. Julia, you are extremely bright. You are capable of attending a university and earning a degree. Do you know what that means?" pressed Blanche.

Julia shook her head, "No."

"It means you can be and do anything you want." Blanche pressed on, "You won't have to wait for a man's permission. You can control you own destiny."

"Destiny? Blanche, Maggie said I'll be going to parties and dances."

"Yes," Blanche chuckled, "that will be part of it. But those parties aren't just so you can have a good time," she continued, seriously, "You'll be given opportunities. Meet people that have influence. People that can help you someday."

Blanche brought her plate to the table and sat near Julia. She cut her toast in half and gently spread it with a thin layer of butter. Taking a small bite, she calmly chewed and swallowed.

"A lady never rushes," she instructed, "at anything. Now, take your dishes to the sink and go get ready. We leave in half an hour."

∽

"Ouch!" Julia cried. Peg was busily pinning a brown paper pattern at her shoulders and sides.

"If you'd hold still, I wouldn't stick you," reproved Peg.

Julia sighed heavily, "Are you almost done?"

"Nearly. Sooner if you stop moving."

Julia tried to stand still. She was so bored! Even reading Melville was more pleasurable than this. They had arrived at Peg's late in the morning and it was now mid-afternoon. Blanche had brought pictures and fabric swatches to show Peg what she wanted. At first, Julia had fun looking at all the drawings of the different dresses and capes. It was hard for her to believe there would be enough occasions to wear them all, but Blanche was adamant. None would go unworn.

"Stand-up straight," Peg's voice broke through her thoughts.

Ugh! Julia was trying to ignore the growing ache in her belly. It was alerting her that she had missed a meal. She pulled up her shoulders and stared straight ahead. She thought, "Maybe if I follow the pattern in the wallpaper, I won't notice my stomach grumbling and the ache in my feet." Her eyes picked up the trail of vines as they wove across the wall with small leaves dispersed throughout. That was when she began to see the patches. Most were rather small, a little larger than the size of her fist. But one looked as if it could swallow a lamp whole. Funny, she thought, whoever had done the mending was very good. If she hadn't been staring directly at those spots for so long, she never would have noticed.

"Ow!" cried Julia. She looked down at Peg accusingly. Peg was busily working, avoiding Julia's eyes. If she didn't know better, Julia would have thought that Peg had stuck her on purpose.

Peg slid one more pin through the paper at Julia's side. "There, all done," she announced in triumph. Peg stood back. Her eyes ran up and down searching for any mistakes. She slowly walked around Julia and smiled with satisfaction.

"Ok, Blanche," said Peg, "you take one side and I'll get the other." The two women carefully lifted the dress pattern over Julia's head. Then, Peg carefully set it aside along with all the pictures and sheets of paper bearing measurements and specific instructions.

"All the material has come in, Peg," said Blanche, "Maggie's holding it for you. Oh, and I almost forgot to ask, will your niece be able to do all the bead work?"

"Yes, Blanche, and thank you!" said Peg, "she's grateful for the work."

Just then, they heard the back door to the kitchen open.

Peg visibly shrunk and her previous smile evaporated. Nervously she began to shuffle Blanche and Julia towards the door.

"You take care and I'll let you know when Julia can come for a fitting."

Blanche stopped at the door and turned. Just over Peg's shoulder she saw the kitchen doorway darken. There stood Phil blocking out the sun. He glared at the women, his eyes moved from one to the next. Blanche felt uneasy when she saw how he looked at Julia. He paused just a little too long and for an instant he reminded her of a wolf, hungry and eying his prey. Blanche stood just a little taller and when his gaze met hers, she didn't flinch. He stared at her with hard, black eyes. It only lasted a few moments. Then suddenly, he turned on his heel and left. The kitchen door slammed shut and they were left in uncomfortable silence.

Blanche looked at Peg with a worried expression, "You don't have to stay," she pleaded, "I can take you away, he'll never find you!"

Peg's shoulders drooped in despair. "I have no choice."

Julia could barely hear Peg's voice, but the emptiness of her words filled the room.

Peg opened the door.

Reluctantly, Blanche walked out with Julia in tow. At the gate, she glanced over her shoulder but Peg was gone. She'd closed the door before they'd even reached the bottom step.

Julia stood at the mirror putting the final touches on her hair. Carefully, she swept back some strands with the silver comb given to her by Blanche, thankful to have the errant curls tucked into place. She looked down at her dress and was pleased to see how the light silky fabric clung to her figure. She ran her hands down the front of her dress, smoothing out non-existent wrinkles. A final turn and she was ready to go.

Tonight was the barn dance. For the farming community, it marked the beginning of autumn. Every year it was the same. Families from miles around came to renew friendships and catch-up with their neighbors. As for Julia, she couldn't wait to see some of her old friends. Tonight would probably be the last chance to visit before she had to head back to the Kimball Academy.

Julia had always found it interesting that the barn dance didn't take place in a barn at all. Instead, the area folks would come together at the County Grange. They would open up the large hall and have a band of local musicians come in to play. The band was well versed in all the traditional favorites, as well as some of the newer songs. The dances would be carried out on practiced feet, and both young and old would take part in the fun.

Julia dashed downstairs and almost bumped into Lou coming out of the kitchen. She had just finished feeding Alfred and was taking him upstairs for his bath.

"Slow down, Julia," scolded Lou, "You'll get there soon enough without knocking me over".

Julia frowned.

"Ok," smiled Lou, "Go on and have a good time. You'll find your Dad and Blanche waiting for you outside."

Julia took a moment to kiss her brothers cheek and ruffle the soft curls crowning his head. Alfred smiled. It was apparent he adored his big sister. But before he could ask for a story, Julia was gone. The shudder of the screen door offered evidence of her hasty retreat.

Julia stood on the top porch step looking for Dad and Blanche. Finally she spotted them standing down near the end of the driveway. Their heads were together and it was obvious they were having a serious conversation.

"It's my fault he's making so much trouble for you," agonized Blanche.

"Nonsense," consoled Will, "He thinks it's his life's mission to make things hard for everyone else. If George spent as much time caring, really caring, for the people in this community, we'd have gotten better roads and services a long time ago."

"Yes, that's true," conceded Blanche, "But marrying me put a giant target on your back."

Will wrapped his arms around Blanche's waist and pulled her in close. "Yes," he said, "But marrying you has also made me a very happy man!"

Blanche smiled and buried her face in his shoulder. Will grinned. It was nice to see he could still make her blush.

All of a sudden, Julia bounded up to them. She was practically percolating in anticipation.

"Ready?" she asked.

Will released Blanche and then took her hand in his. His arm reached out and wrapped around Julia's shoulder, pulling her in for a quick squeeze. Julia allowed Dad his moment of closeness, but then squirmed away. Her excitement was too great.

They walked along the quiet country road, following their shadows into town as the sun set at their backs. When they were almost there, they could see dots of light scattered throughout the trees. The area ladies had hung Mason jars with lit candles inside on some of the lower branches to welcome all who came.

When the trio entered the bright yard, they saw laid out before them long lines of tables. They were covered with a variety of patterned and colored cloths. Some of the tables were bordered by wooden folding chairs, while others formed a buffet and were laden with every sort of casserole, picnic salad or pie. Julia licked her lips in anticipation. She knew the local ladies only brought their finest recipes. It was an unspoken competition with each cook hoping to bring home an empty dish.

Julia broke off from Dad and Blanche just as their neighbors began approaching Will. They wanted to greet him and shake his hand.

Julia wandered to the buffet tables to plan her attack.

"Where should she start?" she asked herself, "With the baked beans or deviled eggs?"

The eggs won out and she popped one in her mouth with about as much grace as a squirrel stuffing an acorn in its cheek. She was in the process of chewing and swallowing when she heard an all too familiar voice behind her.

"Hey, Julia, I've been waiting for you!"

Julia forced herself to chew more slowly so she didn't have to answer right away. She glanced around hoping to see some of her friends, but...no luck! There was no escape.

Julia swallowed the last bit and turned to say, "Hi."

Waiting impatiently was Davy. "So, Julia, what do you say we go in and have that dance?" he asked eagerly.

Julia was confused. It had been nearly two months since she'd seen him last and she had no idea what he was referring to. Not waiting for her reply, Davy grabbed her hand and half-dragged, half-led her into the hall.

Once inside, Julia noticed DJ standing against a wall talking with Bobby, and Jimmy. There weren't any girls nearby and she wondered if Abigail had even come.

Suddenly, she felt herself being propelled onto the dance floor. The song was a lively jig. Davy had one arm wrapped around her waist and held his other arm out to the side. Gingerly, she placed her hand in his and they began to swirl across the wooden floor. Davy led to a beat unfamiliar to the rest of the dancers and her feet suffered from him stepping lively on her toes. There were also a few near misses as Davy almost took out some of the other couples. Soon, they were given a wide berth and much to her chagrin, everyone was watching their odd display.

Finally, the last notes were played and Julia said a hasty, "Thanks." She quickly moved away from Davy and blended into the crowd. Then she wove her way to the door and ducked outside. The night air was only slightly cooler than inside the hall, so she went in search of a cold drink. Off to the side of the building, she took her place in line for some lemonade. But before her turn came, she saw Davy appear in the doorway. He was craning his neck, trying to see above the mass of heads.

"Oh, no," thought Julia. "I need to keep moving or I'll be stuck dancing with him all night."

Reluctantly, she stepped out of line, circled back towards the buffet tables and slid into a small grove of maples that bordered the yard. There were small groups clustered about, chatting and laughing gaily. So Julia began her search for familiar faces, hoping to join her friends before Davy found her. Julia wandered between tree trunks and couples making their way in to the dance or in search of food. Eventually she found herself at the back line of trees where they met a neighbor's cornfield.

The thick stalks stood tall and erect and were heavy with almost ripe ears of corn. Julia was getting tired of searching so she decided to lean against a thick maple's trunk and rest for a moment. She felt a slight breeze blow warm against her face. She closed her eyes and listened to the hum of voices blending with the band's music. That was when she caught snatches of a conversation coming from the cornfield.

"Abigail, stay...just a little longer," a young man's voice pleaded, in a thick whisper.

"You know I can't!" she whispered back, her voice was full of regret, "If he finds us, my father will kill you!"

"Just one minute more?" His request was followed by a long silence.

Julia moved off as quickly as she could without making too much noise. Her stomach ached. She wished she'd never stopped. Perhaps stumbling upon DJ and Abigail was her punishment for ditching Davy.

Julia no longer gave any thought to where she was going. She just pushed her way through clusters of people until she came out on the other side of the grove towards the back side of the Grange. There, she saw a group of boys smoking and swearing loudly. She hoped she could pass by unnoticed, especially when she saw Wally, Phil and Frank Jr. They were surrounded by some younger boys who obviously looked up to them. Julia was so intent on watching what they were doing, that she wasn't paying attention to what was in front of her.

Smack!

Julia walked into a low hanging branch that was thickly covered in leaves. It hit her directly in the face and caused her to stumble.

"Ow!" she cried out, the words escaped her lips before she could stop them. Julia froze. She was hoping the boys were so involved in their own conversation, that her outburst would go unnoticed. Unfortunately, that was not the case. In unison, all of their heads turned in Julia's direction.

Wally scowled, "It's only a girl."

"Yeah," the younger boys agreed, "just a stupid girl."

Julia exhaled with relief. They couldn't care less. She was just a minor interruption, much like an annoying insect. Quickly forgotten as soon as it flew off. They all turned back to each other and resumed their joking. All with the exception of one. Phil.

As soon as Phil realized Julia was "the girl" causing the disturbance, a slow smile spread across his face. He began to walk slowly towards her.

Wally knew Phil was in one of his dark moods and quickly followed. He only hoped he could intercept him before he reached Julia. When he was within reach, Wally grabbed Phil's arm and asked, "Hey, where ya' headin' off to?"

Phil brushed Wally off with a raised fist and some choice curses.

It was then that Frank Jr. joined them. "Come on, Phil," he pleaded, "You don't wanna be messing with her."

Wally nodded in agreement. Julia wasn't just another poor farm girl. Her family had money and her father was a state senator. But they both knew Phil didn't have enough sense to leave her alone, especially since all he'd done lately was complain about all the fancy dresses Peg had been making for Julia. They'd even heard him say she was no different than any other girl once she took her expensive clothes off.

Frank Jr. tried one more time to stop Phil, but made the mistake of stepping in front of him. Phil's eyes narrowed and it was like staring into a dark abyss. His hands were clenched in two hard fists that twitched at his side. More than once he'd beaten an opponent to a bloody pulp and Frank Jr. held no illusions that their friendship would prevent Phil from doing the same to him. Frank Jr. raised his hands and backed off. What did he care anyways? He was about to go find Abigail and show her off on the dance floor. As far as he was concerned, she was the prize and it was time for him to go claim her.

When Frank Jr. stepped off and headed toward the dance, Wally fell in at his side. Phil resumed his course.

Meanwhile, Julia had been trying to slip away unnoticed. She was steps away from ducking into a break in the trees when a hand reached out and grabbed her arm. She winced and instinctively tried to break free but the grip only tightened. Julia felt herself being pulled into the grove. Taken off guard, she tripped on a tree root and lost her footing. Julia landed face first on the hard ground. Slowly, she rolled onto her side and began to sit up. Standing before her was Davy.

"I finally found you," he exclaimed, "And just in time. Come on!"

Davy held out his hand to help Julia to her feet but never got the chance. A shadow swung out from the dark and a strange look crossed his face. Davy let out a soft grunt as his eyes rolled to the back of his head and then, he sank to the ground in a heap. Julia looked up and saw Phil standing over Davy's limp body.

Inflamed, she demanded, "What did you do to him?"

But before Phil could reply, two hands materialized from behind him and grasped his neck. It only took seconds for Phil to lose consciousness and collapse on the ground. His limp hand fell open at his side and a large rock rolled onto the dirt.

"DJ, what did you do to him?" Julia asked.

"Nothing permanent," he answered, "Just a little move that will give him a nice nap."

DJ looked around to make sure no one else had noticed what he'd done. Fortunately, they were far enough away from the rest of the crowd for anyone to have seen. Meanwhile, the young boys were too busy bickering over who could spit the farthest, so there was nothing to worry about there.

"Hurry, Julia, come and help me!" DJ instructed, "You grab his feet and I'll take his head."

"What are we going to do with him," she asked.

"Just move him into the grove," DJ said, "Just enough so no one stumbles across him till after you and I are gone."

DJ linked his arms under Phil's while Julia bent over and grabbed his feet. Together they dragged his seemingly lifeless body into a patch of tall weeds that were skirting the tree line.

Julia wiped her dirty hands on her now soiled and torn dress. Absent mindedly, she brushed a loose strand of hair away from her eyes. She looked over at Davy, still lying on the ground. He was beginning to wake up.

"Ow!" he moaned. Davy pulled himself to sitting and felt the back of head.

"You got a nice knot there, Dav," congratulated DJ.

"Yeah?" he asked, smiling with pride.

"Yeah!" said DJ, and he helped Davy to his feet, "You ok to walk?"

"I think so," he replied, "Hurts like a son of a bitch!"

"Watch your language," DJ admonished, and nodded in Julia's direction.

"Oh, sorry, Julia," Davy apologized, "Are you ok?" he asked her, "And where's Phil?"

"Out of sight," said DJ, "Now let's get outta here before anyone gets nosy!"

Julia took one more look at her dress. How was she supposed to leave without attracting attention?

DJ saw her concern. He thought for a moment and then said, "Hey, Davy, come over here."

Davy did as he was told.

"You and me are going to walk out of here together," DJ directed and stood tight against Davy's side, "Like this, real close." Then he said to Julia, "Now you follow behind us, no dawdling, ok?"

"Ok," said Julia, relieved that DJ had come up with a plan.

The two boys began to head towards the crowd with Julia close on their heels. She kept her head down hoping no one would be able to see her face. Thankfully most people were so engrossed in their own conversations they barely noticed when DJ or Davy nudged them aside. They were almost to the road when they heard a loud voice say, "Hey, isn't that Julia?"

Julia groaned. All night she had been hoping to run into her friends, but not now!

"What happened to her dress?" she heard Sara ask in a timid voice.

"It's torn up past her knees," Bettie replied in a loud whisper.

"I don't know what she did," chimed in Bonnie conspiratorially, "But she's with two boys and looks like she was rolling around in the woods." Bonnie's comment generated a round of laughter. A sly smile appeared on her face. It was clear she loved being the center of attention, so she continued with more one liners all designed to mock Julia and criticize her new life at the Kimball Academy. Soon, a crowd of young people began to form a circle around Bonnie and her three friends. After hearing her wit, they too joined in the fun, all at Julia's expense.

Julia's eyes were glued on the small mob and instead of using this opportunity to retreat, she simply stood and listened. Her torn and muddy dress was now forgotten and replaced with shock from their cruelty. Mostly because she had no idea anyone felt this way about her.

DJ looked back and scowled. He noticed that for the moment, the crowd had eyes on Bonnie and had all but forgotten about Julia. It was time they made their escape. DJ spun around and hurried back to get her.

"Come on," he admonished, then put his hand on Julia's back and pushed her forward. Julia felt the heat of embarrassment wash over her face. Now all she wanted was to leave the barn dance behind. She only wanted to go home. Julia began to walk faster, leaving the crowd of kids, the gaily lit trees, and the sounds of lively music back in the distance. When she finally rounded the bend in the dark road, Julia slowed her pace and began to cry. Hot tears ran down her cheeks and she heaved silent sobs. When DJ caught up to her, he saw her wet face. Gently, he wrapped his arms around her, pulling her to his chest. DJ continued to hold her while she cried, softly rubbing her back. Finally, Julia came up for air.

Abruptly, DJ released her, handed her his kerchief, and asked, "Better?"

"Yes," she replied, sadly.

"Good," then turning to Davy asked, "Hey, Dav, what do you say we drop off Julia and then go meet up with the other fellas?"

Davy had been left standing off to the side and it was clear he'd been feeling left out. Now thankful for the chance to be included, he replied eagerly, "Sure! I can't wait to show them my bump!".

"That's right, Dav," congratulated DJ, "Tonight you're a hero."

Davy stood a little taller. He felt sure he had impressed Julia.

The three of them headed off down the road. DJ and Davy joked about how Phil hadn't stood a chance. But, Julia walked quietly alongside them, lost in her own thoughts. She was still hearing Bonnie's jokes in her mind and it troubled her that her old friends thought she was uppity now that she attended a private school.

When they finally reached the farm, Julia was exhausted, but before she said good night to the boys she had to ask, "Have I really changed that much since I went away to school?"

DJ hesitated, but Davy spoke up, "No, Julia, you're still the same girl I've always known. It's just now you don't have chores like the rest of us." Davy saw Julia wince. He tried again hoping to make things better, "It's just now you have nicer clothes so you aren't outside as much."

DJ punched him in the arm and hissed, "Please shut-up, you're not helping."

"Oh," Julia replied softly, "So it is true. And that's why the girls don't care to be around me anymore." Her heart felt heavy and sad.

DJ tried to console her by saying, "Never mind them, Julia, the only life they know is this town. It's good you're getting out of here. That's what I want to do."

"Really?" she asked surprised.

"Well sure," he continued, "Working for someone else is fine for my Pa, but I have other plans." He saw a question on Julia's face and quickly added, "Not that your Dad hasn't been good to me and my family. We feel fortunate to be here. Your Dad is very fair."

"So what do you plan to do?" asked Davy before Julia could get the words out.

DJ stood tall, clearly he had given his plans a lot of thought. "I'm going to make moonshine." He saw the looks of disbelief on their faces. "Really, it's a good idea. Prohibition won't be around forever. There's already talk of ending it. When that happens I want to be ready."

"But if alcohol becomes legal again," asked Julia, "Who's going to buy your moonshine?"

"Bars, saloons," DJ explained, "Anywhere they serve booze. My shine will be top shelf, expensive. I already have Billy working on a label."

Julia was stunned. It never occurred to her that DJ would be anywhere but here. On her family's farm.

Suddenly two figures burst through the trees across the road. Jimmy and Bobbie wore conspiratorial grins and looked ready to burst.

"Guess who we found passed out in the woods?" asked Jimmy.

"Phil," stated Davy without missing a beat.

Jimmy looked deflated, "How'd you know?" he demanded.

"Cause I put him there!"

"I don't believe you," said Jimmy.

Davy turned around and pointed to the back of his head, "Feel this!"

Jimmy and Bobbie both took turns rubbing the knot on the back of Davy's head.

"Ok," said Bobbie, "but that doesn't mean you had anything to do with putting Phil down for the count."

"It was me!" he stated emphatically, "Ask DJ!"

The two boys turned to DJ who simply nodded his head, "Yes."

Davy looked gratefully at DJ. It wasn't often he had the chance to impress his older brother. So Julia and DJ listened quietly while Davy spun a tale of chivalry and cunning.

Once he was done, DJ had to ask, "So why were you guys so excited when you got here?"

Immediately the sly smiles returned to their faces. They started to answer at the same time, but then Bobbie stopped and nudged Jimmy to go ahead. Apparently the two of them had been searching for DJ and Davy after they'd gotten separated at the buffet. They were heading to the back of the Grange by skirting the edge of the grove when Jimmy tripped over a big log. Only thing was, it wasn't a log…it was Phil. That's when they got an idea! Seems at the time they were both still munching on large slices of fresh berry pie, and it also seems that there was a nosy skunk a little ways off in the woods. So the boys smeared their pie slices all over Phil's face and then waited in some bushes out of sight. It didn't take long for that skunk to wander close enough to Phil to smell the pie and when he did, he began to lick it off. That was also about the time when Phil was just starting to come around.

"Well, you can imagine what happened next," exuded Jimmy with a triumphant finish, "Phil won't be sneaking up on anyone for at least a little while!"

"Good work, fellas," said DJ, "Just don't go mouthing off about it around town. If he finds out it was you..."

Both Bobbie and Jimmy knew what DJ meant without any explanation.

"Hey, guys," interrupted Davy, "Are we gonna stand here all night? Seems like we have a couple things to celebrate."

That was all the prompting needed. The boys said hasty, "Good nights" to Julia, then fell into the shadows.

She watched as they headed down toward the pond, and then went into the house. She passed the living room doorway and saw Lou sleeping in the old rocker. Julia tip toed up the stairs so she wouldn't wake her. She was too tired to do more than a quick wash up at the bathroom basin and then made her way down the hall to her bedroom. The sweet room greeted her when she opened the door. Its simple elegance was a clear reminder that she was no longer like the other farm girls. Her path had changed and there would be no going back.

The next morning Julia went to see Peg. She had one more item to pick-up, a cape made of emerald green brocade with a velvet collar and trim. Of everything Peg had made her, this was her favorite. Blanche had also given her an envelope with the last of the money they owed Peg for all her work.

When Julia got to Peg's gate, she heard her name being called out, "Julia ... Julia, over here!"

It was Maggie at the Mountainside. Julia crossed the quiet street to see what she needed,

"Good morning, Maggie, what can I do for you?" she asked.

"I have your pretty cape inside," she answered.

Julia followed Maggie inside the store.

"This is strange," commented Julia, "I had plans with Peg to pick it up this morning at her place. I even have her money," she said, holding up the plain white envelope that had been stuffed in her pocket.

"I know nothing of your arrangements," stated Maggie, and she disappeared into the back room. "All I know," she yelled out, "Is Peg came over with it yesterday. Asked if I'd be willing to hold onto it and make sure you got it when you came to town."

"What should I do with this," queried Julia, referring to the wrinkled wad of paper that held Peg's payment.

"Not sure," Maggie hollered, "How about you drop it under her mat after you try on the cape?" Maggie appeared with a large box. She placed it on the counter and removed the lid. Nestled on a bed of tissue was a sea of green fabric, "I can't wait to see it on you!"

Meanwhile, across the street, Peg sat waiting. She was in her rocker. The same place she'd been since late the night before.

She'd had a plan, but like so many plans, hers had taken a left turn. At first she'd been angry. She had known that it would take all the courage she could muster to see it through. So to come so close and then have it all fall apart…well, she was past that now. Peg had spent part of the night and into the early morning hours making a new plan.

Above her head, Peg heard the bedsprings creak. Then the heavy thud as John got out of bed. He was hung-over, as usual. She was sure he'd come down in a foul mood.

Normally, she would be busy in the kitchen. She'd have a fresh pot of hot coffee waiting on the stove, and sausages browning in her heavy cast iron skillet. On the counter a warm loaf of bread would be cooling with fresh butter nearby. But not today.

A low rumble of curses announced John's descent and his heavy tread on the stairs grew louder. He entered the living room and stared at Peg in confusion. He couldn't seem to figure out why she was sitting, doing nothing, in the middle of the morning. And what was that odor? Recognition crossed his face when he realized the source of the noxious smell.

"Peg, what'd you do?" he demanded, "Knock over a lamp?"

Peg just sat. Unmoving.

John's bloodshot eyes searched the room until he spotted a dark stain on the wall across from Peg. It took a minute more for them to focus and that was when he saw the broken glass on the floor.

"You stupid BITCH! Get off your lazy ass and clean it up!" he yelled.

Peg didn't move.

"What the hell's wrong with you?" he thundered.

Peg reached under the lap quilt she'd made as a girl with her mother. She extracted a box of stick matches.

The truth was, it had taken every ounce of strength for her to crawl into the rocker late last night. John was already passed out in bed when she'd headed downstairs to investigate some strange noises. She was making her way towards the top of the stairs when she was greeted by the pungent odor of skunk. Peg became worried that one of the creatures had somehow made its way into the house. She quietly made her way downstairs but what she discovered broke what was left of her heart.

She'd found Phil in the living room digging through her piles of mending. He was ripping apart each piece of clothing and throwing it across the room. Peg could only stand in horror watching as he urinated on the now torn scraps of cloth. Then, he stomped on the sewing basket that had belonged to her mother. She could keep silent no more.

"Stop!" she screamed, as the frail wicker crumbled beneath his boot. At the sound of Peg's voice, Phil turned and faced her. He wore a look of utter disgust and began to close the gap between them. His kicks and punches landed on layers of abuse and Peg found it hard to believe he could still hurt her. Finally she fell to the floor and that was when his boot landed a crushing blow to her pelvis. Pain shot through her body and mercifully, she passed out.

When Peg woke it was still dark, but a dreadful silence enveloped the house. Carefully, and very slowly, Peg dragged herself to the rocking chair and with a will that super-ceded pain, she managed to pull herself up and into it. There she stayed, revising her plan and firming her resolve.

Her original idea was to leave town. Of course she knew John would never let her go, and if she left, he would come after her. Even Blanche couldn't hide her far enough away that he wouldn't get to her. So Peg devised another way. For the past few months she had been purchasing and hiding bottles of lamp oil. She knew if John stumbled on her stash, he wouldn't give it much thought. Then she waited for the night of the barn dance. Peg knew the whole town would show up. She also knew John would come home drunk and pass out. All she had to do was wait until everyone around the quiet community was fast asleep, worn out from a long night of eating, dancing and visiting. Then she would work quickly, spreading puddles of kerosene throughout the house. She would waste no good byes, there would be no fond farewells. One match and as far as anyone would know, she, John and Phil would be consumed in a house fire. But her plan was better than that. For she would be on her way out of town. She'd saved all the money Blanche paid her. It was enough to get her across the Canadian border and to a new life of freedom.

What she hadn't anticipated was Phil's tirade. She could have kicked herself for reacting the way she did. For a short time she felt desolate. All her scheming for nothing.

On the small table next to her sat her bible, and an old kerosene lamp that she'd recently filled. That's when she found a new way.

Peg was looking directly into John's eyes. She'd already made her peace with God and now she was ready to take on the Devil.

John was still yelling, calling her the same foul names she'd been hearing for years. She gently pushed on one end of the match box until the inside tray poked through on the other side. She reached in and took out one match. That was all she needed. Holding it firmly between her thumb and index finger, she struck it against the side of the box. The tip burst into flame. John's face was full of horror as the realization of her intent hit him. Peg wore a smile of satisfaction. She let the match go and watched it fall from her hand to the puddle at her feet.

∞

Across the street Julia was standing before a full length mirror admiring her new cape. The force from the blast shook the building so hard that the overhead lamps began to sway and cans fell off the shelves.

"What was that?" exclaimed Maggie as she and Julia ran to the door.

The largest fire either of them had ever seen was consuming the small house across the street. Neither Julia nor Maggie said a word as they watched the flames grow until all semblance of a structure was gone. By the time the men had gathered to start a bucket brigade, the only thing to save were the two houses on either side.

It was hours later when the men finally put their buckets down. All that remained was a black smoldering hole. It wouldn't be cool enough for an investigation until the next day but everyone already knew...there would be no one to bury.

That night, Julia sat on her bed staring at the large box containing the green cape. Next to it lay the envelope with Peg's money. She couldn't feel sorry for the death of Phil. He was a mean, angry boy and she wouldn't miss him. But Peg? All she felt was loss and tragedy.

Julia looked out her window and up at the dark sky. The stars twinkled back at her. They were right where they were supposed to be. She sighed and lay back on her pillow. Tonight she felt especially grateful for her life on the farm. She said a quiet prayer and then fell into a restless sleep.

"Come on, Julia, it's time to leave!"

Billy's voice echoed as he came down the hall.

"One minute more," she pleaded, "I can't find my hair comb."

"You mean to tell me there are no other hair combs in any of your trunks?"

"Well, yes," she conceded, "but not the one I want. It's special. Blanche gave it to me."

"Julia," Billy rationalized, "if it's so special, why can't you find it?"

"I don't know," she answered, "I wore it the night of the barn dance."

"Well, maybe it fell out while you were there. Have you seen it since?"

Julia dropped a handful of hankies back into her drawer. She scowled and replied, "I hate to think that's what happened to it."

"It really doesn't matter," Billy continued, "we have to leave. I have to get you and ALL your things moved into your room at school before dark."

"Ok," Julia sighed.

He saw the disappointment on her face. "Hey, what do you say we go over to the grange and have a look around. Real quick. You never know".

"Really?" Julia perked up, "Thanks, I'd really appreciate it!"

Billy headed back down the stairs with Julia at his heels. He opened the front door and let her through. It was a warm sunny day, perfect for the drive out to Kimball Academy.

The Grange grounds were deserted and quiet. Julia found it hard to believe the crowd that was there just a week earlier. She got out of the car and began to search following the path she remembered taking through the grove. Billy followed behind her keeping his eyes on the ground. He hoped they would find the comb fast and get on their way. He had plans that night and he didn't want to be late getting back.

Julia followed the line of trees at the back of the grove until she came around to the far side of the Grange.

"This must be where it came loose," she thought. Julia began to sweep the tall grass and plants with her foot.

"Did you find it?" asked Billy, hopefully.

"No," she admitted, reluctantly, "but this is the area I scuffled with Phil. It must have fallen out here," she reasoned.

Billy impatiently pushed at some patches of weeds but saw nothing.

Finally, Julia gave up. "I guess it's not here."

"Sorry, Julia. It was worth a try."

As Julia walked back to the car, she felt something odd. She was probably just uneasy because of what had happened with Phil the night of the dance and then the fire the next day.

Billy and Julia drove off leaving a cloud of dust in their wake. Once the car was out of sight a silent figure stepped out of the shadows. Gripped in its deformed hand was Julia's hair comb!

8

The Kimball Academy was a whirl of activities and autumn was quickly giving way to winter. Julia and Izzy fell into a familiar routine while being joined by a new girl from across the hall. Her name was Esther. At first glance she appeared small and shy, but much to their delight, a heart of mischief beat within her soul. Julia and Izzy had found their third musketeer.

Each day, the girls spent engaged in the required assortment of academic classes. Busily they would read, take notes and compute numbers. But once three o'clock arrived, another form of instruction would begin. Gone were the days when they would take walks around the grounds, or harmonize in the common room. Now their late afternoons and early evenings were devoted to learning the finer points of landing and keeping a husband.

It was on one of these days in early winter that all the marketable girls were summoned to the East drawing room. They had been practicing the art of hosting a tea party for weeks and this would be the final test of their skills. Izzy was in a particularily saucy mood and as much as Julia and Ester wanted to stand clear, destiny landed her at their table.

Julia sat at the head of a small rectangular table playing hostess to her five "guests". She was nervously biting her bottom lip and staring down at the starched, white tablecloth with matching napkins, silently rehearsing her duties. Before her sat a steeping pot of English tea and a tiered tray of bite size squares generously coated in powdered sugar. Julia took a deep breath, then turned to her right and asked her first "guest" how she would like her tea.

"Cream, no sugar," was the reply.

Carefully, Julia balanced a small, china cup and saucer in one hand and poured a splash of cream with the other. Then she tried to dispense the piping hot amber without spilling. She watched the cup slowly fill and began to relax.

"I think the weather is quite lovely today, don't you?" she questioned. The air around her was still. Julia was setting the teapot down and handing off the cup when she felt a spray of sugar on her cheek. Immediately she turned and looked. Across the table Izzy sat shaking with laughter, sugar still spittling out of her mouth.

"What are you doing?" whispered Julia, trying to feign disapproval.

"Just wanted a little tea with my sugar, luv," she replied in a fake cockney accent.

Julia and Esther could not contain themselves any longer. Soon they too had sugar cubes stuffed in their cheeks and were carrying on a very un-proper conversation with a very un-proper English accent.

The two other girls seated at their table wore faces of horrified pleasure. They looked as if they were about to join in when they suddenly turned pale and their eyes dropped to their laps.

Julia glanced behind her and saw Miss Stone making a bee line in their direction.

"Shh!" she implored, but Izzy and Esther continued on.

Miss Stone sped past them with an air of purpose – she had spotted a table at the far end of the room that had had a major spill. It seems two of the girls had the notion to give a celebratory toast with the fine china, it being their last lesson and all. In their exuberance, they "clinked" a little too hard shattering their cups. When the hot liquid splashed out, it not only scalded their hands but also the young lady who was pouring out. She in turn dropped the entire pot causing chards of pottery and hot tea to spray everywhere. Ultimately two of the girls were escorted to the infirmary for minor burns and another for a few small cuts on the her lower arm.

It didn't take long for the mess to be cleared away but given the disruption, it was decided to abandon the lesson. The girls were given the evening off.

That was the night Julia learned Izzy's secret. The two girls were sitting in their room trying to study when suddenly, a loud moan erupted. Julia stopped reading. Stunned, she looked across at Izzy.

"It's not my fault," Izzy said, defensively, "I didn't get much dinner."

Julia caught the gleam in her roommate's eye. "How about we go get a snack," she suggested. "We can sneak down to the kitchen and see if there are any cakes left over from this afternoon."

Quickly, they pulled on their slippers and robes, then went across the hall to get Esther. Soon, there were three dark shapes creeping down the back stairs and making their way into the unlit kitchen. Silently, they pushed the door open. On the far counter sat a large platter still laden with tasty treats.

Julia held the door and they quietly tip-toed in. She took one last peek down the hallway and seeing noone, eased it shut.

No time was wasted. The girls ran over to the counter and grabbed a pastry with each hand. They began to gobble them down oblivious of the white powdery mess they were making.

Suddenly, Esther stopped mid-bite. "What's that?" she asked.

"Nothing," scolded Izzy, "just the wind or something."

"No, I hear it too," joined Julia, "Voices!"

The girls scrambled into the pantry and pulled the door shut just in time. Light flooded the room and in came the Head Mistress and a man Julia had never seen before.

"I assure you, she will be ready,"

"It is imperative that she is," the man admonished. "She was sent here to make sure nothing goes wrong! This marriage is essential."

"Your employer placed his confindence in me, I have no intention of failing."

"If you want the balance of what was promised," he warned, "you won't."

"Relax, have a cup of coffee."

The man sat at a small table near the window while a pot began to brew on the stove. Meanwhile, the girls huddled in the pantry uncomfortably. Julia and Ester continued to listen at the door, even though no further information could be gleened. Izzy crouched in a corner against the back wall and was uncharacteristically quiet.

It was over an hour later when the pot was drained of coffee and the small talk had ceased. The man followed the Head Mistress out and the kitchen was again submerged in darkness.

"What's the matter, Izzy?"

"Yeah, you're so quiet."

"That man works for my father. He was talking about me." Izzy slowly rose and moved towards the door.

"You?" asked Julia, "Izz, what's he want with you? Why was he here?"

"He's checking up on me. Wants to make sure I'll be ready for my wedding," she replied sullenly.

"Aren't you getting ahead of yourself," laughed Esther, "You don't even have a beau."

"Don't need one," she answered, and when she turned her head, they could see a tear break away and run slowly down her cheek. "My father has already brokered a husband for me."

Both Julia and Esther stared in disbelief as Izzy shared the details of the business arrangement that was to be her marriage. Her fiancé was the son of a European industrialist, quite the catch she'd been told. The ink had all but dried on the paper and it looked as though nothing could stop their impending union.

"But Izz," reasoned Julia, "you're a debutante, we're just beginning to get ready for our season." Her face scrunched up as she tried to make sense of her friends confession.

"Yeah," chimed in Esther, "the husband hunting has just begun."

"Not for me, all this.....my time here, the classes and dances are just a formality."

"Ok, so you're already spoken for," said Julia, " what's he like? When can we meet him?"

"Will he be at our coming out?" asked Esther.

"Lets see," answered Izzy, "he's a rich bore, you can meet him in boresville and, oh yes, the bore will be there to see me presented and make sure he's the only bore that gets to dance with me."

"Isadore!"

Suddenly the pantry door jerked open. The girls looked up and into the hard face of the head mistress with Miss Stone a few steps behind.

"I don't have to ask what the three of you are doing."

Julia looked down at the bodice of her nightgown. The white powder bib betrayed her.

Izzy opened her mouth to explain, but the head mistress simply raised her hand. She gave a slight tilt of her head toward the door. The girls rose and without a word, filed out of the kitchen and headed upstairs to bed.

Still standing in the kitchen, Miss Stone waited until the girls were out of earshot and then asked, "Is it really true what they say about her young man?"

"Which part," sighed the head mistress, "that he had an affair with an underage girl, or that he impregnated her? Or is it the one where the girl commits suicide when he rejects her? Or the story that he staged the suicide to avoid arrest?"

"Oh, my," exclaimed Miss Stone, " I certainly hope none of them are true. For Izzy's sake!"

"Sadly, by all accounts, they are most nearly all true."

Quietly, the two women left the kitchen. The night had taken a chill, and it was doubtful that either of them would be able to sleep.

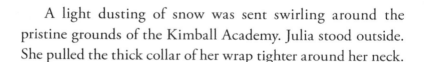

A light dusting of snow was sent swirling around the pristine grounds of the Kimball Academy. Julia stood outside. She pulled the thick collar of her wrap tighter around her neck.

She'd left the warmth of Kimball's grand hall to venture out into the dark and chilly courtyard.

Dejectedly, she dropped onto one of the granite benches and let out a deep sigh. She had just completed her final dance class and was concerned with her lack of progress. She was still struggling with the stiff posture and subtle nuances that each dance style required. What made it even harder was the girls had to practice with each other. One evening she would lead and then the next she would follow.

Waltzes and Foxtrots and Quick Steps.

Julia lifted her head and found comfort in the early winter sky. She smiled back at the small specks of light twinkling down at her. The soft breeze rose again and blew across the courtyard rustling the last errant leaves of autumn.

"You just need to relax," came a encouraging voice from behind the bushes.

Julia jumped! She turned as Peter emerged from the foliage. "You startled me!"

"Sorry," he replied, "I was just about to head home and I saw you here."

"Oh, good! Then you didn't see me waltz across the ballroom with my two left feet."

Peter chuckled.

"You have seen me!"

If it helps you feel better," he consoled, "you're not the worst." Julia grimaced.

"It's not as hard as you make it." he continued, "Really! you're not half bad." Peter could see Julia's frown. "I've been here a lot of years and there's one thing I've learned..." Peter paused.

"Yes??"

"You need to let go."

"Let go?" Julia gasped, "How can I? What does that even mean?"

"Just stop fighting the music."

"You don't understand," she lamented."Apparently my whole future rests on my ability to choose the right fork and not crush my would-be-husband's toes on the dance floor."

Peter began to laugh. She glared back at him with annoyance.

"I'm sorry, Julia, but trust me – I've seen the worst of the worst. You're not even close."

The furrow on Julia's brow deepened.

"Honest," he continued and took a few steps closer with his hand extended. "May I have this dance?" he asked, with a slight bow of his head.

Julia hesitated.

"Don't leave me hanging," he whispered, "You'll damage my self-esteem."

Julia smiled and shrugged. "Ok, it can't be any worse than trying to follow Izzy."

Julia reached out and placed her hand in Peters. She felt his strength and confidence as he pulled her in closer. His other hand slid to her side and before she knew it she was gliding across the smooth stones.The couple waltzed in the enclosed circle with Peter humming softly.

Julia felt her stiff body begin to relax and her movements became more fluid. She was easily able to follow his strong lead and he continued to guide her, his quiet melody playing in her right ear.

Clap! Clap! Clap!

Their waltz stopped abruptly and they spun to see who it was.

"Very good form," critiqued Izzy, as she stepped into the circle of light.

"I didn't hear you, Izz."

"I can be quiet." she replied, with mock offense, "When I want to."

Peter let out a loud guffaw.

"Enough from you," Izzy teased, then turned back to Julia.

"What did you think, Izz?" she asked eagerly.

"It was beautiful," remarked Izzy, transferring her gaze onto Peter, "You looked quite graceful." But her compliment wasn't intended for Julia alone.

Delighted, Julia turned to Peter, "Thank you," she exclaimed, "so much!"

Peter answered with a slight nod, and a "My pleasure, ma'am."

Julia spun happily toward the doors. "I have to go tell Esther!" she exclaimed, her joy and relief obvious. Then, before her friends could say another word, she disappeared inside.

The French doors closed behind her with a crisp, "click", and the courtyard returned to quiet.

Peter hadn't moved, but stood looking over at Izzy. Softly, he offered, "I guess I better get on home."

"Right this minute?" Izzy asked, her eyes pleading with him to stay.

"I can stay…. a bit longer." Peter paused, "Would you care to walk with me?"

Izzy answered by wrapping her arm in his. He pulled her in close, protectively, and they left the courtyard and its circle of light.

A week later the dormitory was abuzz with activity. There was a "casual" affair taking place in the large drawing room of the main house on Kimball's campus. A select group of young men had been invited for the afternoon to join in poetry recitations and light refreshment. It was an opportunity for the girls to practice the fine arts of mingling and conversation. But each girl's real objective was to make aquaintences and begin to scope out their possibilities.

Julia frowned at the small oval mirror tilted up at her face. She had pulled her hair back into a soft knot and one of the girls had arranged tiny silver flowers throughout her curls. But still, there was one errant curl that would not stay tucked in place.

"I give up," she sighed.

Suddenly, a whirl of color flew into the room and demanded, "What do you think?"

Julia turned. Izzy stopped moving and struck a pose in the center of the room. She looked stunning in a pale yellow dress splattered with large peach colored blossoms and a pair of matching low heels. Her powdered face was framed with loose pin curls whose only constraint was a pair of small barrettes at each temple and her lips were polished in luminous pink gloss.

"Wow, Izz," exclaimed Julia, "You look gorgeous!" Then she looked down at her simple and understated gray dress. She'd thought the "silver mist" fabric so lovely back home, but now it just seemed dull.

Izzy saw Julia's face fall and immediately came to the rescue.

"Come with me," Izzy demanded.

"Why?" Julia hesitated.

"Don't argue, just come!"

Julia rose slowly and began to follow. Her mind was racing through her wardrobe, desperately trying to find a quick alternative to the dress she had on. She trailed behind Izzy, across the hall, and into Ester's room. The sight before her made her jaw drop. There was jewelry of all shapes, colors and styles strewn across the bed, along with scarves, ribbons, silk flowers, and bows. The dressing table was littered with pots of color, powders and brushes, a variety of lip glosses and eye shadows. And about the floor, there were shoes of all colors and styles, along with a variety of dresses and skirts. All of which had been rejected.

"Come," commanded Izzy and pointed to a small, cushioned chair positioned in front of a large, round mirror attatched to the back of the vanity. Julia sat obediently and watched as Izzy chose a pot of pale pink rouge. Izzy ran her finger across the surface then lightly brushed strokes along Julia's cheek bones. Pausing for only a minute, she then grabbed a small brush and a tin of lip gloss and told Julia, "Open". Julia obeyed. She felt the soft hairs brush color on her parted lips.

Izzy put the brush and color back on the table, then spun Julia around so she could see her reflection.

"Oh, my!" exclaimed Julia.

"Oh, my," Izzy teased, "You're not done." She went to the bed and poked around until she found a small pair of sparkly, teardrop earrings. She smiled and dangled them at Julia. "Put these on. Then you're almost done!"

Julia took one and carefully screwed it onto her lobe. She could feel its slight swing when she moved her head. Already she felt so special. She put on the other and returned to her reflection.

"Oh, Izzy," she smiled, "I feel so pretty!"

Izzy beamed.

"Let's go girls," Miss Stone called from the top of the stairs. Izzy linked her arm with Julia's and they headed out the door.

"Where's Esther?" Julia asked. It suddenly occurred to her that their third musketeer was missing.

"She already went down," related Izzy. "Her brother is here, he drove over from Dartmouth with some friends. They're on the list of eligible."

Izzy and Julia joined the rest of the girls downstairs and together they excitedly walked over to the reception.

Miss Stone stood in front of a set of double doors leading into the main house. She scanned the assembledge one last time and gave them a final reminder to "carry themselves in Kimball fashion."

Julia and Izzy unlinked arms, gave their dresses a final tug and smooth, and then tried to walk in slowly.

The drawingroom was fairly large and lined with tall windows that were framed by heavy velvet drapes. Today they had been pulled back and the late afternoon sun came flooding in. There was a fieldstone fireplace stoked and blazing, and nearby a circle of chairs artfully arranged around a podium.

Julia glanced around heer and already saw small circles of young men and girls starting to form. She looked to her side expecting to see Izzy but miraculously her chum had disappeared. A surge of panic hit her and was threatening to overtake when she heard a deep voice from behind.

"Would you like a cup of lemonade?" it asked.

Julia's mind blacked out. For the life of her she couldn't remember what she should say,"Yes"- no, that was too abrupt.

"Yes, please" – no, still not right. "If it's no trouble"- yes, that
was it. Slowly she turned toward the voice's owner hoping she
would be able to squeak out the appropriate response. A pair of
ice blue eyes met hers. Their intensity left her feeling weak and
mute. He was already holding two full cups and extending one
in her direction.

"Oh, thank God," thought Julia, all I have to do is accept
it. But as she reached for her glass, an awkward young man
with thick glasses and pimples stumbled into her. He knocked
Julia off balance and despite her struggle to keep her footing
she soon found herself on the carpet staring at a finely polished
pair of brown boots.

Meanwhile, the gangly youth's momentum continued and
with a slight twist of his graceless frame he fell, knocking out
of hand the two full cups of lemonade, and dousing both the
bearer and himself.

"Lewis!"

"I'm sorry, Cecil," lamented the young man, wincing under
the others steely glare.

Immediately, all eyes turned in their direction. Julia felt
her cheeks burn. She pulled herself to sitting and was trying
to decide how best to arrange her dress so it wouldn't tear
when she stood when a strong hand reached down and gently
lifted, helping her up. Before she could see his face, she felt
herself being guided to another part of the room. Behind her,
the crowd was being entertained as Cecil berated his unlucky
assailant.

The pressure on Julia's arm disappeared. "Are you okay?"
questioned a kind voice. Julia turned. Her eyes met a quiet smile
and soft gray eyes.

She looked down at her dress and aside from a few wrinkles that she quickly smoothed out, she discovered that she was "Fine".

His head tilted towards hers for just a second and he tried to tuck her wayward curl back in place. "Almost no harm done," he remarked, "pretty near perfect."

Julia smiled. "Thank you for rescuing me."

"My pleasure," he replied, "but who's going to save poor Lewis?"

They glanced back in Lewis' direction. The lashing seemed almost over with Cecil spewing out a few parting insults and then storming off with his chums. "Poor Lewis" was left to stand alone.

The young man at Julia's side turned his attention back to her and introduced himself, "I'm Jonathan."

Julia couldn't look away from his eyes. They were tender and kind and actually had small flecks of green sprinkled amongst the gray.

"I usually like to know the names of the women I save," he joked, pulling Julia out from her thoughts.

"Oh, my, forgive me," she stammered, "Julia, my name is Julia."

"Nice to meet you," he smiled, "Julia."

The rest of the afternoon became a blur. There was a program with a variety of younger girls performing recitations. Meanwhile, Jonathan politely excused himself to rejoin his friends, then moved away. He blended back into the clusters of lively guests. Julia was left alone again until she heard wild laughter from across the room. She stood on tip toe scanning for "that" familiar face when she finally caught sight of Esther and Izzy.

The rest of the time was spent together and before they knew it, shadows were crawling across the room and Miss Stone was bidding good-bye to their male guests and showing them to the door. Julia tried to get one more glimpse of Jonathan before he left, but it seemed he had mysteriously vanished from sight. Julia decided to give up, but she did take one moment by the fire place. She closed her eyes, feeling heat from the remaining embers, and let herself hold onto the memory of his smile and the warmth of his gaze. But suddenly, Izzy broke in shouting, "Come on girls!", and the dream was gone. Izzy linked her arms with Julia's and Esther's and began to drag them back to the dorm. The only thing Julia could do was grin. She'd learned not to fight Izz. She just had to try and keep pace.

When they got upstairs, Esther went to Izzy and Julia's room and they all flopped on the beds. Izzy reached under hers and pulled out a plate covered with a clean dish towel.

Julia's eyes lit up. "What's that, Izz?"

With great flourish, Izzy whipped off the towel and revealed a large wedge of lemon cake with white frosting. "Where are the forks?" she asked.

Julia ran to her dresser and pulled open one of the small top drawers. She pushed aside a layer of hankies and extracted three forks. After handing one to both of her friends, they began to dig in, indulging themselves on Izzy's contraband.

Between forkfuls, Esther asked, "So, Julia, I saw you met my brother?"

"Your brother?" she questioned, still chewing on a mouthful of cake. "You mean Jonathan?"

"No," she replied, "Lewis."

"Lewis, that can't be!"

"Yup, that walking catastrophe is my big brother."

"Oh, gosh," said Julia, not trusting herself to say more.

"And Cecil is her cousin," added Izzy.

"Oh, really," replied Julia, still not wanting to say too much.

"Leave it to my family to be the center of attention," remarked Esther.

"So, who was that good looker I saw you with?" asked Izzy, slyly.

"Me?" asked Julia, her voice a little too high and eager.

"Yes, you," they said in unison.

Julia put her fork down. "His name is Jonathan."

9

Julia looked down at the painting in her hands and could almost feel every brushstroke as it was being applied to the canvas. Sometimes it was hard for her to believe she had been that girl, so brave and bold. She crossed the room to her bureau and propped the painting against her mirror. The room suddenly felt close and the air hard to breathe. She took a step back, as if a little distance could remove her from a pain she'd thought forgotten. A silent tear slid down her cheek. Ignoring it, Julia reached into her bodice and retrieved the worn and faded note. She sighed and carefully opened its folds. Holding it gingerly between her fingers she examined the beautiful script, faded but still legible. Its meticulous rendering proclaimed the author's care which made her ache that much more profound. In a whisper she began to read, slightly stirring the stillness of the room.

Dear Julia,
You have been a friend to me like no other. Your encouragement pushed me to pursue my dreams and because of that, I met Max. I have learned so much from him and now I am taking the next step. You will probably want to be sitting when I tell you – I am off to Paris. I have heard of a group of artists and writers and they are getting a lot of notice. I feel certain I will have more opportunities there, than I will ever have here.

I am leaving you with the only painting I refuse to sell, and I think it's my best. Honestly, I don't know if I'll ever see you again. Once I leave I can't come back. But I hope someday you'll buy a magazine with a cover I designed. Take care of yourself, and remember, love doesn't always come dressed in a tux with tails.
Your friend, and so far as I know, the first man to ever see your bare shoulder,
Billy

Julia closed her eyes on the tears that threatened to spill. After a moment she refolded his note and tucked it back in her dress, close to her heart. Billy was not here to see who she'd become and what she'd done with her life. But the woman who delivered the painting had, and for today, that was enough!

∽

The parlor room was darkening as late afternoon shadows crept across the floor. Julia wrapped herself in an old quilt and sat on the thick wool rug in front of the warm fire. She felt the weight of the thick envelope in her hands and reread her name and address on the front. She recognized the familiar handwriting and knew Izzy's letter would be worth the wait. It had arrived earlier that morning by special delivery. But Julia had tucked it away until now when she could relax and savor every word.

The girls were on their Christmas break and Izzy's family had sent her to England. She was to spend it in a dusty old manor with an equally antiquated, and severe aunt just outside the city of London. Her parents were keenly aware of their daughter's penchant for mischief and quite concerned that Izzy might do something to derail the plans they had so carefully laid for her future. Unknown to them, Izzy's intended was causing the same amount of consternation to his parents. Thus, he was spending his time sequestered under the watchful but silent eyes of Benedictin monks deep within the Austrian Alps.

Julia turned the envelope over and smiled at the flattened glob of wax that bore the imprint of Forget Me Not flowers.

"As if I ever could, " murmered Julia to herself.

Slowly she began to lift the edge and peel open the flap. She felt the wax relinquish its grip and as it parted she was rewarded with the scent of lavender. Julia had to tug carefully on the thick wad of papers wedged inside. When she finally set them free, a lavender sachet came sailing out as well. It landed on the floor in front of her and clearly printed on its label were the words:

HELP! I am being held prisoner on an old English estate and will surely die of boredom.

"Poor Izzy," thought Julia, "'They clipped your wings."

"Bang, bang, bang!"

Startled by the sudden pounding, Julia cast aside her letter and as she stood her quilt fell to the floor. Hesitantly she tip-toed to the hall where Lou was pulling open the front door.

"What can I do for you?" her question lay hanging in the chilly winter air.

"Where is he?" thundered an impatient George Barnett.

"Who?" asked Lou, calmly.

By now Julia was standing on the threshold that led to the hall. She could see past Lou to the dark figure that was filling the doorway.

"You know," George retorted, "that boy of yours." The barrel of a shotgun poked its way inside followed by George's threat, "either you tell me where he is or I'll search every inch of this property until I find him!"

"Why Mr. Barnett, there's no need for threats. Tell me what happened and I'm sure we can figure things without having to use that gun."

"She's gone!" he bellowed. A shaft of light crossed his face and Julia could see it was twisted in anguish.

Just then they heard the back door fly open.

"Hey, Ma," came a yell from the kitchen. "Okay if we grab a piece of cornbread before going to the barn?"

It was Billy.

George honed in on Billy's voice. He shoved Lou to the side and stormed past her. He took three long strides and entered the kitchen making for Billy.

"Hey Mr. Barnett," greeted DJ.

"Where's your brother?"

DJ pointed to the pantry just as Billy was walking out with a half empty pan of cornbread. By now Lou was at Georges elbow with Julia watching from behind.

From the still open back door, a deep voice commanded, "Put it down, George." By now, Don had entered the room and was standing in the back doorway.

"Not until I get answers," spat George.

"Answers will come, but not this way. Lou," Don spoke without taking his eyes off George, "put a pot of coffee on the stove and bring out that apple pie I saw earlier."

George lowered his gun slightly, he was clearly exhausted. "I can't find her," his words were filled with pain. Then looking at Billy the fire returned to his eyes. "Where's Abigail?" he demanded.

"I don't know, sir," he replied.

"She's been gone since, since….I don't know how long," he stammered. "All I know is she wasn't in her bed this morning when her mother went to wake her."

"Why would you think she'd be here," questioned Don, "Why not at one of her girlfriend's ?"

"Don't you think I already checked with them?"

The room was still and heavy, no one knew what to do and feared saying the wrong thing.

Finally, Don spoke,"I know we can figure this out, we just need to keep our heads," he counseled.

By now there were pie slices waiting on plates, but no one moved toward them. The aroma of fresh coffee filled the air but it held no appeal. Lou began to fill cups and place them around the table, then she went to a cupboard and took out a jar of shine.

"Coffee's better this way," she stated, and set it down.

Don nodded to the boys who pulled back chairs and sat. He motioned for Lou and Julia to leave and then took a seat himself. George was leaning his gun against the wall as they left the room.

Out in the hall Julia whispered to Lou, "What's that all about?"

"Not really sure," answered Lou.

"You look worried," pressed Julia, "Why? What aren't you telling me?"

Lou hesitated, then answered, "There have been strange things happening around here. Ever since the night of the barn dance."

The sun was just cresting the horizon when the search parties began to return. After meeting with George the night before, Don and his boys left to round up their neighbors. Groups were quickly formed and each set off in a different direction armed with dogs and lanterns. At sunrise, everyone was to meet at the Grange where hot coffee and baked goods would be waiting.

"Did you hear that?"

"Is she with them?"

"How many more groups are we waiting on?"

The questions were repeated over and over again. And each time someone new was spotted in the distance, a surge of hope would fill the air. But with each return, that hope was dashed and replaced with a deepening despair.

Finally, the last of the men were heard coming around the bend. "Someone, come quick," they were calling, "Hurry!!"

Before his cup had time to hit the ground, George Barnett took off running with his wife, Millie, close behind. "Where is she?" he yelled to the still unseen men, "Is she okay?"

Bent and walking slowly, three figures apperared in the distance. George's pace slowed as his hope began to evaporate. He couldn't see Abigail with them. The sun began to set a little lower in the sky illuminating the three men. Clearly it shown on a small fourth. She was being carried.

"Abigail!"

"Oh, Thank God!"

The exclamations were heard throughout the yard of the Grange. The small community had joined together to recover a lost member and now it moved as one to reassure themselves that she was truly safe.

George's vigor returned and being the first to reach her, he immediately gathered Abigail in his arms. Her mother was only seconds behind and joined him, losing themselves in the care of their child.

Soon, caring neighbors surrounded the family and Doc Abbott had to push folks aside so he could get through. Doc Abbott was the areas only physician, but he didn't have an office in any of the towns he served. Instead, he drove a buggy with a pair of sturdy, gray mares in a consistent circuit, meeting his patients on their farms or at a common room in their town. In Julia's community, there was a back room at the Mountainside where Doc would see patients every other Thursday.

"Okay, everybody, let's give her some air," he instructed.

On the fringes of the circle were DJ and Billy.

"I can't see anything," lamented Billy, "can you?" he asked, standing on tip toes and craning his neck.

DJ put a firm hand on Billy's arm, "You need to back off," he warned, "We've done our part, now we should head on home."

Billy hesitated, then reluctantly turned away. "Yeah," he said, "the important thing's she's okay, right?"

"Right. Now let's go. We need to let Ma know she's been found."

Billy took one last glance over his shoulder and began to walk away.

"Don't worry," consoled DJ, " we'll know soon enough what happened to her."

"Small towns, no secrets," Billy mumbled miserably.

Doc accompanied the Barnetts back to their home and gave Abigail a thorough exam. Besides a bump on her head and some scrapes and bruises, she was otherwise unharmed. He left her resting in her bed, now sleeping comfortably after drinking a warm cup of tea laced with one of his homemade sleeping potions.

Doc quietly pulled Abigail's bedroom door closed and slowly headed downstairs. He was troubled by some of her bruises, but he would keep that to himself for now. He wanted a chance to talk with the girl once she had healed.

Doc entered the drawingroom where George and Millie were waiting. "Doc, how is she ?" asked George, anxiously, "Will she be okay?"

"Sure," reassured Doc, "Sure, just make certain she gets plenty of rest and fluids." Doc turned to leave but paused in the doorway and added, "And don't tax her with questions."

George and Millie nodded obediently, clearly exhausted.

It was a few days later when Doc stopped by to check on Abigail. She was awake and alert and almost fully recovered. Her scrapes and bruises were barely noticeable and even the goose egg on her forehead was less painful and smaller.

"Good morning, Abigail," he greeted cheerfully.

"Hey, Doc," she answered shyly, "Sorry to have caused all the fuss."

Doc responded with a smile and went to sit on the chair next to her bed. "That's okay, honey, we're all just thankful you were found and your injuries weren't more severe."

Doc re-examined her, then gave the good news. Her recovery was complete.

"So it's okay for me to get up now?" Abigail asked.

"As long as you take it slow," Doc cautioned. Doc began to gather his things when he noticed an antique hair comb on

Abigail's night table. "This is pretty," he stated, picking it up and turning it over in his hand.

"Yeah but I don't know where it came from," she commented, "It fell out of my coat pocket when they found me."

"Humph," frowned Doc, "It looks expensive. And you've never seen it before?"

"Never."

"Well, I'm sure there's a reasonable explanation." He placed it back on the stand and struggled back into his heavy coat. Doc paused for a moment, not quite ready to leave.

"Is there something else?" Abigail asked, pensively.

"No, honey, you seem to have healed nicely."

"Then why do you look like there's more?" she asked.

Doc answered slowly, trying not to alarm her, "I was wondering if you could tell me what happened the night you disappeared? Why were you out in the woods?"

Abigail turned pale and stared down at her covers. Doc reached over and gently put his hand on her shoulder.

Abigail looked up and began, "Well," she chose her words carefully, "the other night I decided to take a walk up to the ridge. It was a clear night and I just wanted to look at the stars… alone…by myself."

Doc immediately understood. The ridge was a long time meeting place for young lovers. "Okay," he encouraged, "so how did you get hurt?"

"Well," Abigail took a deep breath, then continued "as I was sitting there, on this old log, I felt like I was being watched. So I turned around, but there was no one. I called out but all I heard was a few branches cracking."

"Did anyone answer?"

"No."

"So then what?"

"I started to walk back to the path at the edge of the woods," she paused, "that's when I thought I saw a shadow."

"A shadow?" he pressed, " Did you see anyone?"

"I can't be sure. I thought so then, but now I don't know. Anyways that was why I started to run."

"Did you hear any footsteps behind you? Were you followed?"

"I really don't know," she confessed, "I just ran. I guess I wasn't watching where I was going that's when I tripped over a fallen tree branch. All I remember is catching my foot and flying through the air. I hit my head on a rock and everything went black."

"And you don't know how you ended up so far from home? Out on the far side of the Kelly's woods?"

"No," she answered, "I vaguely remember waking up while it was still dark and my head was pounding. I must have wandered around for hours before I passed out again. That bump to my head was pretty bad!"

Doc smiled, "You got that right."

"Is everything okay?"

"Just fine, dear, it all makes sense." At least he hoped it did. Doc took one more look at Abigail. She was no longer a girl and yet, not quite a woman. With a final warning not to wander alone in the woods, Doc took his leave.

∽

Before Julia knew it, it was time to return to The Kimball Academy. Except for the momentary excitement of Abigail's disappearance, the holidays had been quiet. Each day she'd spend time playing with Alfred and she'd read, just for pleasure. She'd even gotten to be in the barns with DJ and Billy and made an impromptu visit to Max's studio.

But now she sat in the living room, impatiently tapping her foot. Julia was anxious to make the drive back to school and catch up with her friends. She'd received several more letters from England and it was obvious Izzy's pent up frustrations would be unleashed during their spring semester. Julia's friend had spent too much time alone. Meanwhile, Esther had been up in mountains skiing with family friends she had long ago outgrown. She too was ready for the return to school and her new circle. There was also the excitement of upcoming balls and parties as the older girls finished out their season. As junior debs, she and her classmates would be attending several of the nearby events and that would give them an idea of what their next year held in store.

Bang! The kitchen door slammed, it was DJ and Billy.

"I don't know why you can't do it!"

"Because I have chores of my own to do!"

"I'll help when you get back…Pleaseee!"

There was a long pause, then finally, "Okay. Fine. But don't make me come looking for you."

The back door slammed again and Julia heard footsteps in the hall. She looked up to see DJ's scowling face.

"Come on," he growled, "I don't have all day."

Obediently, Julia arose and followed him outside. Her bags had already been loaded into the car so she only had to climb in and get settled. DJ was already behind the wheel. He turned the key and gunned the engine. She felt the accelerator hit the floor and with a slight jerk, the car rumbled to life. It sped down the driveway, churning and spitting the packed snow to the side.

In the car's cab, the tension lay thick and Julia's excitement was squashed. A number of times she opened her mouth to start a conversation, but the scowl on DJ's face and his set jaw caused her to change her mind.

Finally, when she could take it no longer she asked, "What were you two fighting about?"

DJ glanced at Julia out of the corner of his eye.

"Humph," he replied, rolling his eyes, "As if you didn't know."

"Yeah, I know, you didn't want to drive me back to school," she said, "But there's more to it than that."

It was a minute before DJ answered, then he spat out, "Girls!"

"Hmm," said Julia, "All girls or just me?"

"The whole lot of you," he ranted, "A fella has plans…good plans, but who comes along to mess up everything? Girls! Oh, they make you think you're something special and get a fella all tied up in knots, then…Wham! They take it all away and leave the poor bastard writhing in pain and worthless. And where are his plans then? Gone. Just like the girl that broke his heart and all his plans!"

Julia reached over and softly touched DJ's shoulder. "Did something happen between you and Abigail?" she asked, concerned.

DJ shook off her hand "Abigail? What the …?"

"Well," continued Julia, " I know you've been sweet on her for a while and after what you just said, well, it sounds like she dropped you or something."

DJ began to laugh. He continued laughing loud and heartily until Julia demanded that he stop.

"I don't know why you find me so funny."

DJ drove silently for a few minutes. Finally, he said, " I'm sorry, but how did you ever come up with the notion that Abigail and me were 'anything'?"

"From a lot of things," Julia replied, defensively. "I know you were with her back in the grove during the barn dance."

"Me?"

"At least I thought it was you."

"Not me! Not her!" he declared. He looked at Julia sideways, and quietly added, "Not just any girl."

"Sorry, my mistake."

Julia sat back in the seat and thought on his words. "Not him…not with Abigail…but there was definitely someone."

The solid oak door flew open and Julia burst into the room she shared with Izzy. She'd barely dismissed DJ with a hasty, "Bye," when she jumped out of the car in front of the stone walkway leading to Kimball's entrance. She had raced inside and up the wide staircase, all but forgetting the farm and her family. She couldn't wait to reconnect with her schoolmate.

A pile of neatly stacked cases greeted Julia when she entered the oddly still room.

"She's not in."

Julia turned around and saw Esther's smiling face. The girls hugged before Julia asked, "Where's Izz?"

"She arrived earlier," replied Esther, " but as soon as her 'guardian' left, so did she."

"Humph," commented Julia, her brows furrowed. What could that girl be up to?

"...And don't expect your things anytime soon," Esther continued, "Peter's off on some errand so our bags won't make it up here until he gets back."

Julia plopped onto her bed. The reunion she'd been imagining had disintergrated before her eyes.

"Come on then," encouraged Esther, "let's not mope around."

"What do you have in mind?"

"Bundle up," Esther encouraged, " let's get a change of scenery!"

"What are you up to?" Julia asked.

Esther never answered. She just spun on her heel and returned a few minutes later wrapped in warm layers with a fur cap and muff. Julia, still in her traveling clothes, followed Esther who was sneaking down the back staircase.

It was a sunny afternoon and the snow was glistening brightly. The girls squinted as they headed across the back patio and then continued down a winding set of stone steps.They walked a short distance to the now dormant rose garden and passed under a carved granite archway. Off to the right they heard muffled voices from behind a border of thick bushes. Esther put a finger to her lips and motioned for Julia to stop. They both froze in their tracks and strained to hear what was being said.

"...it will be enough..." protested a deep voice.

"Are you sure?...my only hope...die if it doesn't!" a young woman adamantly proclaimed.

Julia mouthed to Esther, "Izzy?"

Esther simply nodded then took Julia's arm and quietly led her back to the dormitory. Silently, they reentered through the back door and tiptoed upstairs. It wasn't until they were in Esther's room with the door shut that either girl spoke.

"What's going on?" demanded Julia, "Who was she with?"

"Peter."

"Peter?" Julia's eyes widened. She couldn't believe what Esther was saying. It didn't make sense.

"Sit," Esther commanded, "I'll fill you in."

For the next hour, Esther explained how Izzy and Peter's friendship had begun and later, turned to love. It started the year before Julia had come to The Kimball Academy. During that time, many of the girls had been warned off Izzy by their parents. She'd come with a reputation for trouble and Kimball was her parent's last hope. Those first months had been extremely lonely for her. It was not much better for a poor, young man trying to make enough money to support his widowed mother. Peter was all she had since they'd lost his father in the war. Sadly, Peter's father had died along with so many others in the trenches. Then, for years after his death, Peter's mother labored long hours in a nearby factory. Her job was already barely sustaining them when she had an accident at her machine. Her machine took her right hand and also her job.

Peter was only twelve when faced with the responsibility of supporting them both. And his mother was adamant about keeping him out of the factory. So, armed with her good reputation and the determination only a desperate mother knows, she went to the Kimball Academy. She had an appointment with the Head Mistress who was known to be stern yet fair. She begged for her to give Peter a job, and that day, charity won out. Peter was hired and assigned to the aging groundskeeper. He was to help with any chores that needed doing. It was a decision neither woman ever regretted making.

When Peter began working at Kimball he was virtually invisible to all of the students and teachers. But he had an eager mind and it wasn't long before the Head Mistress noticed Peter's inquisitive nature and gave him permission to borrow books from their expansive library. She was also sympathetic to the limitations poverty had placed on his education and began to assign him duties that included classtime.

Peter did not disappoint and proved to her that he was a more than capable student. Ultimately, he was rewarded for all his hard work and granted the opportunity to earn extra money by tutoring some of the less than capable girls. That was when he and Izzy met. It wasn't that Izzy couldn't do the schoolwork required of her, it was that she wouldn't do it.

Izzy's parents were frustrated and acting apon the recommendation from the Head Mistress, they engaged Peter as a private tutor. They hoped to prevent their daughter from flunking out of yet another school. To their delight, Izzy's grades began to miraculously improve. They began to see Peter as their daughter's savior and rewarded him with monetary bonuses. They also continued to employ his tutorial services and that was when the teens friendship was forged.

Over the next two years, Peter and Izzy became close and their friendship grew into love. So also did their savings. Peter was wise and took all of his bonuses and began to make investments. He trusted Izzy to help him because her family was connected in the business world. Izzy did her part, also. She started saving all the monetary gifts she was given by wealthy family members and quietly sold off expensive pieces of jewelry. With their monies combined, she too started investing. In the course of those two short years, their assets grew handsomely. Their plan was when they'd made enough money, they would buy a few thousand acres of land just across the border into Canada. Peter didn't trust the stock market. For him it wasn't tangible. But he knew the value of land and knew that it was a resource that could be developed. His years at Kimball had also taught him that the wealthy class could be sold any idea as long as it was considered fashionable. He'd also learned that they would pay unreasonable prices for anything they deemed exclusive. So, he and Izzy devised a plan to build a hunting resort in the Canadian wilderness. They would offer to ferry small hunting parties in and back. Once there, they would provide their guests with the finest of everything. Luxurious accommodations, world class chefs serving the finest cuisine, and of course, the ultimate big game experience. Each party would be led by an experienced guide into the deep woods to track and hunt elk, moose and black bear. Success was guaranteed and with a taxidermist on staff, they would leave for home with the promise of a professionally mounted trophy and many evenings worth of bragging rights.

Julia sat in stunned silence. How was it she knew nothing about any of this?

A sharp knock brought her out of her thoughts. Esther opened the door and allowed Peter to bring in her things.

"Just leave them there," she instructed while pointing to the empty space in the center of the room. "Thanks!" she added.

Peter touched his cap and then hurried off to get his next load.

Julia told Esther she'd see her later, then walked across the
hall and entered her room. Izzy was surrounded by open boxes
and was busily shoving clothes into her dresser and wardrobe.

"Ahem!"

Izzy whirled around. "You're back!" she exclaimed and
hurled herself at Julia, wrapping her in a huge bear hug.

"Yes," Julia managed to squeak out, "some time ago."

Izzy took a step back and looked Julia over, "You've grown,"
she stated emphatically.

"What? That's all you've got to say?"

"Well, you have. You must be a half inch taller."

"Izz," Julia began, but was cut off with the arrival of her
belongings. Peter carefully stacked them on Julia's side of the
room and then turned to leave. For an instant, Julia saw them
share a secret smile, but it quickly disappeared.

How had she missed it before?

Julia's spring semester seemed to be flying by. Amidst
her usual studies there was also the constant flow of social
engagements. Much to her relief, she was becoming more
comfortable in her role as a socialite. The timidity that had
previously left her feeling awkward and inept was now all but
gone. She'd even had numerous encounters with Jonathan and
was beginning to suspect they weren't by accident.

"Oh, bugger!"

"Izzy," Julia admonished, "what's gotten into you?"

It was the last party of the season and both girls were
perilously close to missing their ride.

"I can't get this clasp" Izzy sputtered.

"Come, let me try." With deft fingers Julia easily secured the bracelet on Izzy's wrist. It was a chunky gold band inset with sparkling blue gems that were surrounded by small diamond studs. "This is lovely," commented Julia, "I don't think I've ever seen it before."

"Just came yesterday," stated Izzy, flatly, while she inspected her latest manicure.

"Yesterday?" frowned Julia, "From who?"

Izzy turned and answered with a scowl, "Him."

"Oh, 'Him,'" remarked Julia, knowingly.

'Him' was the code word they used when referring to Izzy's soon to be fiancé. And while many pretty boxes arrived on a regular basis from 'Him', both girls knew that 'Him' had never laid eyes on the gifts that were sent and the signature on the card had never been touched by 'His' pen.

"His parents will be attending," Izzy continued, "They're friends of our hosts." She looked down at her wrist, sniffed dramatically, and put her hand to her cheek , "I must make a good show," she intoned with a nasally voice. Julia merely laughed while Izzy gave a last turn in the mirror. Satisfied, she grabbed Julia's hand and announced, "Let's go!"

An hour later, they arrived in front of a stately home tucked away on a small bay on Lake Winnipesaukee. A warm breeze greeted the girls when they stepped out of the car and loud music from the back lawn gave promise of a lively evening. Julia and Izzy followed a long walkway up to an open set of double doors where a bored man stood, waiting to greet them. He was wearing a starched, white shirt with a bright, red bow tie, a short waisted, black jacket and matching slacks. Silently, he ushered them in and with a simple nod of his head to the left, indicated the direction they were to take.

Julia and Izzy took their cue and headed down a long, wide hall towards the main lounge. They stood for a moment in the doorway surveying the scene inside, but before they could enter, a tall, severe woman descended upon them.

"You're FINALLY here!" she admonished, "Why are you so late?"

"I'm not late, mother," Izzy replied, clearly annoyed. She turned to Julia and said, "My mother."

Not to be distracted, and clearly ignoring Julia, Izzy's mother reached out and wrapped a firm hand around Izzy's arm. She began to drag her through the lounge full of guests milling about and towards a stiff couple seated on the other side of the room.

"Help!" Izzy mouthed over her shoulder, then, was gone.

Julia was suddenly alone. She scanned the room hoping to see a familiar face. Normally, Esther would have been with them, but her brother was graduating from college and she had no choice but to join her family and attend that day.

"Punch?" came a soft, familiar voice from behind.

Julia smiled. She took a slow, calming breath and turned.

Jonathan was waiting with his arm extended. Julia graciously accepted. With an easy confidence, he expertly led her through the large room, weaving his way between small groups that were happily chatting. Finally, he led her through one of five sets of French doors which led them out onto a large patio.

Julia looked around. The lawn was beautifully landscaped with pristine flower beds, climbing trellis's dotted with pink roses, and shapely topiaries sitting in plaster urns. Artfully staged across the deep, green carpet were tables piled high with every sort of food. There were platters of fresh fruits, tiered pastries and cakes, roasted meats at a carving station and scores of waiters milling about with various trays of finger friendly delicacies. On the far left side, where the band was playing, a dance floor had been laid down and couples were already twirling about it in rhythm to the music.

Jonathan leaned in close, "Your voice is quite pretty," he whispered in Julia's ear.

Julia felt a quiver run through her. She assumed it was embarrassment for being caught humming out loud to the music.

"How about we take a stroll," he suggested quietly. "There's a path that runs along the water."

Julia raised an eyebrow. Normally he wasn't this forward. Without waiting for an answer, Jonathan gently touched her elbow and began to lead her out of the light and down the hill.

On the other side of the bay the sun had almost set. Its last streaks of orange and pink were sending rippling splashes of light across the lake's surface.

The path turned out to be a brick walkway and for a few minutes, Julia and Jonathan followed it along the shore. Neither of them spoke and the only sounds were distant strains from the orchestra and the gentle lapping of the waves.

When they had gone a short distance, Jonathan stopped. Julia looked up at the darkening sky. There were clouds moving in, crowding out the stars and the warm breezes were turning strong. She turned to the young man beside her and marked his profile as he stared off into the early twilight shadows.

Finally, he began in his soft, gentle voice, "You must have noticed...", he paused and cleared his throat. "You must have noticed that I've been seeking...your...you out at parties."

Julia waited. She wasn't sure what she was suppose to do or say.

"I just want you to know," he continued uncomfortably, "You're the only girl I've found interesting"

"Interesting?" she questioned, hoping there was more.

Jonathan laughed uneasily. "Perhaps that's not the right word." He fumbled, then forged on, "Julia, you're different from all the others, and ...I find that refreshing."

Silence.

"Damn," he muttered, "I'm really making a botch of this." Jonathan turned to face her. Julia lifted her eyes and was startled to see his were darkened with pain. She looked down and saw his hand tremble as it reached to gingerly hold hers. "I want you to know, if you approve, that I will be pursuing you next fall."

He waited a moment more, then added hastily, "When you start your season."

Julia felt her cheeks flood with warmth and was grateful for the shadows. She desperately wanted to reply in a calm, appropriate way that would not leave her feeling foolish. Instead, she heard herself blurt, "I'd love that!"

Instantly, the heat on her face intensified.

Jonathan relaxed and grinned, "Good!" he replied, then, just above a whisper, "that's settled."

Spontaneously, he lifted her hand to his lips and gave it a quick kiss. He laughed lightly. "Come on," he encouraged and began to lead Julia, pulling her back to the party.

When they reentered the brightly lit lawn, a group of Jonathan's chums immediately descended apon them. They seemed to be a nice sort, but all Julia could think about was finding Izzy. She couldn't wait to tell her what had just happened.

Reading her thoughts, Jonathan spoke softly, "Go find Izz." Then, quickly added, "Just be sure to say good-bye before you leave."

Julia grinned and hurried off.

She wove her way between clusters of young men and women now flirting happily under twilights canopy. When she finally got to the patio, she realized she had no idea if she'd still find Izzy inside. But since this was the best place to start, she slide past a couple deep in conversation and went inside.

Thankfully, the lounge was less crowded than when she'd arrived and Julia began to scoot along the room's perimeter. She circled her way around straining in all directions hoping to catch a glimpse of her friend. It wasn't until she was within earshot of a small group having a heated discussion that Julia realized she had found Izzy's mother. She was seated across from the stiff couple perched on a pale blue settee. Only the gray haired gentleman wearing a pinstriped suit with an overly bright green bow tie was speaking. His voice was low and terse and although Julia knew she should walk away, she found her feet wouldn't move.

"I thought by now you'd have the situation under control!" the gentleman admonished Izzy's mother. With a sidewards glance, he gave his wife a steely look that withered any thoughts she might have had about speaking. "We need to use leverage," he seethed, more to himself than anyone else. "Nothing has worked so far...for either of them!"

Izzy's mother opened her mouth to say something. Then, clearly thinking better of it, shut it back again.

"A baby!" he declared, a little too loudly.

"A baby?" both women asked in unison.

"Yes," he restated emphatically, "and not just a baby. An heir. An obligation. A noose around both their necks!"

"How?" Izzy's mother asked, "and to what end? Is this really how they should start their marriage?"

Clearly unconcerned with her doubts, the now animated gentleman began to lay out his plan.

"They've never actually met one another," he started, "so we arrange an 'accidental' meeting. My son is such a whore, he'll fornicate with any pretty thing he sets his eye on."

"But," Izzy's mother interrupted, "She's a virgin. Are you suggesting ... force?"

"No, no, not that," he reassured her, unconvincingly, "we'll just help Izzy relax into my son's bed and into the relationship she was intended for.

Julia felt sick to her stomach. Slowly, she inched away from the heated conversation and retraced her steps back to the patio doors. She pushed her way through and once she was again outside, she took a huge gulp of cool evening air.

"Poor Izzy!" she thought, "I've got to warn her!"

"There you are," said a deep voice at her side.

Julia turned, "Oh, Jonathan, it's you."

"Were you expecting someone else?" he laughed.

"Oh," she cried, "No, no one else."

Jonathan smiled and took her hand, "I think you owe me a dance."

"I'd love that," Julia stuttered, "normally, but, Izzy…I have to tell her something."

"You didn't find her?"

"No," Julia stammered on, "I tried."

"That's okay," he consoled, leading her towards the music, "You'll see her later."

Julia's feet were moving toward the dance floor but she kept looking over her shoulder hoping she'd catch sight of Izzy.

Suddenly, she felt Jonathan's arm wrap around her waist, her hand was in his and they were moving in rhythm to a slow, sultry song with bluesy undertones. All thoughts of Izzy began to drift away as she was led around the dance floor. When the last notes died off, an announcement was made that the party was over. The guests began to leave, moving towards the main house.

Julia felt Jonathan's arm slip away from her back and he quietly said, "I'll walk you out front."Julia simply smiled and allowed herself to be led across the cool grass.

Once they'd managed to navigate their way through the house, they emerged outside and stood with the others on the front walk waiting for their rides to come around. The crowd thinned as more and more cars pulled away from the curb, and it wasn't long before Julia saw some of the other Kimball girls she'd ridden with.

It was only a few minutes later that Jonathan saw his buddies getting into a large, shiny black car. "Hurry up!" they yelled and waved to him. Jonathan held up one finger, then turned to Julia, "This was nice."

"Yes," Julia blushed, not knowing what else to say.

"I'll see you soon," he added, then ran off to catch his ride.

Julia watched as the car disappeared into the darkness. She felt so happy and kept playing the night over and over in her mind.

Suddenly, she felt a jab in her side.

"What are you doing?" she exclaimed.

A tall, pretty brunette scowled and asked, "Where's Izzy? Our ride is here and we've got to go!"

A wave of panic flooded over Julia, "I don't know!" she cried, "Isn't she here?"

"Would I have asked if she was?" the brunette was clearly annoyed.

Julia scanned the few remaining guests, hoping to see her, but there was no sign of Izzy.

"Should I look inside?"

"No. The car is here. You can get in or get left behind."

Reluctantly, Julia followed the others to the vehicle that was quietly idling in the driveway. She gave one last look over her shoulder, then slowly slid in next to the brunette.

The drive back to Kimball seemed to take forever, which made the knot in Julia's stomach grow tighter.

Back at the school, she headed into the dorm and silently went upstairs. Julia was wracked with guilt and on the verge of tears. She only hoped she could get into the comfort of their room before she started to cry. When she was nearly there, she heard the sound of muffled laughter. She could see a sliver of light shining from beneath Esther's door. Julia walked up to it and knocked softly. The laughter ceased and she could hear soft footsteps approaching.

The door barely opened and Esther's nose peeked out, "Oh, thank goodness!" she exclaimed, "It's only you!"

The crack widened, her hand reached out and grabbed Julia's arm. Quickly she was pulled inside and heard a firm, "Click", from behind. The light was low but Julia could see propped up on a bed of pillows, balancing a plate of yellow frosted cake in one hand, and a fork in the other…Izzy.

"What? How?" she exclaimed.

Esther gave a loud,"Shhh!"

"But when?" Julia asked in a loud whisper. "I thought you got left behind."

Izzy smiled and waited, allowing her dramatic moment to play out. Then, when Julia looked like she was ready to lunge at her, Izzy began to explain. Apparently the entire evening had been going horribly. The parents were planning her entire summer. Where to visit and who to make an impression upon. Of course she had been resistant, in a polite, passive aggressive way. She could tell they were losing patience with her and just when she thought the parents would blow their tops, her mother sent her to "powder her nose". "I tell you, Julia, I was so steamed I almost left. I was ready to walk back to Kimball. In the dark!"

Julia didn't doubt for one moment that Izzy was capable of such a reckless decision.

"But," Izzy continued, " As I was leaving for the door, my mother met me in the hall. I've never seen her so mad, not even at me. I don't know what they did or said, but she grabbed me by the arm," at which point Izzy stuck her chin in the air and adopted a nasally tone, "Isadore, it's time we left!" Izzy lay back a little deeper into the pillows with a satisfied smile. "She said the engagement plans are off! I'm not to have anything more to do with those depraved people."

Julia was both relieved and stunned. She hadn't looked forward to telling Izz about the conversation she'd overheard. Still, she found it hard to believe that Izzy's mother told her what had really happened.

"I won," beamed Izzy, "I wore them down. I'm finally free!"

Julia realized the truth. Thankfully, Izzy's mother hadn't spilled all the details. If Izzy ever knew what that diabolical man intended, well, that didn't bear thinking about. Now, all that mattered was her friend was safe, and Julia was relieved to know there were lines even Izzy's mother wouldn't cross.

The following weeks passed quickly as the girls struggled to focus on studying for their year end exams. When the term was finally over Julia, Izzy, and Esther had already made plans to meet in Boston at the end of the summer. Esther's parents had a brownstone where they usually spent the winter and it had been agreed that all three girls and their mothers would stay there. The plan was to do some sightseeing and then hit some dress shops to round out their wardrobes before going back to school.

Julia stood looking around at their near empty dorm room. Peter had already taken her bags out front and it looked rather sad without all of her and Izzy's belongings scattered throughout. Reluctantly, she turned to leave. She wasn't sure who would come to get her, and for once, it didn't really matter. The year had changed her, and now Kimball felt more like her home than the farm did.

"Ready to go?" Esther's cheerful voice broke into her thoughts.

"Yup," answered Julia, forcing a smile.

Esther bounded to her side, grabbed her hand, and they began to walk down the hall.

"Don't look so glum," Esther encouraged, "the summer will fly by! We'll be in Boston before you know it and just wait till you see what my mother has planned! She's already made appointments with some of the finest dress makers and there'll be so many other wonderful things to do!"

"Oh, I know," Julia exclaimed, longingly. "I can't wait! I've never been to the city, you know."

"Really?" Esther feigned astonishment.

Julia gave her a playful push. "I know, I've told you many times."

"Have you? I can only think of thirty, forty…certainly not more than fifty."

Julia blushed and gave Esther another nudge with her shoulder. The two chums continued downstairs chatting and laughing gaily.

Miss Stone was sitting at her post in the main hall, clucking over the girls as they left and wishing them a restful summer break. Esther and Julia passed through the wide entry doors which were propped wide open and Julia could feel a warm breeze swirling around her ankles, rustling her skirt. When she first stepped into the bright sunshine it left her momentarily blinded. She had to blink a few times before her eyes adjusted to the light. When she could finally see, she looked ahead and saw DJ standing at the end of the walk talking with Peter. They had their heads together and were speaking in hushed tones. It seemed serious. Then, DJ slipped a small jar out of his pants pocket and passed it to Peter, who then slid it inside his shirt.

"What could that be about?" she wondered.

"Hey!"

Julia nearly fell over as Izzy plowed into her. Julia just grinned. Ever since the night of the cocktail party, Izzy had been happier than ever. Once the weight of her impending engagement had been lifted, she had a joy that couldn't be contained. In fact, some of the other girls had begun to complain that they liked the "Old Izzy" better. This seemed strange to Julia since these same girls had been the ones complaining about Izzy getting into mischief and playing tricks. Now they went about the dorm with their hands covering their ears because Izzy was singing too much and too loud and altogether too off key. Julia didn't care. She was fond of her friend and much preferred a happy Izz to a forlorn one.

By the time Julia reached DJ, Peter was gone and DJ was putting the last of her trunks in the car. He looked anxious to go. Esther's ride was waiting a few cars behind but she made it wait while she took a minute to run over and say "good-bye". The three chums wrapped their arms around each others shoulders. They vowed to have no fun until they met up in Boston and promised to share any "new developments" by letter.

After they separated, Julia sat in the car next to DJ. Her heart felt empty. An air of sadness enveloped her. Meanwhile, DJ sped back to the farm along the well worn roads, a smile at the corners of his mouth. Julia took a moment and glanced over at him. She was startled to see the subtle changes in his appearance. Changes that made him look less like a boy and more like a man. His jaw was more defined and chisled. There was even a shadow left behind from his mornings shave. His brow had faint creases and even his eyes seemed wiser. She started to look away but not before she noticed his shoulder and arm muscles straining against the fabric of his shirt. Much to her chagrin, Julia could feel herself blushing and was annoyed at the flutters that now filled the hollow in her stomach.

Julia laid her head back against the warm upholstery and closed her eyes. She could feel the sun beating on her face and she forced herself to think of Jonathan. She dreamed of beautiful gowns swirling at her feet and his hand on her waist as they glide across a dimly lit dance floor.

She knew it was important for her to remain realistic and not get distracted. Her future lay elsewhere, far beyond the farm.

The trip home had tired her out, so that evening, Julia allowed herself the luxury of soaking in a long, hot bath. The scent of lavender filled her nostrils and she relished the soft suds that clung to her skin leaving it smoothe and tender. When she was finally done, she stepped out of the tub leaving only the brown water and a light film.

Julia changed into a light dress and then threw a sweater over her shoulders. In bare feet she went out onto the porch intending to go visit Gert. Will was sitting on the steps looking out across the field to the mountains beyond. The sun had already set and its last rays were quickly fading into the hills. A soft wind blew, rustling Julia's curls and she pulled her arms into the sleeves of her sweater.

Dad patted a place on the stoop. Julia stepped down and sat beside him. She felt her Dad's arm wrap around her shoulders and gently pull her in for a hug. Julia let herself lean in. She could hear his soft breathing and feel the rise and fall of his chest. They stared into the shadows watching for the first stars. After a bit, Julia began to move away. She still wanted to see Gert before it got too late.

Dad's arm tightened.

"I'm sorry, honey," he began, "Gert's not here."

"What?" Julia asked in alarm.

"I'm guessing that was where you were headed."

"Yes," she answered, "Where is she?"

"We had to put her down."

"No," argued Julia, stunned. "Not Gert, no!"

"I'm sorry, Julia," Dad continued, "She was old. Too old."

"But Dad, she was fine when I left for school."

"She was old, Julia," Dad consoled, "And tired. It was a kindness to let her go."

Julia slumped. The emptiness that had followed her all day deepened and she was unaware when a deep sigh escaped her lips. Dad tried to rub her back but she moved away, his touch offered no comfort.

Julia sat a little longer and watched as dark shadows began their nightly trek across the pond and slow ascent up the hill. When the porch was finally enveloped in the nights black haze, Julia mumbled a consolatory, "Good night," and went inside leaving Will.

Later that night, Julia lay in her bed. She felt so alone without Izzy and Esther. There was even one point when her stomach let out a loud groan. She thought about sneaking downstairs for a piece of pie, but there was no sense in doing it. She was at home so she could help herself to whatever she wanted at anytime. And without her best friends and the risk of getting caught, well, she wondered, where was the fun?

So instead, Julia rolled over and pulled Mum's quilt a little closer. She pushed her face deep into her pillow and allowed the tears she'd been holding back to flow. Eventually, despair turned to exhaustion and with that, she drifted off into a restless sleep.

∽

Julia slept late the next morning and no one bothered to wake her. By the time she had washed up and dressed, it was well past breakfast. Despite the ache of hunger, Julia decided to make do with some fresh strawberries. She reached into a deep bowl on the counter and grabbed a handful as she passed through the kitchen. Once outside, she paused to lift her face to the sky and breathe in the summer's heat. Then with the resolve of a new day, she walked to the barn and stepped inside.

Julia went straight to Gert's stall fully expecting it to be empty. But, much to her surprise, there was a new resident filling Gert's space.

"Who are you?" Julia demanded.

A beautiful brown calf looked up at her with large, moist eyes. Immediately Julia was smitten.

"Her name's Bea."

Julia smiled and scratched the calf's head. "Why Bea?" she asked.

Billy was now standing next to Julia holding a warm bottle of milk. "Well," he began, "the day she came here Alfred was playing outside. When he saw her, there was a small bumble bee sitting on the end of her nose. He got real excited and began pointing and screaming, 'Bee, bee!! No one thought much about it until later when he saw her again and yelled, 'Bee!' From that day on, that's what we've called her."

Julia reached out and took the bottle Billy was handing her. She held it out to the hungry calf who began to suck noisily.

"How'd we get you?" asked Julia, absently.

"Her mother didn't survive her birth," answered Billy, "and she was too stubborn to take a bottle. Just skin and bones when your Dad brought her home."

"Poor girl," consoled Julia.

"Yeah, if it wasn't for DJ, I think she would have died."

"DJ?"

Billy chuckled. "You should have seen him talking all sweet to this cow." Billy shrugged slightly, "I don't really know what he did exactly, but Bea wouldn't be here if he hadn't."

Suddenly, the bottle gave a sharp tug as a disgruntled Bea tried to coax out a few more drops of milk.

"Well," exclaimed Julia, "I guess we don't have to worry about you starving anymore!"

Bea's brown dewy eyes looked up and she reluctantly let go of the nipple. Her chin was wet with milk and she gave her tail a contented 'swish'.

Billy grabbed the empty bottle out of Julia's hand. He gave a quick wave, and was out the door to continue his chores. Julia took another glance at Bea then reluctantly left the barn. She looked around the yard wondering how to spend her day. Dad and Blanche had left early that morning with Alfred to spend a couple days at the shore and everyone else on the farm was busy working.

Julia stepped out of the barn's shadow and into the sunlight. Mum's locket felt warm against her chest and she decided to go up to the North pasture. It had been a long time since she'd brought flowers to Mum and Will's graves. She also felt an almost desperate need to find something on the farm that was the same as when she'd left.

After picking a bouquet of bright yellow daisies and some pale blue corn flowers, Julia began the short walk up to the pasture. With no shoes to protect her tender feet, the tall meadow grass felt slightly prickly and scratched her bare ankles. All around her she could hear the steady buzz of insects and even from a little ways off she could see a small patch of Queen Anne's Lace growing near the headstones.

Julia took her time. She had nowhere else to be and wanted to savor the sounds and smells of her childhood. By the time she reached the small cemetary, the sun had climbed high in the sky. It shone down brightly and caught the edge of something hidden in the low grass at the base of Mum's gravestone. The small flash of light caught Julia's eye.

"What can that be?" she wondered.

Her pace quickened and a minute later, Julia was stooping down to see.

She gasped! Her small bouquet fell to the ground. Julia pushed aside a few blades of grass and picked up a familiar piece of jewelry. It was the silver haircomb she'd lost last fall. She held it in the palm of her hand and ran her finger over the dark blue gems.

"There's no dirt on it," Julia observed.

A soft breeze began to stir and the hair on Julia's neck stood on end. Despite the heat, a shiver ran down her spine and the pasture was suddenly quiet. Julia stood up and looked around. Nothing. Despite an uneasy feeling that she was not alone, there was not another human in sight. Julia looked down at the comb again.

"How did you get all the way up here?" she asked, as if she'd get a response.

Suddenly, a flock of blackbirds erupted from a nearby thicket. Julia dropped the comb and ran. She didn't stop until she was by the barn and only then did she turn and look back toward the pasture. Even though there was no one in sight, she still couldn't shake the feeling that she was being watched.

Later that afternoon, Julia waited for Billy to come to the barn.

"Um," Julia hesitated, "Hey, Billy, can I ask you something?"

"Sure, Julia, but when have you ever had to ask if you could ask me anything?" he laughed.

"It's just that something weird happened today. I don't know what to make of it."

The grin on Billy's face melted. "What happened?" he asked, serious now.

Julia told him all about her earlier visit to the North pasture. She finished by asking him to go back with her so she could retrieve her hair comb.

"I know I'm being silly, but…"

"No, you're not," he assured her, "We'll go as soon as Bea's done eating. Then," he grinned, " you can help me with the rest of the stock."

Bea made quick work of her meal and it was only a few minutes till they were setting off across the meadow. It was still bright out, but an early evening breeze was beginning to blow and the crickets were chirping loudly. When they got within sight of the headstones, both Julia and Billy's pace slowed. They approached cautiously, looking in all directions.

Nothing. There was nothing that seemed out of the ordinary. Julia crouched down next to the dropped bouquet of flowers, but there was no sign of the haircomb. She spread her fingers and ran them through the grass. Still no comb.

Julia looked up at Billy questioningly. He shrugged his shoulders. But then, his eyes widened with understanding.

"The comb you lost," he began slowly, " was it silver...with blue stones?"

"Yes," Julia answered, "It's the one I lost at the barn dance last summer."

"I've seen it."

"I know, that night in my hair."

"No," he countered, "I didn't see you that night. I was with Abi....busy. I never went to the dance."

"Then when did you see it?"

"Do you remember when Abigail went missing?" he asked.

"Sure," Julia answered, impatiently, "The whole town was looking for her."

"Yeah, well, when they found her....that comb, YOUR comb, was in her pocket. She had no idea where it came from or how it got there."

Slowly, Julia asked, "Where is that comb now?"

"Gone."

"Gone?"

"Gone! Abigail brought it by the barn one day to show me."

Julia raised an eyebrow. "Abigail came by the barn? Here?"

Billy blushed; ignoring the implication, he continued with his story. "She forgot it on the rail outside the door. Next day, I looked for it but it had disappeared."

"And you think it was mine? The one I lost?"

"I'm sure of it. What I'm not sure of is who has it and why they're playing around."

∽

The days were flowing into one another at the lazy pace found only on a country farm in midsummer. Every day the heat would hang thickly in the air so that even a late afternoon shower could only manage a slow crawl across the valley.

During this time, Julia remained close to home. Her visit to the North Pasture had left her feeling uneasy, so instead of venturing off on her own, she spent most of her time with Alfred. They would read stories, play games like Hide and Seek, and eventually, go on visits to see Bea.

The calf was growing fast and displaying the same gentle patience as her predecessor. Even when her silky hair was being tugged on by an energetic toddler, she showed no sign of irritation. She would simply gaze up at Julia with a look that communicated love and understanding.

Most days while Alfred napped, Julia would grab a book, go out to the porch and gently rock in the swing. She found it very relaxing but wasn't sure if the energy she was expending was worth the small breeze it created.

"Looks like it's gonna be a doozy," Lou observed from the doorway on one especially humid day.

Gazing at the sky, Julia noticed dark clouds gathering and could hear the soft rumble of thunder echoing off the distant hills.

"I guess we're due,"she commented.

Lou scowled at the approaching storm and turned to go back inside. She paused, "How about you help the boys finish up with the stock. I want everyone in before this starts."

Julia pulled herself to standing, shook off her sluggishness and went to visit the biddies and see if they had any eggs for her. Thankfully, it hadn't taken long for Julia's bare feet to toughen up so she was surprised when she felt cutting pain as she approached the coops.

"Ow!" Julia cried out and brushed the bottom of her foot. Small slivers of glass clung to her damp, sweaty hand. "What's this from?" she muttered.

Bending down, Julia looked closely at the path. There amidst the small rocks and pebbles were pieces of clear broken glass. She continued on to the henhouse, careful to avoid stepping on any of them. As she approached, Julia was struck by an unnatural quiet and when she reached for the latch, she noticed fingerprints and a long, dark smear.

Julia looked around uneasily. The thunder was growing louder and the sky had turned black. Quickly, she flipped the latch and peeked inside. The biddies were softly clucking and nervously shifting in their nests.

At first, Julia didn't see him; she was too busy checking for eggs. Then a dark shadow in the bed of hay let out a soft groan. Julia reached over and pushed aside a thin layer of straw.

"Oh, my goodness!" she exclaimed, "Billy!"

Julia stuck her head outside the door and yelled for help, but her cries were lost in the strengthening winds. She felt bad, but she had to leave Billy and run to the barn for help. She went as fast as she could, nearly colliding with DJ as he came around the corner.

"Watch where you're going," he admonished.

"Come with me," Julia demanded, "Billy's hurt!"

"Hurt?" DJ exclaimed.

"Be careful," she warned "There's glass on the path."

"Okay," he answered and hurried after her.

It took both of them to maneuver Billy out of the coop. Without hesitation, DJ hoisted his brother's limp body onto his shoulders and began to carry him to the barn. Julia ran ahead to find Lou. By the time DJ got to the barn, the rain was pouring and thunder was shaking the timbers. Lou and Julia were waiting with the door open and quickly ushered DJ in. They had him lay Billy on a small cot in one of the stalls.

"Get my kit," Lou ordered.

DJ flew back out into the storm and headed up the hill to their cottage.

"I need hot water, Julia," Lou commanded, without looking up. "The kettle's on in the kitchen. Fill me a pan and bring some clean rags."

✿

Billy's eyes fluttered open. A soft groan escaped his lips and his hand instinctively reached to the gash on the side of his head that was now covered with a thick layer of bandage.

"Don't pick," Lou scolded softly.

At the sound of his mother's voice, DJ appeared from a dark corner of the barn. His brow was creased and he tapped the side of his leg impatiently. Finally he blurted out, "What happened to you?"

"Leave him for now," Lou snapped.

Reluctantly, DJ backed off.

"He'll be okay, won't he, Lou?" Julia asked quietly.

"He just needs a few days rest," then added, "It's good you found him when you did."

Julia shuffled her feet uncomfortably and winced.

"What's wrong with your feet?"

Julia held one up, revealing jagged, bloody gashes.

"Oh, Julia!" Lou pointed to a small stool. "Sit here." She turned, "DJ, rinse out this pan and get me some more hot water."

DJ took the pan from Lou and left.

It was early evening and all that remained of the recent storm was a light gray haze. DJ strode toward the house, the white enamel dish swung pensively at his side. From the corner of his eye, he noticed a shadow creeping under the kitchen window. He slowed his pace slightly and tightened his grip. Just when he was about to charge and deliver a well placed blow, Davy called out, "Wait!"

DJ stopped in his tracks and lowered his arm. "What are you doing?" he demanded, clearly annoyed. "I almost clocked you!"

"Sorry, we were s'pose to meet up, remember?"

"Yeah," DJ paused, "Sorry, Dav, we had a little trouble here. Tell the fellas I'll catch up tomorrow." He was about to walk off when two more figures rose from behind a nearby cluster of lilac bushes. They cautiously came forward. It was Jimmy and Bobby.

"Is everything okay?" asked Jimmy.

DJ turned and answered emphatically. "No. It's starting up again."

"Do you still think it's tied to Julia?" Bobby asked.

"Has to be. Someone's been coming around ever since she got home. Coop's been getting raided, and not just eggs this time. We lost two of the biddies." DJ took a breath, "And today Billy went early to try and catch him in the act." DJ paused for emphasis, "Got hit from behind."

"Bastard!" exclaimed Bobby.

"With one of our jars!"

"Rotten bastard," added Jimmy.

The group stood silently for a moment, contemplating what this meant. Finally Jimmy put into words what they were all thinking, "So if whoever is doing this only comes around when Julia's here. Why?"

DJ shrugged, "I have no idea, but clearly...he's dangerous."

"And now he knows where our still is, too!" added Davy.

Later that night, Will arrived home with Blanche and Alfred. Don was waiting on the front porch steps. "Hey," he greeted as they walked up toward the house.

"Hey, Don," responded Will with a smile that quickly faded when he noticed the 12 gauge at Don's side. He motioned for Blanche to take Alfred inside and then asked, "Trouble?"

"A bit," answered Don, evenly.

Will stopped and turned aside. He looked out toward the pond, straining into the dark shadows.

"Let me put on some coffee and you can fill me in."

"Lou's already got a pot made," Don responded.

"And I'm guessing something sweet to go with it?"

Don gave a soft chuckle. "Wouldn't be much good without a warm piece of Lou's blueberry buckle."

The two men entered the house and quietly went to the kitchen. Will turned up the lights while Don grabbed cups and began to pour the coffee. On the kitchen table was a large tin with a blue checked cloth draped over the top. Will slowly pulled it back and breathed in its sweet scent. Lou had conveniently left two plates, a serving knife and a couple of forks along side the pan.

Will picked up the knife and slowly cut into the thin top layer, savoring the soft, sugary crunch. Then he sank his knife into the dense layer beneath. Carefully, he carved out two large squares and placed them on the plates. Will could hardly wait as deep purple juice from the blueberries began to stain the pale yellow cake and pool around the sides of the plate.

Don walked over and placed two steaming cups down on the table. They both sat, not speaking a word until both of their plates had been cleaned and their cups drained.

Finally, Will leaned back in his chair and asked, "So, what's going on that you're waiting for me on the front steps instead of home with your wife?"

Don began to relate the events of the past few weeks ending with the assault on Billy at the coops. Will's brow furrowed.

"What do you make of it?"

Don hesitated, then answered evenly, "It appears to be starting again."

Will's eyes remained fixed on a nonexistent stain on the tablecloth. He exhaled slowly, his gaze met Don's. "I'll get her out of here," he stated firmly, "tomorrow."

"That would be best," agreed Don, "Where will she go?"

"She and Blanche have plans to go to Boston in a couple weeks, they can just go early. I know a nice place to put them up. They can catch some sights until it's time to meet up with Julia's friends."

Don began to speak but caught himself, choosing to remain silent.

"What else?" questioned Will, "Don't start going quiet on me now!"

"You just need to know," Don paused, "Barnett's in Boston right now."

Will's brow furrowed deeper. "Hmm," he murmured. "What would you think about DJ going with them? I don't want Blanche worrying about that man."

"Sounds good," agreed Don, "the next month or so will be slow until crops start coming in."

"I'll have Blanche take him to get a couple nice suits first thing," thought Will out loud.

"He won't like it," Don chuckled, "But he'll do it - to keep her safe."

The next morning Will drove Blanche, Julia and DJ to the depot. The air was heavy and stale. The sun was barely up and a haze was already hanging over the mountains. It was sure to be another hot and breezeless day. Two small leather trunks with bright brass buckles and a small cardboard suitcase sat at their feet. There were no other passengers on the platform so they stood quietly, waiting to hear the soft whistle that would announce the train's approach.

Toot, Toot.

Finally the whistle was heard and within minutes a dark engine came into view chugging out black puffs of smoke. Blanche turned to Will and forced a small smile. He gave her hand a reassuring squeeze. A cloud of dust billowed down the tracks and the slow screech of metal announced its arrival.

As the train braked alongside the platform, a smallish man sporting a tidy gray handlebar and wearing a dark blue conductors uniform appeared at the top step of the passenger car. His gold brass buttons matched the gleam in his eyes and it was clear to all that he loved his job. With a slight florish he dropped down a set of steps and disembarked. Then at the bottom, he turned to take the hand of a corpulent woman whose bodice begged for a couple more inches. Her pudgy fingers engulfed the conductor's hand and his smile waned as he helped steady her descent.

"Come along, Abigail! Don't dawdle!" She beckoned to the shadow of a girl trailing behind.

"Coming, Grams," reassured Abigail Barnett, who now stood in the car's doorway. She watched as the older woman extracted her hand from the conductor's, leaving him with a sniff of disdain.

Not waiting to see if her granddaughter was following, Mrs. Barnett simply muscled her way past the conductor and plowed straight into Blanche. First to recover, the older woman sneered and exclaimed, "You! What are you doing here?"

Blanche was taken aback but before she could respond, Will stepped forward.

"Good day, Mrs. Barnett," he offered with a slight nod of his head.

Mrs. Barnett recoiled slightly. She glared at Will and then turned on her heel and began to stalk away, all the while muttering, "A well-dressed tramp is still just a tramp!"

Abigail trailed few steps behind. As she passed Blanche she mouthed, "Sorry!"

Blanche answered with a soft smile and mouthed back, "Thank-you!"

It was mid-morning when the train pulled into Boston. As they disembarked into the subway, Julia didn't know where to look first. Her head began to spin. There was so much. So many people walking briskly past her. Pushing. Eyes straight ahead. And the noise. So many new sounds! The screech of the subway cars. The constant hum of conversations. And the smells. So many assaulting her nose! Grease and oil. Perfumes and aftershave. All fighting for dominance.

Julia tried desperately to keep up with Blanche, who was effortlessly weaving her way through the throng. Once Julia made the mistake of being distracted by a colorful poster boasting the finest chowder in all of Boston. When she looked back, Blanche was gone! Thankfully she felt DJ's strong hand on the middle of her back, gently pushing her in the right direction.

Finally, Julia took the last step up and out of the subway. When she entered the bright, sunlit day she was ready to fall on her knees and kiss the ground. But before she could breathe a sigh of relief, she heard Blanche beckoning, "Come along."

"Oh, Blanche," moaned Julia, "Can't we please stop for just a minute?"

Blanche paused and looked back. Her eyes softened as she remembered that for Julia this was all new. "Can you walk a bit further?"

"Just a bit?"

Blanche smiled. "I promise. Not much farther…and it will be worth it!"

Julia tried to perk up but when she heard DJ chuckling behind her, she felt her back stiffen. Fortunately, Blanche hadn't lied. They only had to walk a short block and along the way they passed a large, open park.

Julia found herself entranced by its rows of tall maple and elm trees and felt welcomed by its lush, green lawn. She couldn't take her eyes off the small clusters of people milling about. There were colorful parasols bobbing to and fro and young children laughing and running about with playful pups hard on their heels.

"We're going to cross here," Blanche directed.

Julia turned from the park and looked across the cobblestone street. A long, narrow ten story building stared back at her. Its windows sparkled and gleamed in the noonday sun and there was a large green canopy hanging over a set of perfectly polished double doors that bore the name, R.H. Stearns. Just on the other side of the glass stood a man in an impeccably pressed suit, erect and ready to serve. As they approached, he eyed Blanche and Julia with mild interest and, with an imperceptible movement, swung the door open. As they entered, he nodded slightly to the ladies but his nose of disapproval raised slightly higher when DJ passed through.

Once inside the department store, its enormity hit Julia. She slowly turned and for a few moments, could only stare in unbelief at all the merchandise.

Quietly, Blanche instructed, "Julia."

"Hmmm?"

"Close your mouth."

Julia blushed, but before she could feel too embarrassed there was a sudden burst from across the store.

"Miss Blanche!" the greeting echoed. "I thought you'd never get here!"

It wasn't until a full minute later that its owner appeared from around a display of brightly colored men's trousers. Like the greeter, he was sharply dressed and moved with a practiced efficiency. His name was Samuel Schneider and he had long been a trusted employee of R.H. Stearns. Also, but not quite as long, he had been a trusted friend of Blanche's.

Blanche and Samuel exchanged a quick hug.

"It must be something special to bring you back to Boston?" Samuel probed, gently.

Blanche glanced over at Julia. "Yes, very special."

Samuel acknowledged with an imperceptible nod and then got down to business. "Is this the young man you wired about?"

Blanche smiled, "This is DJ."

Without missing a beat, Samuel stepped over to DJ. He gave him a quick head to toe, then stated, "First, we should assemble some outfits. Day and night?" he asked with raised brows.

"Yes, and perhaps one nice suit…casual, for evening."

"Very good. And you'll be wanting a full grooming?"

"Yes," Blanche replied, hesitated, and then added, "But only a trim. Leave it long."

Samuel took his eyes off DJ, questioningly.

"I'm sure," she stated.

Satisfied, Samuel turned back to DJ, "Follow me," he instructed.

Then, he was off, quickly disappearing into the depths of the men's department. DJ simply strode off in the same general direction.

The store became quiet and still. Now Blanche and Julia were alone.

"Okay," Blanche said, turning her attention to Julia. "Let's go to the third floor. They have a marvelous coffee shop."

"Coffee?" Julia wrinkled her nose.

Blanche chuckled. "That's just the name, Julia, they also have sandwiches and desserts."

Julia's eyes lit up and as if on cue, her stomach emitted a low growl. Blanche and Julia laughed. Then they linked arms and headed off in the direction of the elevator.

Later that day the elevator made its return to the first floor. The ride was quiet except for Julia's soft sigh of contentment. She was still full from their lunch of egg salad sandwiches and fresh lemonade. She and Blanche had even splurged and split a thick slice of Raisin Spice cake with buttercreme frosting.

After they finished eating, they ventured into the ladies department where Blanche selected a number of outfits to "round out" Julia's wardrobe. In all honesty, Julia didn't see the need for a tennis outfit and in her opinion most of the dresses defied modesty. But Blanche had insisted that in the city it was not only quite fashionable but within the bounds of propriety to expose ones ankles and even ones lower calves. Julia wasn't convinced and had even begun to stubbornly dig in her heels. It wasn't until she saw the adorable matching shoes that she, a bit less reluctantly, abandoned her cause.

Once Blanche and Julia finished making all their purchases, the clerk carefully wrapped everything in brown paper and tied it up with twine. Then, Blanche made arrangements to have it all delivered to the nearby brownstone where they would be staying.

"Ding, ding"

The elevator stopped with a soft thud and the doors slowly parted. Its operator pulled the heavy black gate to the side and held it open so Julia and Blanche could depart. Stepping out into the mens department, they were easily able to locate Samuel and DJ simply by following the melodic chatter of Samuel's voice. As Blanche had told Julia over lunch, "He's a dear man who believes his greatest gift is his ability to speak to anyone at anytime about anything."

As they approached, Samuel turned. He wore a quizzical look and with a slight shrug of his shoulders indicated that perhaps today, for the first time, his gift had failed him.

"Hi Blanche," Samuel greeted. Then with a slight grimace, he prompted, "Okay, DJ, show your transformation."

Slowly, DJ turned. His eyes were slightly narrowed and his hands twitched at his sides. He waited.

Blanche took a few minutes to study Samuels work. She nodded approvingly. DJ's face had been shaven clean. His hair was trimmed neatly to just above his shirt collar, his sideburns cut short and square. Samuel had dressed DJ in a light gray shirt with rose colored stripes and a white collar. His crisp gray trousers clung to his hips, accentuating his athletic build and the maroon suspenders were clearly just for show.

Julia scowled. She found it hard to reconcile the young man before her with the same boy that mucked stalls and pitched hay on her father's farm. Even his nails gleamed even and white.

"Thank you, Samuel," complimented Blanche.

"To your liking?"

"Yes," she assured, "You never disappoint."

Samuel stood a bit taller, his eyes sparkled. Clearly he valued Blanche's opinion.

Julia and DJ waited patiently while Blanche finished up with Samuel. The tension had vanished from DJ's face and he now stood more at ease. It wasn't until he caught Julia staring at him that his jaw clenched and he hissed, "What are you looking at?"

"Nothing," Julia retorted, and before she could take it back she snipped, "Just a dandy looking boy."

DJ snorted, gave a final tug on the collar of his shirt and moved off toward the doors to wait for Blanche.

⚬⚮⚬

By late afternoon, Julia had settled in and was sitting quietly in the intimate library of the stylish townhouse. She closed her eyes and breathed in deeply. The scent of lemon oil and aged wood filled her nostrils, reminding her of the large, dark halls at Kimball Academy. Her fingers rested lightly on a small book of poetry, as yet, unopened.

"Emily Dickinson. Good choice."

Julia looked up. DJ stood before her. His shirt collar was unbuttoned and the suspenders were hanging at his sides. He crossed the room and plopped into a large overstuffed arm chair covered in green brocade. He tucked his bare feet underneath himself and leaned back.

Julia's mouth gaped open. "How do you...?"

"Know about poetry?" he finished for her.

"Yes!" she snapped.

"Humph," DJ, shook his head, and closed his eyes.

Julia waited for his response but when it became clear he had no intention of answering her, she flung open the cover of the book and noisily flipped the pages.

The tension was finally cut when Blanche entered the library a few minutes later.

"DJ?" she inquired.

DJ opened his eyes and quickly uncurled his legs. "Yes, Blanche, what do you need?"

"I feel silly asking," she began, "but could you please accompany me across town?"

"Of course," he answered quickly. "I just have to get my shoes." DJ was already across the room, buttoning his shirt and pulling up his suspenders as he went.

"Where are we going?" asked Julia.

"No where," replied Blanche. "You stay here and relax. I just have a quick errand to run."

Julia frowned. Where could Blanche be going that would exclude her?

DJ reappeared in the doorway. "Ready whenever you are, Blanche."

Blanche nodded and reassured Julia, "We'll be back within the hour." She turned to leave and added, "I think I'll get some sweet cakes from a bakery I know for after dinner."

Julia smiled and by the time the door clicked shut she was already lost in the first poem.

∼∞∽

The next couple of weeks passed quietly. Each morning they would venture out for a leisurely stroll before the heat of day set in. Often they would visit the park they'd passed when first arriving in Boston. Julia had now discovered that this was the Boston Commons, and of all the places they'd explored, this was her favorite. It also didn't take long for her to realize that she wasn't the only one who started each day on the Commons. It was host to a sea of regulars. Afternoons when the day heated up, they usually spent sitting in the darkened library of the spacious apartment, occupying themselves with reading, board games and puzzles.

Julia was surprised how different summer was in the city. She had only known the open fields where breezes blew freely down from the mountains, cooling the air long into the night. In Boston, the tall buildings of brick and stone not only kept the air stagnant but also held onto the sun's fire. The city would continue baking, even after dark, with only a short reprieve in the very early morning before the sun rose up.

The evenings were always different. All around the city there was always something special going on. Any night they might enjoy a bandstand concert on the Commons. Then on another, penny night at the marquee.Wednesdays were always the same, fresh churned ice cream on Samuel's front porch with his wife, Maisey. And one time they caught a magician performing outside Quincy market. But the last Friday before they moved to Esther's house was unforgettable. They went down by the waterfront and watched fireworks explode over the water. Standing amidst the thick crowd, watching as streams of light were sent screaming up into the darkness. And then, joining in with "Ooohs!" and "Ahhs!" when after a sudden

"BOOM!", colors flashed and began to cascade down. They were so bright she couldn't even see the stars. More and more rockets were shot off and a smokey breeze began to fill the air. It mingled into the fog lifting off the water and blended into the oceans saltiness burning her nose.

"Julia," Blanche beckoned.

Julia was so enthralled with the display, she barely heard Blanche call her. Then when she felt a firm hand at her elbow directing her to turn and leave, she moaned, "Do we have to, Blanche?"

"Yes, Julia, we must."

The fireworks weren't yet over and with another, "BOOM", Julia was again lost in the magical display.

"Julia, Now!" commanded Blanche.

Stunned by her harsh tone, Julia complied and began to slowly follow Blanche away from the piers. Off to her left she detected a small scuffle but Blanche kept a brisk pace that prevented her from turning to see what was happening.

Once they were several blocks away from the piers, DJ trotted up from behind them. He was breathing hard but still managed to wave down a cabbie. When it stopped, DJ opened th back door, then extended his arm to help both Blanche and Julia into the carriage.

"I'll meet you back at the apartment," he said to Blanche. She nodded and watched him slip into the darkness.

Julia's back bristled and she crossed her arms. Clearly it was not fair that she had to leave the fireworks while DJ got to stay. The ride was short and silent, and once inside, she began to head upstairs without a word.

"Julia," Blanche stopped her.

Julia stood on the staircase but refused to turn around.

"I'm sorry you're disappointed," Blanche consoled.

Julia waited. Surely Blanche would give her some sort of explanation. But when she realized one wasn't forthcoming, she angrily continued upstairs and began to wash up.

A little while later, Julia lay on her bed staring at the ceiling. She heard DJ come in and go to the library. Quietly, she stole down the stairs stopping just short of the bottom step.

"Are you sure he knows?"

"No doubt about it, Blanche. Your uncle sent those thugs with a message."

"Here, sip on this while I get some salve and bandages."

Blanche rounded the corner before Julia could make her escape back up the stairs.

"Oh, Julia!" Blanche exclaimed, "What are you doing there?" Her eyes narrowed slightly, "How long have you been standing there?" she questioned, "And what did you hear?"

Julia should have felt ashamed but her irritation from earlier hadn't worn off.

"More secrets?" she accused. "Private papers, and sneaking off at night. And now, tonight, DJ gone for hours and when he does come back, it looks like he was in a fight."

"Julia," Blanche began, "There are explanations. But none that you need to be concerned with. The best thing you can do tonight is go to bed. After all," she said, forcing a smile, "we have a busy day tomorrow."

"Grr!" Julia clenched her fists at her sides. With that she spun on her heel and stomped her way back upstairs. When she reached her room, she slammed the door behind her.

Julia strode to the open window and stood looking out. The air was stale and thick. Down below, she heard the back screen door moan open, and then close with a soft thud. DJ stepped out onto the dimly lit patio. His shirt was off and even in the dim light she could make out his hard muscles and lean torso. He had a glass of dark liquid in one hand and a round jar of ointment in the other. DJ sighed and took a long sip draining his glass. He set it down on a small table and began to unscrew the jar's lid. Slowly, he dipped his fingers in, then, carefully began to rub the white cream onto the gashes covering his shoulders and side.

Julia wanted to move away from the window, but her feet wouldn't budge. Why couldn't she pull herself away? "Ugh!" she thought, "I can't wait for tomorrow. I just want to join my friends."

———

The next morning everyone got off to a slow start. And despite the continued heat and humidity, there was a marked chill at the kitchen table during breakfast.

"Good morning, Julia," greeted Blanche. "Did you want toast this morning?"

Julia glanced in Blanche's direction and answered curtly, "Yes. Please."

Blanche chose not to notice and delivered a plate to the table and set it in front of Julia.

"More coffee, DJ?"

DJ could not contain his smirk. He glanced over at Julia and responded, sarcastically, "Yes. Please."

Blanche brought the coffee pot over and poured DJ and herself another cup. She returned it to the stovetop, then took her seat at the table.

"I think we should walk over to Esther's later this morning," she announced, gaily.

"Do you think that's wise?" asked DJ.

"After last night? I feel certain I'll have no more problems this trip."

Julia quietly munched her toast and laboriously wiped the corners of her mouth. She didn't care how they got to Esther's, she was just glad to be going.

"Is that okay with you?" Blanche was asking.

"Hmm?"

"Walking to Esther's. Is that okay with you?"

"Fine," Julia replied drily, "Just fine."

∼∞∽

It was late morning when they were finally leaving the Brownston. Blanche locked the door behind them and they started down the walk. It had been arranged for DJ to escort Blanche and Julia to the Gilman's Boston residence on Beacon Hill, then catch the train back to the farm.

"Let's go through the Public Gardens," Blanche suggested, looking aside at DJ. "I love to look at all the pretty flowers."

Julia groaned, and shuffled along behind them.

"Come on, Julia," admonished Blanche, "pick up those feet and walk like a lady."

Obediently Julia straightened up and began to walk with a lady-like precision that even Miss Stone wouldn't fault. Within seconds, she was glad she did. Just as they were entering the gardens, a familiar face caught her eye. He had seen her first and was already making a bee line towards them.

"Julia," Jonathan greeted, with an easy smile.

"Hello," she answered, color flooding her cheeks,

Jonathan turned his attention to Blanche. "Good afternoon, maam, I'm a friend of Julia's," he paused slightly, then held out his hand. "Jonathan Ashcroft."

Blanche glanced at Julia with slightly raised brows, while extending her hand. "Pleased," she replied. "I'm Julia's step mother, Blanche Kelly."

Jonathan reached out and took her hand. He held Blanche's fingers gingerly and responded, "The pleasures all mine."

Then, with all the subtly of an elephant at a garden party, DJ stepped forward and thrusting out his hand announced, "And I'm DJ." But then, clearing his throat, corrected, "Donald... McGrath."

Julia stared at DJ in disbelief. Why was he acting so strange?

"Donald?" Jonathan put his hands in his pockets and looked DJ straight in the eye, "Nice to meet you... Donald."

Julia quickly took a side step around DJ and asked, "I didn't know you came to Boston, does your family live here?"

Jonathan gave her a warm smile. "Just a small place on the South Slope. Really not that far from the Gilmans."

Julia's eyes shot open and her heart began to pound. But before she could say anything more, DJ interjected, "That's really quite interesting, but we have to be on our way."

"What?" asked Julia, "Why?"

DJ answered her, never taking his eyes off Jonathan, "We are expected...elsewhere...and then, I have a train to catch. So, really, we must be going."

At that point Blanche stepped in. Graciously she told Jonathan, "It was lovely meeting you. Perhaps one day you could meet us for tea." And turning to Julia, "The day is getting away from us."

Julia took her cue, "This was a lovely surprise."

Jonathan smiled again, "Yes, it was, and while you're in the city, we really should meet for tea." Jonathan touched the side of his cap and began to step off, but as he passed DJ he murmured, "Have a safe trip, Donald."

The rest of the walk was spent in silence. They decided to forego the gardens and go straight to Chestnut street. It was only a few blocks, but the smile on Julia's lips didn't fade nor did the dark cloud over DJ.

Once they reached Chestnut street, they didn't have to search long or read each green placard to locate Esther's townhouse. Before they'd even arrived at her walkway, a shiny black door was flung open and two lively young women came racing down the steps crying, "Julia!"

Julia's eyes widened and dropping all pretense of decorum, she ran to meet her friends. Blanche and DJ hung back, waiting. They couldn't help but grin watching Julia and the girls all chatting at the same time.

Once the intial excitement had worn off, Esther broke free and came over to introduce herself. "Mrs. Kelly," she began, "I'm delighted to have you here." Then, she turned to DJ, "Welcome, you are DJ? Julia's told me all about you."

DJ's brow creased slightly, surprised that his name had ever come up at all. He nodded once in affirmation.

"Please come inside, both of you," Esther offered, "We have a late lunch already prepared."

"That's kind of you to offer," replied DJ, "but I have to get back to the farm." He turned to Blanche and added, cryptically, "I'll make sure everything gets put in Will's hands tonight."

"Thank you," said Blanche, "I'm so grateful for all your help!"

DJ turned and started off in the direction of the station while Blanche turned back to Esther. Smiling graciously, she said, "Lunch sounds lovely."

The next couple of weeks were spent in a flurry of activity. The girls were shepherded around to some of Boston's finest dress shops in search of the perfect ball gown. It was imperative that it accentuate the wearer's most desirable features while masking any perceived flaws. The evening of their coming out was just the beginning of a year filled with opportunities to meet and secure a favorable union.

Since French designs were all the rage, their search ultimately led them to a tiny shop in Cambridge named and owned by a petite middle aged woman, Madam Chambeau.

A small brass bell above the door tinkled gailey when the tired but excited trio entered followed by their cautiously optimistic mothers. This was the last good option on their list and with the fall semester fast approaching, they all hoped each girl would find what they were looking for.

The racks were filled with every color and fabric imaginable, and on the walls hung shawls, feather boas, furs and caplets. At the back of the shop sat a large glass display case. Inside, drapped over mounds of crimson velvet were long strands of pearls, ostrich feather fans, bejeweled butterfly and dragonfly broaches and hair clips, along with writhing gold snake pins. On top of the case to the left, was a silver pole and from each branch hung a small beaded bag with a long strap. On the other side to the right on a small set of tiers, sat pairs of the most beautiful shoes Julia had ever seen. Shiny satin, embroidered, spangled and bowed. One pair on each step.

"Julia," Blanche called, "Julia!"

"What?" she asked, turning around.

Blanche stood with her hands on her hips and in the background, Izzy and Esther were giggling. They had already begun their search through the forest of dresses.

"Oh," she cried, realizing she had better get to work. Julia hurried over and began pushing hangers aside, barely examining each dress. By now she had seen enough gowns to know what she wasn't looking for.

"Got it!" yelled out Esther, parting the sea of fabrics. Carefully, she lifted out the hanger and extricated a powder blue velvet gown. Madam came out from behind her counter. A tape measure hung from her neck and a short, stubby pencil was wedged behind an ear.

"Come with me," she commanded. She led Esther and her mother to the back of the store and pushed aside a dark, heavy curtain. Inside was a small room with a pedestal in the center of a half circle of mirrors.

"Please, try it on in there," she said while pointing to a small stall in the back corner with swinging doors. "Call me when you are ready, okay?"

Esther nodded. She disappeared inside while Julia and Izzy continued their search.

It only took a couple more minutes before Izzy cried out in triumph, "This is the one!" She held in her hand a hanger supporting the most dramatic gown Julia had ever seen. It was soft beige velvet with gold accents. Izzy beamed, clearly she believed this to be perfect.

Encouraged by her friends success, Julia pressed on.

"Ta da!" Esther announced from the back of the store. The curtains had been tucked to the side and she stood waiting on the pedestal. All eyes turned.

Julia's jaw dropped. The shimmery blue material gave warmth to Esther's normally pale skin, and her dark brown hair appeared thicker and richer. The style was more feminine than most of the ones they'd already seen, but Esther's curvy figure needed it to be. This dress had sheer capped sleeves and a low scooped neckline. The bodice was criss crossed with iridescent beads all the way down to the bottom of the dropped waistline. The skirt was unfashionably full, but because it was made of chiffon in the same powdery blue with dramatic slits, it hung fairly straight.

Marion let out an audible gasp and her eyes began to mist up. Her daughter was a very pretty girl, but the young woman before her was beautiful!

"Now it is your turn," Madam instructed, pointing at Izzy and directing her towards the changing room.

"Come on," encouraged Esther. "You can help me out of this and I'll help you get into yours!"

The curtains closed and Julia resumed her quest, now tackling the last rack.

Marion and Bitsy were fondling clutches and comparing accessories when the drapes reopened. This time the pedestal showcased an almost unrecognizable Izzy. The way she was posed, she could easily have been a Greek goddess looking down from Mount Olympus. Julia was mesmerized by the delicate folds cascading over her friend's body and airy layers floating around her ankles. The color of the fabric next to Izzy's porcelain skin and platinum blond hair, appeared to be gold white instead of simply beige and the over all effect gave Izzy a sophistication and sensuality beyond her years.

"Well," Izzy stamped her foot and demanded impatiently, "What do you think?"

Without realizing it, they had all fallen silent as though under a spell. But the real Izzy had broken it and in a cacophony of apologies, they quickly reassured her that she looked beautiful and had indeed found perfection.

Julia looked back and fingered her way through the last few dresses. Her heart sank and she could feel tears threatening to spill. How was it that her two best friends were able to find the exact, perfect choice and in this whole shop, there was nothing for her.

Julia felt a hand on her shoulder and was about to tell Blanche to leave her alone when a brusk voice demanded, "Look over here. This one is special."

Julia turned and followed Madam around behind the counter. She watched Madam push aside an array of cloaks and wraps and pull out a garment bag. Julia's fingers twitched nervously as Madam slowly pulled down the zipper, releasing the fabric within. Gently she slid the gown out of the bag and held it up for Julia to see.

Her hand flew to her mouth and her eyes grew large. Behind her, Blanche encouraged, "Take it, Julia, this one was made for you!"

Julia's hand was shaking when she reached out to take the hanger. Gingerly she carried it to the fitting room.

"Here, Julia," offered Esther, "Let me hold it while you get undressed."

Julia wasted no time shedding her summer frock and slipping it on. The fabric clung to her as if providing a second set of skin. And when she walked to the mirror, it added grace to each step.

Julia admired her reflection. This dress was the same light-weight velvet as her friends, but in a deep emerald green and for the first time, she thought her auburn curls lovely. The neckline barely skirted the tops of her shoulders then plunged down her back to just above her waist. She ran her fingers down the unadorned bodice until they reached her right hip. An ornate dragonfly encrusted with sapphire blue stones and tufts of pale green ostrich feathers sat holding folds that had been gathered and draped across her front. Then, instead of leaving her legs exposed, the gown had a sheer under layer which provided an ample hem.

"Ta da!" declared Izzy, and with great florish, she threw back the curtains allowing the mothers to see what she and Esther already knew.

The rest of the afternoon was spent picking out accessories and shoes and having Madam do some pinning for minor adjustments.

When they finally left, they all agreed they were exhausted and hungry. So Marion suggested that they treat themselves to dinner out. "I know the best place for lobster," she announced. "It's not in the best part of the city, but by no means the worst. What do you think?"

Julia had never tried lobster but she figured if she was going to, she should at least go where she'd have the best chance of liking it. Blanche also knew of the restaurant and so it was agreed, they would hop a cab to down near the piers and celebrate the day's success.

Everyone was already in a good mood, and the maneuvers required just to eat made for a light and joyous time. At the meal's close their waiter began to remove their dishes, piled high with claws and shells. Suddenly a familiar face appeared at their table.

"Good evening, ladies," greeted Jonathan.

Izzy kicked Julia from under the table and raised her brows. Julia shot her friend a warning glance while trying to appear calm and unaffected.

"Why hello, Jonathan?" Blanche queried.

"Yes, maam, thank you for remembering."

"Of course," Blanche replied, "I always make it a point to take notice of Julia's friends."

Jonathan shuffled a little uneasily but mercifully, Marion came to his rescue. "I think I know your mother," she suggested. "Laura?"

"Yes, maam," he replied, thankfully. "You do!"

"Of course," she continued, " We've played bridge together."

"Yes," he responded, "she does enjoy a good round."

"Hmmm," smiled Marion.

The table fell silent and poor Julia was at a loss of what to do.

"Well…" Jonathan stumbled, "I really should be going. It was nice…a pleasure running into you." He ventured a small smile at Julia, nodded to Blanche and took his leave.

Once he was out of earshot the mothers erupted in laughter. Julia was aghast! "What's so funny?" she wanted to know.

"Oh, sweetie," explained Bitsy, "never let any man get the upper hand."

"Clearly he's taken with you," added Marion, "but a least make him work for it. Besides, his mother's a horrid bridge player and a sniveling bore."

"How can you speak this way?"

This time Blanche spoke up, "Julia, you haven't even started your season. Half the fun is getting dressed up, meeting lots of young men and attending all sorts of events."

But what if I don't want or need to meet a lot of young men?" she asked.

A soft chuckle was heard around the table.

"We've already checked him out," Esther assured her. "He's okay."

"You can thank us anytime," joined in Izzy, grinning broadly. "And in case you were wondering, good family. At least good in the sense that they brought their wealth with them when they crossed the Atlantic."

Julia couldn't believe her ears.

"Lawyers," added Esther. "His ancestors were up to their ears in powdered wigs and Parliament."

"Don't be surprised if he does the same, minus the wig," giggled Izzy, "I hope," she added slyly.

"Stop it!" blushed Julia, "This is really too much!"

"Sorry," soothed Blanche, " we really shouldn't tease. It's just that this is the first time you've been smitten."

Julia's cheeks were burning.

"Oh, dear," teased Izzy, and in a high pitched tone, "She's turned as red as our lobsters!"

With that, Julia finally began to laugh. She realized this was only the first of many ribbings. She also knew it was only a matter of time before her friends received their share as well!

Later that night, Julia lay in bed staring up at the shadowy ceiling. She kept picturing Jonathan standing beside their table. He always looked so neat and stylish. Pristine. Even in the hot, crowded restaurant, his hair was perfect. And his shirt and trousers were starched with crisp creases. He was so different from the farm boys she'd grown up with. So different from DJ. Clearly, Jonathan had never done a physical days work in his life. Why would he? She was sure he'd grown up with servants. Probably lots of servants. Was that how her life would be?

Her thoughts continued to turn over and over until finally she fell into a restless sleep. A sleep filled with thoughts of Jonathan. And DJ.

10

"You look like perfection!" Izzy reassured.

Julia bit her bottom lip and continued to stare at her reflection. Something was off, just didn't fit.

Izzy moved behind her and slowly unclasped the delicate chain at the base of Julia's neck. Mum's locket fell limp and disappeared from view. Julia heard the snap of a jewelry box closing and watched as Izzy deposited it into a bureau drawer. Then, Izz went to her own bureau and pulled out a large black laquer box with gold inlay. Izzy lifted the lid and pulled out a dark green velvet choker with rhinestone studs. "Here," she announced. "This is what you're looking for." Julia felt the narrow band circle her throat and tighten slightly while Izzy secured the clasp. "There!"

Julia reassessed herself and nodded. "Thanks Izz!"

Izzy frowned, "Now what?" she prodded.

"Why aren't you nervous?"

"Because, first – I know how good I look," Izzy grinned and batted her eyelashes, "and second, because none of this matters. I've found my love and all of this is just for show."

During their time in Boston, Izzy had finally come clean and confessed all. Of course, both Esther and Julia feigned shock, but then let her know they supported her romance with Peter and would cover whenever she needed them to.

But for Julia, tonight would be different. Tonight she would be announcing her availability for marriage. And if Jonathan followed through on his promise, he would make his intention to begin courting her known.

A short time later, Julia was standing backstage with the others, waiting. The minutes dragged on as she fought the urge to tug at her dress, one more time. Or play with the delicate ostrich feather on her hip. Then, after she had checked herself in the full length mirror for the fourth time, she finally heard Miss Stone loudly clear her throat and announce, "Ladies, attention, ladies! Please line up."

The shuffling began as each girl lifted skirts and tottered into her preassigned spot. On the other side of the curtain, the music swelled, then lowered, carrying a soft, rhythmic beat that was easy to walk to. The curtains parted. Each name was read and that young lady stepped forward. With pose and grace she joined her waiting father. Then, taking his outstretched arm, she allowed him to escort her to the dance floor.

The voice in Julia's head kept rehearsing Miss Stone's instructions, "Don't bite your lip" "Don't fidget." "Keep your chin up and your eyes straight ahead." "Smile but don't grin like a buffoon." And, "Make sure you don't rush and fall on your face!"

"Julia Louise Kelly." She barely heard the soft hum of applause. Her large green eyes looked at Will hoping to see approval. Blanche had kept her dress a secret and this would be the first time he'd ever seen her this elegant.

A smile played at the corners of Will's mouth and his eyes grew soft and teary. Julia placed her hand on her father's arm and they began their descent to the ballroom floor. Casually, he leaned over, just a little, and whispered in her ear, "You've never looked more beautiful."

Julia glanced at him sideways, "Really?" she whispered back.

"Stunning!" he replied, "I almost don't recognize you."

Once all the couples had taken their places, the band let loose and began to play in earnest. The fathers took their daughters in their arms and began to lead them around the dance floor. Round and round without a single misstep. Finally, the music began to trail off. This was their cue to leave the floor and take their seats alongside the mothers. Will led Julia to a table where Blanche was already seated along with Marion and Bitsy. He helped her get settled and then, only moments later, they saw Esther and Izzy approach, perched on the arms of their fathers.

The tables quickly filled up and the room quieted to a low hum. Conversations played back and forth as plates of food began to appear and disappear. Almost unseen, practiced waiters seamlessly moved about the diningroom balancing an array of tempting dishes. But this was all lost on Julia. She barely tasted her dinner. It was all so much and she was far too excited to eat.

It was just after dessert when the band began to warm up again. That was when all the young men that had been biding their time, now began to make their move. Dispersing throughout the hall, hands were extended to eager young ladies who were then escorted onto the dance floor. Within minutes, there was a sea of satin and taffeta swirling in time to the music.

Julia recognized the deep voice from behind her. She turned and was met by a pair of familiar, icy blue eyes.

"May I have a dance?" he stated, ready to pull out her chair.

"Why, yes," Julia responded, politely and with much more confidence than the last time they'd met.

Cecil put his hand lightly at the small of Julia's back and gently guided her to the floor. Then, in one fluid movement he gently spun to face her and took her other hand in his. Before she knew it they were gliding across the floor in practiced ease. Julia tried to look around and see who else was there, but Cecil seemed intent on monopolizing her view. Just as the song was coming to a finish and she could feel an offer of punch on the horizon, a soft, gentle voice came to her rescue.

"Excuse me, I'd like to cut in."

Cecil scowled and reluctantly released his hold. Jonathan looked down at Julia appreciatively, "You look stunning," he complimented.

Julia felt her knees weaken but somehow managed to murmur, "Thank you."

Jonathan took Julia in his arms and gently began to lead her across the floor. She became so lost in his soft gray eyes that she didn't realize she was being danced outside onto the patio. The night air was still and warm. Jonathan released all but her hand and they began to walk. There were other couples milling about through the gardens, so with a tilt of his head, Jonathan led Julia away from the patio and down an almost hidden set of steps. Silently they strolled along a narrow, stone path to a small bench beneath a trellis of pink roses. Jonathan lightly brushed the seat with a pale blue hankerchief that suddenly materialized from his back pocket. Julia smiled, made a minor adjustment to her skirt, and perched herself on the edge of the bench. Jonathan, joined her. "It's a lovely evening." He ventured.

"Yes," Julia responded, then continued, "And the band is really quite fantastic."

"Sure, sure," he answered, "They play a lot of these parties."

"Really?" Julia felt a slight tinge of disappointment.

Jonathan noticed her eyes fall and quickly recovered, "Not that I attend a lot of these events."

"Oh," she smiled slightly.

"They just have a reputation of being good. And reliable. Never late. And don't steal." He stumbled on.

Julia smiled a little deeper. "Well, that is good news."

Jonathan began to fidget with his cuff links. Facing her, he began again, "Julia,"

Julia looked up and into his deep gray eyes. "Hmm?" she replied.

"Julia," Jonathan wet his lips. " I ... I can't stop thinking about you. And I realize you don't know me ... or really anything about me, but I .. " he paused, "Well, I, really from the first time we met, I felt ... something."

"Something?"

Jonathan took a breath. "Yes, something that makes my stomach flip and my knees weak and," he paused, "and makes me sound like an idiot," he laughed.

"Me too!" Julia chuckled softly, "I mean, that happens to me too!"

Jonathan stopped fidgeting. "That's good," he said. "And since it seems unreasonable to expect anyone else to want us, stomach and knee ailments and all, perhaps we should stick together?"

"Yes," agreed Julia. "It seems only fair. To all the others."

Jonathan smiled and took her hands in his. "So, Miss Julia Kelly, because clearly we are perfect for each other and since no one else will have us," he paused dramatically, "From this moment on... if I have your permission... I am making my intentions known."

"Oh," responded Julia. "And that means...?"

Jonathan cleared his throat. "That means I would like to spend more time with you. Get to know you better."

"Ok,"

"And," he continued, quickly, "When the season is over, I will ask you to marry me."

"Oh," Julia exclaimed.

"With your permission," he reiterated, then, added softly, "And I'll do it right. Not like this."

"Okay," answered Julia.

"Okay you understand, or okay I have your permission?"

"Okay to both."

Jonathan exhaled and smiled. "Okay. Good!" He paused for a moment as if he'd forgotten something, then leaned in and softly kissed Julia's cheek. "Let me take you back," he said, still smiling.

Jonathan slipped his hand in Julia's. The music grew louder as they slowly retraced their steps back to the patio. Just as they were about to reenter the hall, they heard Izzy cry out, "Where have you been?"

"We just stepped out for a minute."

Izzy looked annoyed. "Your parents are getting ready to leave. You need to go over and say good-bye."

"Okay, Izz," Julia placated. She turned and gazed up into Jonathan's misty eyes, "Good night!"

"Good night, Julia," he answered and walked away, fading into the crowd.

Julia turned and followed Izzy inside to join her parents. She caught up with them just as Will was helping Blanche with her wrap.

"There you are!" he teased, "I thought you'd danced off into the night never to be seen again."

"Oh, Dad," she blushed, then, more seriously, "Thank you for tonight!"

"It was Blanche," Will reminded.

"And you too, Blanche."

Will hugged her warmly, "You carried yourself like a lady. I'm very proud of you."

Julia beamed. She and Izzy watched as Dad and Blanche made their way to the front hall, then disappear.

Clearly tired from the excitement of the evening, Julia and Izzy ducked out a side door to head to the dorms. "Let's walk the back way," suggested Izzy, "The air feels good...less stuffy."

"Okay," Julia agreed. She didn't really care how they got to their room, she just wanted to savor the way she felt right now.

The girls carefully picked their way along the manicured path that wound its way around the rear of the school buildings. They were just about to come out past a row of hedges when they heard a heated discussion up ahead.

"Please understand, I have no other choice!" a deep whisper pleaded.

"But what about us?" questioned a low woman's voice.

"Nothing has changed! I promise!"

Izzy and Julia heard muffled sobs. Slowly, they emerged from their cover and a little ways off they saw a young woman in the shadows. She was wiping tears from her face when she noticed the girls approaching. Startled, she held up her hands and backed away. Then, lifting up the hem of her dress, she turned and ducked down a side path. Julia and Izzy tried to follow but she had already disappeared into the dark.

The girls turned back and continued to their dorm. Once inside their room, Julia began to change. She took great care hanging up her dress, lovingly running her fingers down the front and playfully flicking the ostrich feathers. Dreamily, she slipped into her cotton nightie. She knew from this moment on her life would never be the same.

11

The hard wooden pew offered little warmth and Julia sat hunched and shivering in the dimly lit chapel. She pushed curls, damp and knotted, away from her face and stared down at the torn hem of her dress, wet and caked with mud. She had no idea where she was. She only knew that she hadn't cared about that when she blindly raced out of the club and into the night. She'd been in such a hurry she hadn't even thought to grab her heavy cloak.

In the corner of the chapel a small stove glowed, and slowly, Julia began to thaw out. A soft cry escaped her chapped lips and she sank deeper into the pew. Exhausted and alone.

"How?" she thought, "How had this happened?"

She began to replay the past four months in her mind wondering, where had she missed the signs? After the night of their coming out, the girls had been flooded with invitations to parties and dances, as well as concerts, afternoon teas, and poetry readings. Izzy was, of course, taken. But she played her part most convincingly and adeptly garnered just enough attention without ever attracting any serious suitors. Esther on the other hand, always managed to find herself surrounded by no less than three prospects at a time. Whatever the occasion, she had a loyal band of followers competing for her attention. As for Julia, Jonathan was true to his promise. From that night on he made it clear to her and every other young man that his interest lay only with Julia.

Julia lifted her head and gently rubbed her temples. Blinders on. She had been so swept up in all the activities – the glamour and gaiety – and oh, oh so naïve! She'd never been in love before. Never been loved before. Maybe if she had…maybe then she would have realized. It had always been there. She could see it so clearly now. Julia's hand flew to her mouth, "Her!" She suddenly remembered.

The image of the young woman fleeing from her and Izzy the night of their coming out. Her…it had been "her" that night. And the man with her, Julia now knew for certain that man had been Jonathan.

Julia leaned back and rested her head against the high back of the pew and watched the dark shadows play across the ceiling.

She had loved dressing up for every dance. Each time pulling out a new gown, shoes, and accessories. She'd learned how to apply blush, lip gloss, and eye shadow. Then, each time before heading out, she'd stop at the top of the staircase to take one last glance, admiring herself in the large, gilded mirror.

Then, off she would go. Go to whereever that night's event was being held. At first, she would blush each time Jonathan met her at the door. Smile shyly when he took her arm and lead her to "their" table. And from then on, they'd spend the rest of the evening swirling around the dance floor.

Julia's stomach did a little flip when she thought back to how just the touch of his hand holding hers, the slight pressure on the small of her back, and the faint smell of his cologne made her knees weak. She'd get so lost in his movements, his breath on the base of her neck. Then, as the evening drew on, he would always slow down their dance and lead her off to a quiet spot outside. They'd always talk a little – usually about the next time he'd see her, nothing of consequence. And then, just before they headed back inside, Jonathan would lean in and gently kiss her. And Julia would feel like her insides were about to explode!

"Don't trust him!" warned the harsh, imposing voice. She could still see Cecil's intense blue eyes boring into her own.

"But why?" she had protested, arguing that Cecil didn't know Jonathan. That he was jealous! Now, when she recalled her arrogance … she was flooded with shame.

Of course, Jonathan played his part well, and up until two months ago she'd had no reason to think otherwise. But that was before he had introduced her to Patrick.

"Hmmm," she thought. "Not really introduced."

Patrick had just appeared one night. It was a lovely evening with the usual crowd. Izzy and some stray she'd allowed to follow her, Esther and her current companion, and herself and Jonathan. Then, a slender young man with blond waves and pale blue eyes materialized at their tableside.

"Greetings, kids!" Patrick had announced, and pulling a chair over from a nearby table, he squeezed between Esther and her date. Patrick sat directly across from Jonathan, staring and waiting.

She remembered thinking, "He's so ill-mannered. Who is he and why doesn't Jonathan have him removed?" Now she knew. She'd seen the panic in Jonathan's eyes. Only for a few seconds and then he'd quickly recovered. Hid it by introducing Patrick as a childhood friend. "Yes," she thought, "That's when it started." From that moment on, Patrick would just "show up" and soon became a permanent fixture in their group.

Julia shook her head, "I remember at the time noticing something odd about Patrick. Yet familiar, too. But the feeling passed so quickly," she reasoned, " I never gave it another thought." Julia paused," No...wait," she reproved, " That's not true. I never let myself."

"Well, it doesn't matter now," sighed Julia, and recalled how abruptly things had shifted. From that night on, Patrick was everywhere. No matter where they went, he would be there. Izzy had even referred to him as the third musketeer. "I passed it off as nothing," Julia muttered, "Even when others joked about our chaperone."

No wonder she had been so eager about tonight. Julia would have been willing to go anywhere just to have it be her and Jonathan, just the two of them. She could still hear his voice. He'd sounded so excited when he'd asked her to go out that night. He'd told her about an exclusive club in Boston. "Perfect," she'd responded, without hesitating. She had already made plans to spend the weekend with Esther and her family. The fact that she had to sneak out to meet him only made it more thrilling!

Earlier that evening, Esther and Julia sat in the library reading while they waited for the mantel clock to strike eight. Feigning exhaustion, they excused themselves and went upstairs to prepare for bed. But while Esther donned her nightie, Julia dressed for her date. Carefully, she slipped into her green gown. The one she hadn't worn since the night of her coming out. Jonathan had told her this would be a very special evening and she wanted to look her best.

Then, shortly before ten, Julia left Esther and quietly scooted down the back staircase. By now, the house was still and dark so Julia was able to duck out a side door unseen. She ventured out into the chilly night air and watched as a few light flakes of snow tumbled down around her, sticking to her hair and lashes. Julia pulled her thick, heavy cloak tighter and carefully made her way around to the front of Esther's house. She saw a cab already waiting at the curb, its engine idling. As she approached, Jonathan stepped out of the shadows. Julia smiled up at him and taking his extended arm, allowed him to lead her to the car. Once he had helped her inside and they were settled, the driver began accelerating slowly and the cab pulled away from the curb.

"You were so cryptic when you asked me out," ventured Julia. "Can you tell me where you're taking me?"

"I think you're going to like it," smiled Jonathan, mysteriously. "I'm taking you to a Drag Ball."

"A what?" she asked, having never heard of such a thing.

"They've been happening in Harlem for some time and now they've come to Boston."

"Okay. But why is it called a Drag Ball?"

"Don't worry, you'll see when we get there." Jonathan was lightly tapping his foot and fidgeting with his cuff links.

"He seems anxious," Julia mused, "I wonder why?" But then reasoned, "It's been so long since we've had time alone. That must be it." So rather than think on it anymore, she chose to snuggle in closer and enjoy the ride.

The cab wound its way through the narrow streets of Boston, skirting the state park and making its way down the southwest corridor. If Julia had looked out the window, she would have noticed the garishly painted women standing beneath the gas lights. And men with their hat brims pulled low executing transactions then disappearing under the awnings of older buildings. About half way down the street, they finally arrived in front of a stately, old building that had, at one time, been a chic hotel. The sign over the entrance was worn and drooped to the right, but Julia could still make out the words, The Starlight Ballroom.

The cab sat still while Jonathan handed the driver his fare. Then, pushing the door open, he ducked his head and slid out. Jonathan stepped onto the lightly coated sidewalk, then turned, "Come on," he urged, holding out his hand. Julia took it and emerged from the cab. She wrapped her arm in Jonathan's and allowed him to steady her as they carefully made their way toward the faded red, double doors.

The outside of the building was bathed in dull, gray light. Julia could just make out figures lurking in the shadows and the air was thick with hushed voices and cigarette smoke. Julia clutched Jonathan's arm a little tighter and tried to ignore the quickening of her pulse. At the doors, Jonathan paused for a moment to look around and then gave three sharp raps. A low moan was heard as the right hand door slowly opened a crack. Jonathan reached into the inside breast pocket of his beige, cashmere overcoat and pulled out two tickets. The bouncer widened the crack and his big, meaty hand reached through and plucked them out of Jonathan's fingers. Suddenly, the door opened all the way and Julia felt Jonathan's hand rest on her lower back. Gently he pushed her forward, into the club.

The foyer was only slightly brighter than the outside street with a worn, red carpet and chipped, gray walls. Off to the side was a large alcove with a counter in front. Jonathan led Julia over and then helped her with her cloak. He handed it to a very attractive hat check girl, along with his overcoat. For a moment, Julia stared at the woman's lavish make up, absolutely flawless and a bit theatrical. But before she could notice the pronounced lump at the girl's throat, Julia felt herself being steered toward another set of double doors.

Jonathan paused only a moment and then, pushed them open. Julia's mouth gaped when loud music and bright lights greeted her. She felt a sudden rush of air, heavy with perfume, assault her nose and when she looked up, she saw a dense layer of cigarette smoke hanging high up on the ceiling, drifting lazily amoungst large, crystal chandeliers. Off to the right on a semi-circular stage, she saw an orchestra of black musicians swinging to the latest Ragtime tune while couples danced gailey across the floor. Julia watched awestruck as women with short-cropped hair and dangerously short dresses dance with tuxedoed gents; high kicking and swinging their arms to the Charleston.

"Come with me," Jonathan directed.

Julia followed him to a small cluster of round tables each with a crimson tablecloth and a set of shiny, black chairs. Jonathan chose one near the back and pulled the chair out for her.

Julia sat and he said, "Stay here, I'll get us drinks."

Julia watched as Jonathan disappeared into the sea of partygoers. Her eyes ran to and fro taking in the action and without realizing it, her foot had begun to tap along to the hum of excitement.

Suddenly from behind, Julia felt a hand on her shoulder and a deep, effeminate voice emote, "So glad you came!"

Julia spun around in her seat and looked up, "Patrick?" Her mouth fell open. She tried to form words but could only manage, "You???? ... A woman???"

Patrick threw back his head and laughed through scarlet painted lips. "Of course, neophyte, this is a Drag ball! Now where's that delicious side of meat you came with?"

Julia recoiled. Up until now Patrick had been a little bit sarcastic and a wee bit fussy. But the creature before her looked like a sideshow act. On his feet were a pair of red, velvet pumps that increased his stature by three inches. From there, Julia's eyes traced a pair of black fishnet stockings. They ran all the way up his well-toned legs to a mid-thigh party dress sporting a deep slit. The bodice of the sequined dress had long fringe and with each toss of his hips it swayed menancingly. Finally, her eyes rested on his throat. There, encircling his neck, sat a horrid red smile of crushed velvet that bobbed mockingly each time he chuckled.

Patrick ignored Julia's shock and kept glancing over her shoulder. His eyes lit up when from behind she heard Jonathan say, " Julia, I have your punch."

Gratefully, Julia turned to face Jonathan. When he leaned over to hand her her glass, she asked."Why have you brought me here?"

Jonathan's eyes met hers, "I thought this would be fun." Then suggested, "Can't we just stay, at least for a little while?"

"Okay," she agreed, quietly and began to take a small sip from her glass. She could sense Patrick watching and then, felt his hot breath on the back of her neck.

"Bottoms up, Julia," he cajoled, "The night is young!"

Her skin bristled and only wishing for him to leave her alone, Julia swallowed a large gulp of the sweet, pink liquid, almost draining the glass. She felt it's warmth burn as it slid down her throat and realized too late, the punch was spiked with alcohol. "Oh, dear!" she thought as the music and vibrant colors began to grow louder.

Julia looked down into the near empty glass and could hear Patrick laughing from behind her. Slowly, he moved to her side. and lightly ran his finger down the side of her cheek. "Have fun tonight!" he hissed. Then, giving Jonathan a wink, he sauntered off, disappearing into the crowd of dancers.

Jonathan sat in the chair next to her. "Are you okay?" he asked, "Why did you drink that so fast?"

Julia placed her hand on his, "Please take me back," she pleaded, "I want to go back to Esther's."

"But it's still so early," Jonathan lamented, "Look, I know a private place where we can go. It's quiet." He waited a moment, then asked, "What do you think?" Julia nodded her head. All she wanted was to spend time with Jonathan. Just Jonathan.

Gently, he helped her stand and began to lead her toward the back of the ballroom. Deeper into the crowd they went, weaving through the throng. On the far side of the room was a small elevator. "Easy, Julia," Jonathan encouraged, "I'll have you there soon."

The elevator's cage door shut with a dull, Clang. It began to whirr and with a small jump, started its ascent. Two floors up, it slowed to a stop. Jonathan unlatched the cage and swung the door open. Julia didn't move. She was reluctant to leave the elevator. Something didn't feel right.

"It's okay," Jonathan reassured, and taking her hand, led her out. They made their way down a dimly lit hallway. After passing a series of numbered pink doors they finally stopped in front of number 325. Jonathan reached into his pants pocket and pulled out a brass key. With practiced ease, he slid it into the gold lock, gave a slight turn to the right and gently opened the door.

Fresh tears rolled down Julia's cheeks. Absently she swiped at them with the back of her hand. She felt a light scratch and looked down at the perfectly round emerald ring that only hours ago had been placed on her finger. She held out her hand and turned it back and forth, watching how it caught the light. There was a circle of small diamonds surrounding the sizable stone and each time her hand moved, they shot prisms of light across the wall.

It was just as he'd said. Jonathan had promised to do it right, and in that moment, it was.

Fresh tears rolled down Julia's cheeks. Absently she swiped at them with the back of her hand. She felt a light scratch and looked down at the perfectly round emerald ring that only hours ago had been placed on her finger. She held out her hand and turned it back and forth, watching how it caught the light. There was a circle of small diamonds surrounding the sizable stone and each time her hand moved, they shot prisms of light across the wall.

It was just as he'd said. Jonathan had promised to do it right, and in that moment, it was.

The pink door swung open and inside was a huge suite, beautifully appointed. Julia took a step into the the softly lit room and felt welcomed by a whoosh of warm air. An inviting fire was already burning on the hearth of a large, white marble fireplace and carefully arranged in front of it was a white linened table for two. In the center sat a silver bowl filled with fresh strawberries and next to it, a bowl of ice with a smaller bowl of fresh, whipped cream set into it. Off to the side a silver bucket sat in a pedestal with a bottle of champagne already chilled and opened.

Julia felt like she was in a dream and after she looked around the room she asked, "What is this? It's beautiful."

Jonathan's gray eyes looked pensive. "And romantic?" he asked, "I was trying for romantic."

"Yes," she blushed, "And very romantic!"

Jonathan beamed. Then becoming more serious, he asked, "How's your head? You really threw down that punch."

"Better," she responded, "It really helped getting away from the crowd and loud music." Julia paused a moment, then ventured, "What is this place?"

"Here?" he answered, "An old hotel. Used to be quite posh. But now it runs a speak easy."

"And tonight? What was that downstairs?"

Jonathan casually walked over to the table. Holding one of the flutes, he took the bottle of champagne and poured a glass. "You?" he asked.

Julia shook her head, "No".

Jonathan raised the glass to his lips and took a long sip, then swallowed. "Tonight is a Drag Ball. As I told you earlier, they started in Harlem. It's a party where the men dress as women and the women as men." He took another long sip. "It's called dressing in drag."

"Why?" Julia asked bewildered, "Why would anyone do that?"

The corners of Jonathan's mouth twitched. "It's just for fun."

Julia hesitated. "Have you?"

"No. No. Not my thing," assured Jonathan.

"But Patrick...he seems so...so comfortable."

Jonathan drained the glass and set it on the table. Without answering, he turned toward her. "How about we sit?" he asked, and taking Julia's hand, he led her over to a small settee. Carefully, she sat. But, before she could get comfortable, Jonathan was bending down on one knee in front of her. Gently, he took her hand and began, "Julia, I think I've made my feelings known for some time now...and rather than wait, until later in the spring....I feel the time is right...now...to ask if you will do me the honor of becoming my wife?" With that, Jonathan produced a white velvet box from his inside coat pocket. Slowly, he cracked the lid open. Sitting on a bed of silk was the most beautiful ring Julia had ever seen.

"Oh," her mouth flew open, "It's lovely!"

Jonathan smiled. "It was my grandmother's. She gave it to me a while ago. Hoped I'd find the right girl to give it to." Julia blushed. "I spoke to your father," He blurted out.

"Really?" Julia queried, "What did he say? Does he like you?"

"He gave us his blessing."

Julia bit her bottom lip. She couldn't believe this was happening. Now.

"So? Do you have an answer? Please don't keep me waiting," he pleaded.

"Yes," Julia answered, beaming.

A smile broke out on Jonathan's face and plucking the ring from it's nest, he slid it onto her finger. "I love you," he blurted, and then, with a passion he'd never shown before, Jonathan cupped Julia's face in his hands and kissed her lips. Long and hard.

When they parted, Julia let out a gasp!

She reached up and took his hands from her cheeks. "What are you doing?" she asked.

"I'm sorry," he apologized, "I thought you loved me too."

Julia continued to hold Jonathan's hands, "I do," she answered, in a low whisper. "You just surprised me."

"Oh," he responded, hoarsely, "Then let me give you full notice. I am going to kiss you – again."

This time when Jonathan leaned in, Julia met him halfway. She felt the soft pressure of his lips and with this kiss, a growing urgency.

"Swept up in the moment," she reprimanded herself. "What a little fool I've been. Didn't even question the lie." Yes, she'd tried at one point to pull back, slow things down. Stop and think. Clear her head. But he'd promised so much. Pledged his love. Assured her he'd be gentle.

And the betrayal. Her own body had sold her out. Because if she was honest, and to her shame, tonight she was finally being honest – her body had responded to his caresses and she had enjoyed the heat they evoked.

Julia stirred. Her eyes fluttered open and she was still laying on the thick, fur rug in front of the fireplace. "Mmmm," she murmured. The last thing she remembered was drifting off to sleep in Jonathan's arms, her head resting against his bare chest. Slowly, she sat up and rubbed the side of her temples, surprised at the slight headache. Then, carefully, she pulled herself to standing and looked around.

Her gown had been shed, discarded on the floor. And one of her shoes was peeking out from underneath the settee. Julia grabbed her dress and slipped it over her head. Looking down, she frowned. The ostrich feather at her hip was bent and broken. "Phoey!" she exclaimed. Then, feeling around beneath the table, she produced her other shoe. Slipping both onto her feet, Julia stood, watching the smouldering embers on the hearth.

"Grrr!" her stomach began to rumble. Julia glanced at the empty bowl where the strawberries had been and the smaller dish next to it, filled with soupy cream. "They were delicious," she mused, smiling. "And the champagne – did we really drink it all?" she laughed, to herself. Inside the bucket, a dark, green bottle lay, tipped over and spent.

"Where is he?" she asked, half outloud, as she looked around the large room. That was when she noticed, at the other end of the suite, a set of closed, double doors. "Funny, I didn't notice those before." Julia walked over, her footsteps muffled in the thick carpet. When she was just outside, she thought she could hear voices.

Julia reached down and gently turned the knob. Slowly, she inched the door open, just a crack, and peeked in.

"Oh, my!" thought Julia, "This is the bedroom." She eased the crack open just a bit more and was shocked to see Jonathan sitting on the edge of a massive, four poster bed with Patrick. Her hand flew to her mouth, he hadn't even bothered to redress.

And there was Patrick. Still in his fishnet stockings, but little else.

"I got it out of the way. Just like I told you I would."

"I hope it wasn't too awful," Patrick consoled.

Jonathan put his hand on Patrick's thigh, and crooned, "Not too bad, besides, I had this to look forward to."

Patrick purred, then added, " And now all that remains is the wedding. Once that's over, your parents will be satisfied and we can finally be together."

"Thank goodness she's so naïve. She would have believed anything."

"Virgins!" Patrick mocked. Then pausing he asked, "Are you sure you haven't feelings for the little priss?"

Jonathan shifted uncomfortably, then, reached out and held Patrick's chin, "Now you're insecure?"

Patrick batted his heavy dark eyelashes, leaned forward, and allowed Jonathan to draw him in closer.

Julia quickly turned away. She didn't want to see. Hot tears began to fill her eyes and her stomach felt ready to retch. Without thinking, she ran from the door and flew out of the suite. In the hallway she paused briefly. "The elevator? No! I'm not going back down there." In the opposite direction she spied an exit that led to a back staircase. Julia flew down the hall, past the hideous pink doors and into the stairwell. She ran down taking steps two at a time, almost tripping, but never stopped until she had pushed her way through the heavy door at the bottom.

Julia stepped, falling out into a dank, smelly alley lined with trash cans and litter. A harsh wind whipped her face. She looked to her left and saw it led to the street, still occupied by shadowy figures. With only a moments hesitation, she turned to the right and began to dash further into the night. Julia kept going and going. Her feet got wet and frozen but she never looked back. It wasn't until she saw the old Brownstone church that she slowed her pace. But even then, she didn't stop until she had climbed all sixteen steps and pulled open the thick, oak door. After stumbling into the sanctuary, Julia leaned back. The heavy door closed easily under her weight and clicked shut.

Grateful. So grateful the church had been unlocked. Mustering a last burst of strength, Julia had dragged herself into the chapel and slid into a pew.

⚯

"Young lady,"

"Miss," A gentle, deep voice beckoned through the fog. "Are you alright? Please wake up."

Julia groaned and began to slowly open her eyes. A large, plump hand was gently shaking her shoulder and a round face with deep lines and worried eyes watched patiently as she became fully awake.

At first, she couldn't place where she was. But as she pulled herself to sitting, the events of earlier that night came flooding back.

"Oh, dear," she cried, in almost a whisper. Her hand flew to her throat, instinctively reaching for Mum's locket. The locket she had removed the night of her coming out. The locket she had not worn since."It wasn't a dream," she murmured, and fresh tears began to fill her eyes.

"Did you lose something?" the older man inquired.

"Yes," Julia replied, her hand beginning to shake, slightly.

The large hand patted her shoulder. "You've had a tough night?"

Julia nodded her head.

"A hot cup of tea and a chance to wash up will change everything."

Julia lifted her eyes, wide with despair, "I know you're being kind, and I can see you mean well, but nothing can change what I've done."

"No," he continued, thoughtfully, "the past is set. But, there is nothing so bad that God can't turn it around."

Julia's bottom lip quivered. She wanted to blurt out her transgressions. Desperately wanted the guilt and shame to be wiped clean away. But what she'd done was too great!

"I don't need to know what's happened. What I do know is that God is faithful and He forgives." The man took a breath, then continued, "And I know Jesus paid for all of it when he died on the cross."

Julia sniffed and began to relax. His words held truths she had learned as a child. Mum had made a point of reading to her from the large, family bible in their living room. Every night they had prayed together and Mum had always encouraged her to talk with God on her own. She was ashamed thinking about how many values she had let slip, especially in the past few months.

The old man's voice broke through her thoughts, "Come with me." He pulled himself to standing and held out a hand. Julia looked up into his kind eyes. Taking his hand she raised herself and followed him out of the pew. He led her to the front of the chapel and slowly knelt. Julia joined him and for a few moments, they bowed their heads in silence. Finally, the old man began to speak. His deep voice sounded stronger than before. He prayed with confidence, lifting the young woman beside him up to the Father and entrusting her to God's care. He thanked Jesus for his sacrifice and the new life available through him.

Julia felt her burden ease. Silently, she echoed the pastor's words and added her own, expressing her desire for forgiveness. By the time they finished with "Amen", the weight she had carried into the church was gone.

"Thank you."

The Pastor patted her hand.

"I need to be going."

"My offer of a hot cup of tea is still on the table."

"You're too kind. But there are people who will worry about me if I don't leave soon."

"Alright," he replied. "At least let me give you a wrap and arrange a ride to where ever you need to go."

Julia looked down at her soiled dress and nodded.

A short time later she watched the cab pull away from Esther's house. Cautiously, Julia stole around to the side entrance and returned the way she had left. Once in Esther's room, Julia changed quickly, hiding her dress in a ball at the bottom of her case. Then, without a noise, she pulled back her covers and slipped underneath.

Julia rolled onto her side and noticed pale, yellow sunlight just beginning to streak through the window next to her bed. It wouldn't be long before Esther began to stir and her household awaken. She closed her eyes, hoping to get a little sleep before she had to face the day.

∽

"Brrring, brrring," the doorbell chimed incessantly.

Esther lifted her head, scowling, "Who can that be? The sun is barely up."

Julia poked her nose out from the edge of her covers, "They sure are persistent," she mumbled.

Suddenly, there was a sharp rap on the door. Marion pushed it open a couple inches. "Julia?"

Julia pulled the covers down off her face, "Huh? What is it?"

"I'm so sorry dear. We've tried to put him off but he's positively frantic. Not making any sense at all. Something about losing you?"

The haze began to clear and Julia pulled herself to sitting. She didn't need to ask who or even why. "Please tell him to come back later."

"I have but he's not listening. Mr. Gilman has even threatened removal but still, he remains, ranting like a loon out front."

Julia sighed deeply. "I'm sorry, please give me a minute to dress and I'll be down."

The door closed. Julia dragged herself out of bed and began to change. She pulled on a simple blouse with a long wool skirt and cardigan. Throwing her hair into a knot, she slipped into a pair of shoes and began to walk out.

"Julia," Esther was now sitting up in her bed. "What's going on?"

"Oh, Esther," Julia replied, "It's a long story. Please, just let me take care of this and I'll tell you everything." She paused in the doorway a moment longer, "But it needs to be later, when we get back to school. I can only do this once and I have to tell you and Izz at the same time."

Julia went down the front staircase and rounded the corner heading into the parlor. The maid followed her in carrying a wooden tray with a small pot of hot tea and two cups. The woman quickly set the tray down onto an oval coffee table and with a nod from Julia, left the room, leaving the doors half open.

Jonathan sat perched on the edge of a small sofa, pale and haggard. From a set of red, swollen eyes he looked up at her and asked, "What happened to you?"

Quietly, she walked over to where he was sitting and dropped down beside him. Wordlessly, she slipped the emerald ring off her finger and taking his hand, placed it in his palm.

"I saw you with Patrick," she stated, simply.

Jonathan's face fell and tears began to pool in his eyes. "I'm sorry," he finally choked out, "I never meant for you to find out."

"You asked me to marry you. How were you planning to keep it from me?" she asked.

"You don't understand ... "

"You're right," she interjected, "There is so much about last night, this past year, that doesn't make sense. But the one thing I'm certain of, we can't build a marriage based on lies."

Jonathan opened his mouth to protest but Julia stopped him. "You're not the only one. I'm guilty as well. All along I've been playing a part. The truth is, you've never met me, the real me." Julia's tone softened, "And the thing is, I know why you did it," she paused, "but I can't understand why I did."

Jonathan eyes, tired and turbulent, met hers and she felt a sadness wash over her. His fist wrapped around the ring and he hoarsely whispered, "So there's no going back?"

Julia shook her head, "No."

Jonathan nodded.

Julia began to rise but stopped. She reached out and lightly placed her hand on Jonathan's arm. "Yes?" he asked.

" … I'd appreciate it if last night, you know, if what we did, stayed between us. Please?"

"I can do that," he assured.

"Thank you," she said, rising from the couch. Julia turned to leave. A single tear rolled slowly down her cheek and she walked out of the parlor.

Julia couldn't wait to return to school. She only wanted to finish out the year. She wasn't sure what she would do after graduation. She wasn't sure of a lot of things. But there was one thing she did know for certain, and that was what she was not going to do!

12

Julia watched as tall strands of grass blew gently across the hillside. She closed her eyes and lifted her chin so the sun's warmth could kiss her cheeks. She was sitting in the north pasture, surrounded by the hum of insects and distant din of farm life. She breathed out a long sigh and reopened her eyes. She sat watching Blanche as she began to make her way up the lower slope of the hill. Julia waited, squinting into the sun, expecting to see the top of Alfred's head bobbing alongside of Blanche.

"Strange," she had thought, "Why is she all alone?"

When Blanche finally appeared over the last crest, her face was flushed and tense. Julia noticed Blanche pause slightly and then, with a deepening resolve, cover the last stretch, plopping down in the grass next to her.

Without a preamble, Blanche began, "I want," she corrected herself, "No, no ... I don't ... I need to tell you a story. My story."

"I grew up around here....," she started.

Julia could feel the vulnerability in Blanche's voice. It troubled her when she glanced to the side, and saw a tear slowly roll down Blanche's cheek.

"Blanche, what's ...?"

Blanche held up her hand to stop Julia from asking and continued, "I grew up in these mountains on a farm in the

235

next township. When I was about fifteen, my parents died. It was a horrible accident. One day as they were heading to town in their carriage, the horses got spooked. Tore off, crazy with fear. When they hit a narrow stretch the wheels veered, taking the carriage down a ravine. At the bottom, the carriage slammed into a huge boulder and tipped over. My parents were crushed." Blanche took a long breath, then resumed. "I was an only child with no other family in the area. But, I did have an uncle and aunt living in Boston and it was they who agreed to take me in." Blanche let out a soft chuckle, "Their house is only one street over from the Gilman's brownstone. They were, are, quite wealthy. And it was from them, I learned a new life." Blanche rolled her eyes and looked up at the sky. She gently shook her head and continued, "I didn't know any better."

"What didn't you know?" asked Julia.

"My uncle and aunt had no children of their own. I suspect they never really wanted any. So it's no surprise they made the decision to have me attend a finishing school. Very much like Kimball, so I could be educated and suitable for marriage. And I, still in shock over losing my parents, obediently allowed myself to be sculpted and shaped. I turned out quite well. I am bright, so I achieved academic honors and at the same time, caught the attention of many suitable young men. I fulfilled my role perfectly." Blanche's voice grew quiet and harsh, "Even to the point of not fighting back."

"What do you mean?" Julia asked, almost in a whisper.

Blanche sighed, "It happened at a party, no different than so many others. But at this one, there were a lot of politicians. My uncle made large contributions to various officials campaigns.

At least that was what he called them. Really, he just gave them bribes. Anyways," she went on, "It was on this evening that I met George Barnett and his wife."

Julia's mouth fell open but she waited quietly for Blanche to continue.

"George arrived drunk. Not unusual for him, but that night he and his wife had had a big blow on the way over. He arrived angry and rather than spend anymore time with Mildred, he chose to head upstairs to a private lounge and wait for some of his cronies. My mistake was wandering in thinking it was the powder room." Blanche turned to look Julia straight in the face. Pain was etched into her eyes and tears began to flow freely. "Julia, he forced himself on me." Blanche began to sob. Julia fumbled in her skirt pocket until finally pulling out a small white hankie. She handed it to Blanche and waited while she dabbed at her eyes and face.

"I felt so ashamed!" Blanche divulged, "Later that night when I arrived back at my uncle's, I threw out my clothes. I wanted nothing to remind me of what had happened. I wanted to pretend that everything was the same as before he ... well, that didn't work!"

Julia was stunned. Blanche had never let on.

"It was a couple months later when I discovered I was pregnant. I didn't know what to do. When I finally went to my aunt and uncle, they didn't believe me. George and Mildred are close friends and my confession only confirmed what they had believed about me all along. That I was farm trash like my mother. My aunt said no amount of education or class could overcome poor breeding. " Blanche shook her head, "I needed her help!"

Julia waited until she couldn't stand not knowing, "Blanche, where's your baby?"

A fresh rush of tears ran down Blanche's cheeks. "Gone!" she choked out. "My aunt's idea of fixing my problem was to take me to Chicago. Far enough away from Boston that my "problem" could be resolved quietly. She took me to a small shabby boarding house and left me with a midwife that performed abortions." Blanche paused for a breath. "That woman cut into me and caused a miscarriage."

Julia's hand flew to her mouth and her eyes grew wide with disbelief.

"Then, that butcher left me ... alone, bleeding and feverish." Blanche paused for a moment before going on. "Luckily, the landlady found me and got a doctor. He was able to save my life. Unfortunately, I was so damaged, I can never have children."

"Oh, Blanche!" Julia cried out, "I can't believe such things happen! I'm so sorry for you!"

They sat in silence, watching as a bumble bee landed on a fluffy clover. He rolled around lazily gathering pollen and then flew off, his underside coated in yellow powder.

"Blanche," Julia finally spoke, "Why did you tell me this?"

Blanche turned, now facing Julia. She looked straight in her eyes and stated, "Because I know you're pregnant."

Julia's face flushed with anger. "How can you say such a thing?" she demanded.

Blanche softened. "You don't realize it, do you?"

Julia paled. Her hand flew to her abdomen and she stared back at Blanche, questioning.

"Your stomach's been upset, and you've been sensitive to smells. And haven't you noticed your frocks are getting snug?"

"I just thought … "

"I know," Blanche consoled. "I'm sorry, Julia, I thought Kimball would be different."

"Different. How?"

"These schools," Blanche, shook her head slightly, "They're designed to keep the wealthy rich. Allow families to arrange advantageous matches between their children. But only they know the rules. You can't. Not unless you grow up in that environment."

Julia's brow furrowed. "If that's true," she asked, "Then why did you convince Dad to send me to one?"

"Not me, Julia," Blanche answered, and looked at Mum's headstone. "Her."

"Mum?"

"Yes, Julia. It was your mother's dream. You don't know it, but your mother grew up in France with many advantages, and she wanted that for you." Blanche sighed, "When your Dad told me her wishes, I cautioned him, told him of my concerns. Told him everything."

"You told him everything?"

"Everything. Even before I would accept his offer of employment, I felt he needed to know. Especially living in the same town as Barnett. I was sure the rumors would make their way up here – how I threw myself at George. Seduced a married man."

"But you let me go - to Kimball - with all you knew?"

"I thought it would be better. Better than Boston. And they assured me that all the young men invited to the school were carefully vetted." Blanche waited. Julia sat quietly. Finally, Blanche asked, "What happened with Jonathan? You haven't mentioned him for months now. And Marion told me you stopped attending all of the social gatherings."

Julia looked down at her lap. "I thought he loved me," she stated simply.

"And you?"

"I got swept up in the romance of it all."

"That's not so bad. But, what happened?"

"I forgot who I am. And he pretended to be someone he's not. And then when he told me he'd spoke to Dad ..."

Blanche interrupted, "Spoke to your Dad? Julia, he never spoke with your him."

Julia paused, she thought hard for a moment and then decided to tell Blanche everything. She knew if Blanche was brave enough to share her story, then she could too. Julia began at the beginning and didn't stop until she reached the small church. When she had finished, Blanche put her arm around Julia's shoulder and pulled her in close.

"I had a feeling about him," she confessed, "But Bitsy assured me I was wrong. I'm sorry. But, I won't let you down again – starting with this baby!"

Baby!

Julia's head began to swirl. What was she going to do? But she needn't have worried, Blanche already had a plan.

It had only been a matter of days since Julia had her conversation with Blanche and already they were leaving to spend the duration of her pregnancy and birth of her baby in the house where Blanche had grown up. She felt a dull ache in her heart as she watched the farm fade in her side view mirror.

The car was silent. Will drove with his eyes fixed on the road ahead, while Blanche snuggled in close, her cheek resting, pressed against his shoulder. For Julia, the drive seemed to go on forever, but in reality, it was only about an hour. When the car began to slow, Julia saw an obscure opening in a long neglected field with only a worn, faded signpost to give it distintion. Will swung the wheel and turned into a narrow, deeply rutted driveway.

"Blanche?" Julia ventured, "Are you sure we're going the right way?"

Blanche chuckled softly. She took Julia's hand and gave it a gentle squeeze. "Only a few more minutes."

Bump, bump, bump!

Will slowed even further to accommodate the loose gravel and pot holes. His knuckles began to whiten as he clutched the wheel harder, fighting to stay within the tall grassy borders. It wasn't until they rounded a sharp bend to the right that he was able to relax his grip. Now on smoother ground, he continued on until finally rolling into an expansive clearing Will pulled up alongside an old shed, eased off the gas, and let the car's engine chortle to a stop.

Julia let out an audible sigh of relief.

"We're here," Dad announced, swinging his door open and exiting the car. Blanche followed his lead and slid out behind him while Julia got out on her side. She stood for a moment, scowling at the gray, weathered shack before her when Dad's voice broke through, "Come on, Julia. The house is this way."

Julia followed Dad and Blanche around to the other side of the shed. Her mouth fell open. Rising before her was a large, yellow Victorian with white and biege trim. There were black flower boxes hanging beneath each window that were overflowing with pink and purple petunias. A welcoming porch wrapped around the front and sides with wicker rockers and small tables.

A hand lightly touched Julia's shoulder, she turned to see Blanche with a contented smile on her face. "I haven't been here in years. But thanks to your Dad and DJ, it's mine again."

Julia looked at Blanche questioningly.

"Oh, that's right, you didn't know," began Blanche. "When we were in Boston, DJ was able to secure the deeds to my parents property." Blanche paused, then gave Julia's shoulder a squeeze and said, "I know it's not your home, but it was mine."

Julia said nothing.

"We will be comfortable here, I promise," Blanche consoled. Then, beginning to head inside she encouraged, "Come with me, you can look around."

Julia followed Blanche inside to the front hall, open with a high ceiling. From there she wandered around the first floor. In each room, she was struck by the tall, gleaming windows where rays of light flooded in. She stopped for a moment in the diningroom and watched as the sunlight danced on the recently polished surfaces and floors. Julia began to feel her mood lift.

"Julia." It was Will.

"Yes, Dad?" she answered without turning to look at him. Things the past few days had moved so fast. They hadn't even had time to talk. Now she realized, she didn't know how he felt. About her or the baby.

"You know I love you, don't you?" he asked, quietly.

Julia bit her bottom lip, then answered, "I know, Dad."

"Julia," he waited, then walked over to her. Will spoke tenderly, "Nothing can ever change that."

"Okay," she replied, her voice unsteady. "But, Dad, I'm so sorry."

"For what?" he asked, "Making a mistake? Trusting the wrong person?"

Julia turned to face him and nodded.

Will took her in his arms and hugged her warmly. "Those things can never change how I feel about you," he stated, emphactically, "You are my girl and this baby is family. How it came to be is irrelevant. All that matters is God has blessed us with one more person to love."

Julia sank into Will's embrace and another layer of shame fell from her heart.

Later that evening, Julia sat on the porch watching as lights began to flicker across the fields. She heard the screen door open and shut. Blanche walked past and then sat in the rocker next to hers.

"Feeling a bit more settled?"

"Yes," Julia answered, silently rocking. Off in the distance they heard an owl hooting softly, his nightly hunt about to begin.

"Did you notice I brought your Mum's quilt?" asked Blanche, "It's on your bed."

"Yes, thank you," Julia replied, then added, "I saw it earlier. The room is lovely."

A cool breeze began to stir. The owl continued to call into the shadows. Finally, Blanche ventured, "You have a lot on your mind, don't you?"

Julia continued rocking. She reached for Mum's locket and smiled, it was right where it belonged. Then, needing to know, Julia asked, "Blanche, what do people think? Where do they think we've gone?"

"As far as our friends and neighbors are concerned, you and I are off on a holiday. Traveling before you leave to start college."

"Oh, okay," Julia acknowledged.

"What else?" asked Blanche, "I can tell by the crease in your brow there's more."

Julia's heart began to ache, "The baby," she whispered, "What about the baby?"

"Oh, Julia," Blanche soothed, "I had hoped to put off discussing that till later."

"But I need to know," Julia pressed, "Now."

"All right," Blanche began, "I can tell you our idea. I actually came up with it, but your Dad agrees. And no matter what, the final decision is up to you. It's all up to you."

Julia held the metal oval between her fingers. She waited.

Slowly, Blanche began, "If you want, your Dad and I would like to be your baby's parents." Her words hung heavily between them and Blanche began to wish she hadn't said anything. Not yet.

From off in the distance, a chorus of frogs began their nightly serenade and the whirr of the crickets played along. Finally, Julia spoke, her words slow and measured, "So you and Dad want this baby?"

Blanche's voice trembled, slightly, "It's just, we thought this way you would still be free to go to college, do whatever you want with your life. And your baby would be cared for. In our family."

"And you would love her? Like your own? Like you love Alfred?"

"Her?"

"It's just a feeling. But, would you?"

Blanche simply nodded.

"Okay," Julia stated.

"Okay what?" Blanche asked, quietly.

"Yes," Julia answered, unwaveringly, "I want you and Dad to be her parents."

Blanche sniffed loudly and swiped an errant tear from her eye. Clearly her attempts to remain detatched were failing. Now, it was Julia wrapping her arms around Blanche's shoulders. And Julia realized, as she held this woman, that this was part of God's plan. She could feel His peace soothing the ache she'd been carrying since Mum's death and within the depths of her heart, she knew that this was His answer to both her and Blanche's prayers.

Throughout the following months, Blanche and Julia worked together preparing for the baby's arrival. One warm day they spent empting the smallest upstairs bedroom. They filled buckets with soapy water and scrubbed it clean. On the next day, they painted the walls a pale green with bright white trim. Then, on another day, after Blanche discovered an old bureau out in the shed, they sanded it down and painted it the same green as the bedroom walls. For rainy days, Blanche had asked Lou to send over yards of material that they could stitch into clothes and blankets. And each clear day they would try to venture outside for at least a little bit. Blanche said the sunshine was good for both Julia and her baby.

Of course, there were folks from the farm that came to visit and help out. Will would stay over on his way to Concord, sometimes leaving Alfred and then, pick him up on his way home. Lou made sure there was always something sweet in the pantry and Don kept the wood box filled. Even DJ and Billy popped out a couple times a week, bringing fresh milk and eggs.

At the beginning, Julia felt awkward when the McGraths came around and usually managed to disappear, especially from DJ. But the day came when she could no longer hide. DJ came by to take care of a chore. Will had asked him to clear a path to the old barn, give it a good sweep, and check out the structure.

DJ had been whacking away at the tall grass most of the morning when he took a break and discovered Julia sitting out on the porch. "Whew! It's a hot one," DJ exclaimed, and wiped the sweat from his brow with the bottom of his shirt.

"Blanche set out a pitcher of lemonade," Julia responded, "Go ahead and help yourself."

"Thanks," said DJ, and he strode up the steps and over to a small table where the pitcher and a few glasses waited on a tray.

After pouring himself a tall glass and taking a long drink he said, "Hey, you should come with me to the barn and see what I found."

"I don't know," said Julia, shifting uncomfortably and trying to rearrange the folds of her frock. She was six months along now and even if she could've forgotten the life inside, the tiny hiccups and kicks wouldn't let her.

"You do realize I know," stated DJ.

Julia could feel her face flush and stomach lurch.

DJ took another long drink from his glass. Draining it, he set it back down on the tray. "Julia," he ventured. She looked up into kind eyes. "You're not the first girl to get pregnant."

Julia bit her bottom lip and fought off the tears that threatened to spill. After a minute she was finally able to choke out, "I was so gullible."

DJ said nothing.

"And, I was horrible to you!" she continued, "DJ, I'm so sorry!"

DJ shrugged and stated, simply, "It's okay, I knew what he was the first time I saw him."

"You did?" she questioned, no longer caring if DJ saw her bump.

"Sure," he answered, grinning, "I knew he was a fool."

Julia grinned back, "And how did you know that?" she asked.

"He had to be if he thought he could ever be good enough for you."

Julia laughed.

"So, you want to see what I found," he asked.

Julia hopped up, "Sure, let's go."

DJ led Julia through the swath he'd cut in the waist high grass. When they reached the barn, the door was already pulled part-way open.

"I haven't done anything in here yet," he warned, "So watch yourself."

Carefully, they stepped inside. Julia stood just over the threshold and looked around. There were lacy webs hanging thick in the corners with long, wispy strands floating lazily from the rafters. Light was breaking through the dirt encrusted windows only to reveal clouds of dust rising from thick floorboards.

"There's a lot of work to do," DJ commented, "But first, look up. Do you see it?"

Julia squinted and looked up into the rafters. There, perched almost directly above her, was a cradle!

"Oh," she exclaimed, "It looks to be in good shape. Can you get it down for me?"

Even before the words had left her mouth, DJ was scrambling up the ladder that led to the loft. Within a few seconds he was at the top rung and Julia watched as he disappeared over the edge. She didn't have to wait long before DJ reappeared. Carefully, he began to ease out onto the rafter where the cradle lay.

"Please be careful!" Julia warned.

"Don't worry," he assured her, "I'm almost there."

Julia held her breath until DJ reached the cradle. Slowly, he bent down and lifted it out from the beams. "It's not heavy, "he remarked, "If I hand it down, can you hold it?"

Julia nodded and said, "Yes!"

Carefully, DJ turned the cradle on its side and eased it down to Julia. Waiting with outstretched arms, she grabbed hold and yelled up, "I've got it!" DJ let go and Julia set it down on the dusty floor. "Whew," she exclaimed, and brushed some loose strands from her eyes.

DJ was already down off the ladder and walking toward her when he began to laugh.

"What's so funny?" she asked.

" Your face," he answered, "You have dirt smeared across your brow and cheeks."

Julia frowned and looked down at her hands. Thick black dust covered her palms and fingers. DJ walked over and pulled a kerchief from his pants pocket. "Don't worry, it's clean," he assured her. Then, lifting Julia's chin, he began to wipe her cheeks.

Julia closed her eyes. The soft cotton cloth slowly moved across her skin. Her pulse began to quicken and she could feel her breath catch in the back of her throat. "How can this be?" she thought to herself, "Haven't I learned anything?"

"Did you say something?" DJ asked.

"Hmmm? Oh, yes," Julia stammered, "Is it coming off?"

DJ's voice lowered. "Most of it," he answered, gently wiping the last few smudges away. Julia could feel the pressure of his fingers, still resting under her chin. A strange shiver ran through her body. Slowly, DJ leaned in. Julia could feel his lips gently brush against her own.

A moment. It was only for a moment that they hung suspended, barely touching.

DJ's lips parted slightly, then pulled back. His hand fell from her chin. Suddenly self conscious, he murmured, "I'm sorry, I shouldn't have done that."

"I'm glad you did," Julia replied, hoarsely.

"No," stated DJ, "You're carrying another man's child. You may not want him now, but that can change." DJ turned to walk away from her.

Julia caught his arm, "Please, stop." DJ paused and Julia continued. "Nothing will change. He doesn't want me." She took a breath, "He will never want me …. because … he wants to be with a man."

DJ turned back toward Julia. His brow furrowed and eyes narrowed. "And what about me? Can you ever… why would you ever consider a life with someone like me?"

"Like you? What does that mean?" she asked.

"I'm not educated like you are. And in case you haven't noticed, I don't fit into high society – galas and socials and all."

"I'm beginning to wonder if I ever fit into all that. I really made a mess of things trying to," Julia's hands fell to her small belly. "No, this is my home," she sighed. "Well, not here," she looked around the barn, "but on the farm, in the mountains."

DJ's voice became low and serious, "I'm half Indian. I've watched my parents struggle because of my Ma. There are a lot of people that would make things hard for you."

Julia's mouth gaped open, "Do you really think I'd care about that?"

DJ shifted uncomfortably. "Why now?" he questioned, "Surely you've known how I felt?"

Julia shook her head.

"Well, you were the only one."

Julia remained silent, stunned by this new revelation.

"Come on," said DJ, abruptly, "We should get this to the house."

"Oh, okay."

DJ bent down, "Here, I'll carry it for you. It should be easy enough to scrub clean if I get you a basin of water."

"Okay, thanks," mumbled Julia, distractedly.

DJ swung the cradle up, onto his shoulder and waited for Julia to exit the barn. Silently, he followed her back to the house and once she had everything she needed for cleaning, he left her to finish his chores.

Later that evening Will stopped through. DJ had waited to pull him aside and together, they walked out to the barn. He needed to show Will the pile of bedding, balled up and shoved in a far corner of the loft.

The next morning when DJ returned, he was accompanied by Don and Billy. That day the three men worked mowing down the rest of the tall grass surrounding the house and barn. From then on, anytime Will wasn't there, he had DJ stay the night.

13

Julia's hat barely contained her curls, much like her heavy coat was no match for her expansive belly. She was nearing the end of her nineth month and no matter how hard she tugged, the thick wool refused to stretch further.

Julia hadn't been back to the barn since the day DJ had showed her the cradle. And since that day, DJ had kept busy away from the house, away from Julia.

"Oh, well," she frowned, "Not much longer."

Julia trudged through the knee deep snow. White flakes continued to swirl all around her making it hard to find the path to the barn. The early storm was unexpected and after coming in hard, it still showed no sign of letting up.

"Uhh," Julia groaned, another contraction. She'd felt the first shortly after breakfast. Same as every morning for the past two weeks. Each time she would have a few rounds and then they would simply stop.

"Just your body practicing," Blanche would say.

"But not today. No, today you decide to make it real," Julia reproved. The barn door was now in sight. "Two more steps." Julia fell on the handle and pulled hard. A gust of wind rushed head on and fought her efforts. "Aghhhh!" she cried, holding the handle, trying to make it budge. The wind let out a howl, then died down. Julia tried again. This time the latch released its hold and the door slid to the side. Julia fell through the opening, thankful to be out of the storm. She leaned back against the door, trying to catch her breath before another contraction came on.

"Wood," she reminded herself, "I just need to get a couple logs. Only two and I can keep the house warm till Blanche gets back." It had been a couple hours since Blanche had left. Just a quick walk out to the orchard to grab some cider from the apple house. But then the storm had rolled in. So fast they never saw it coming. Julia went to the stack and grabbed one, and then another nice size log. Wrapped in her arms she turned to venture back out into the snow. "Aghhhh!" She dropped the wood and doubled over. "No, no, no! This can't be happening! Where are you?" she cried out. Cried. To Blanche. To DJ. To anyone.

A rustling was heard in the far corner of the barn. Julia turned to look. Out from the shadows a form emerged. She pressed her back against the thick door. Despite her coat, she felt a chill run up her spine. "Who are you?" she asked.

It was a man, bent and dark. He began to approach, his black eyes staring out from a face scarred pink and brown. Slowly, he held out a hand, shriveled and deformed. In it was something, something that looked familiar. Julia gasped! Her hair comb!

"How did you get my comb?" she demanded.

The man rasped, harshly, "Don't you recognize me?"

Julia knew that voice. But from where? "Aghhhh!" she had no time to think about who this man was. Her baby was coming. Now.

"Please, I need your help," Julia pleaded, "I'm sorry, I don't know who you are but I'm about to give birth."

"Serves you right," the man mocked, "You, the self-righteous bitch delivering your bastard in an old barn. Why would I help you?"

Julia's eyes widened, "Phil?"

The sneer on Phil's face deepened and he threw back his head and howled. The gray knit cap he was wearing fell to the ground, exposing patches of matted hair intermingled with more pink and brown scarring. Julia gasped, horrified to see that one of Phil's ears was completely gone leaving only a small dark hole.

"The fire destroyed everything. We thought you were dead."

"Not me. I wasn't that lucky. Barely made it outside before the place blew up. Flames were shooting out the windows. Bits of hot glass melted into my skin. Yeah, and that was before my hair and clothes caught fire."

Julia's hand flew to mouth. She began to say something when another wave of pain hit. "Aghhhh!" she cried, clutching the door handle.

Phil scowled, "Why should I care anything about you? Always thought you were too good for the rest of us."

Julia began to understand. All the attention Peg had given her, all the time spent making her expensive wardrobe for school. Phil had been jealous. And she had been a worthy target. She could still remember the night at the Grange. The things she'd heard the girls say about her.

"You're right. I've never given you any reason to want to help me. But Phil," she begged, "I need you! This baby is coming. Now! And you're right, she wasn't planned. I've lived selfishly and been foolish, but I realize that now. And I'm sorry I hurt you."

"Words! They mean nothing!" cried Phil vehemently.

"No, Phil, not just words." I had to ask for God's forgiveness. And now, he's turning my mistake into something good."

Phil balled up his fists and began to scream, "Noooo! Look at me! God can never turn this into something good!"

"Please, Phil, I need your help.... I need Blanche."

Phil's fists opened. Her haircomb fell to the floor. Then, shaking his head he howled, "No! Not me!" And in a hoarse whisper he cried, "I'm too far gone." Phil looked back at Julia. A sneer spread across his face, and reaching out, he grabbed Julia's arm. Roughly, he tossed her to the side and ducked out the door, disappearing into the storm.

Julia lay on the floor clutching her belly. A wave of despair threatened to wash over her but another contraction was starting to build and suddenly her only thought was protecting this baby.

"Julia?" DJ's face appeared in the doorway. "What are you doing out here? Are you okay?" he demanded.

"No," Julia panted, heavily, "I came to get wood. The baby's coming," she cried.

"Where's Blanche?"

"Getting cider, but the storm snuck up on us."

"Come on," said DJ, "I need to get you back to the house." Gently, DJ helped her up, but just as they began out the door, another contraction started. DJ lifted Julia and carried her in his arms over to a soft bed of straw. Carefully, he lay her down then, dropped to her side. "I won't leave you," he reassured.

"Aghhh ... " she moaned, "I need to push!"

"Okay, Julia," DJ encouraged, "Push!"

For the next hour, Julia felt waves of pressure build, prompting her to push. Her face and hair became damp with sweat, her body grew fatiqued, and it seemed her labor would never end. Then, they heard the barn door creak open. In stepped Blanche, carrying an armload of warm blankets and her nurses' satchel. She ran over to Julia, dropping her load in DJ's lap.

"Okay, sweets, let's take at look and see how long before this baby makes its entrance."

Blanche positioned herself at Julia's feet. Gently lifting her skirt she remarked, "Just in time, this little one's beginning to crown." Blanche could see how tired Julia was. She glanced at DJ and directed, "Hold her hand, she just needs a couple more good pushes."

DJ grabbed Julia's hand. "You're doing great," he encouraged. "Just a little more and you'll see your baby." Julia's brow creased. Summoning her last bit of strength, she took a deep breath and bore down hard.

The next thing she knew, Blanche was announcing, "She's here!" And a heartwrenching wail echoed through the barn.

Julia dropped DJ's hand and fell back in the hay. She let out a deep sigh and closed her eyes. "Thank you," she mouthed. A few minutes later, Blanche placed the swaddled baby in Julia's arms. Julia looked down at the small creature, cradled at her breast. "She's perfect," she murmured.

Hours later Julia lay in her bed, the newborn by her side. She knew she should use this time to sleep, but she just couldn't take her eyes off her little girl.

Tap, tap!

"Come in," Julia answered, quietly.

The door eased open and Blanche tip toed in. She came next to Julia and smiled. "How are feeling?"

"Fine. Tired and a little sore, but fine."

"Good. Can I get you a snack?"

"No, thanks," Julia paused. the baby was beginning to stir. "Would you like to take her?" she asked. Blanche busied herself, straightening Julia's covers. "She needs to meet her mama," Julia encouraged.

Blanche lifted her eyes, wide with hope, "Really? You're ready to let me hold her?"

Julia reached out and took Blanche's hand. She gave it a soft squeeze and said, "You are her mother. I will nurse her for a few months, until it's time for her to be weaned. But from here out, I will be her sister."

Blanche was at a loss. Gratitude swelled within her chest and for a moment, she couldn't speak. When she finally could, she asked, "I was wondering if you have a name picked out?"

Julia shook her head. Funny, but that was the one thing she'd never considered.

"Well," said Blanche, "If it's okay with you, I think she should be named Elizabeth."

"But that was mum's name," Julia argued, "People will think it odd."

"Not if we call her Lizzie," suggested Blanche, her eyes twinkling.

Julia smiled. "Yes, Lizzie. I like that, it fits!"

14

It was only a few months later but already Lizzie was taking a bottle. Julia and Blanche had ridden out the worst of the winter on the estate. Will had continued to make trips out, but with the senate on break and nothing to do in the fields till spring, he spent more time with "his girls" than on his farm.

Then, when the snow began its spring thaw, they decided it was time to go home. Wedged into the front seat of Will's car, Julia could feel Lizzie's little feet pressed against her side. She could hear Blanche gently humming and Dad whistling, quietly under his breath. Julia stared out the window. Watching and marking each curve and bump in the road. Mentally noting that nothing had changed. A year had passed but everything was where she had left it. Where it should be.

She knew the town had been buzzing with the news and awaiting the arrival of Blanche and baby Lizzie. Their friends had been stunned when they heard of Blanche's unexpected pregnancy. And at such an inconvenient time. Right in the middle of her and Julia's big trip. But now, Will was bringing them home and the community had rallied to welcome its newest member. Already, trips had been made out to the farm to drop off baskets of hand sewn blankets, knit booties and assorted baked goods.

The car began to slow and gingerly, Will turned the wheel easing the car into the driveway. Coasting up to the front, he pushed down on the brake pedal and glided to a stop. Will shut off the engine and turned to Blanche, "We're home!" he smiled. Then, turning to Julia he said, "All my girls are finally home!"

Blanche glanced over at Will and mouthed, "I love you!" But Julia already had her door open and was stepping out into the sunlight. She only took a moment to look around before she headed to the house.

She'd played the scene out in her mind a hundred times. What she would say, how he would respond. She'd had months to make sure she knew how she felt. She wouldn't make a mistake. Not again. Not this time.

Taking a deep breath, Julia pushed through the front door and headed into the kitchen. Lou was right where she'd expected, working at the sink with her back to the doorway.

"Hey, Lou!" Julia called out.

Lou spun around and grinned. She shook off her hands and grabbing a towel began to wipe them dry. Then tossing it on the counter, came over to greet Julia.

After giving her a warm hug, Lou pulled back and looked Julia up and down. "You've changed," she remarked.

"Oh, Lou," teased Julia. "It's been a year. I should think so."

"No," answered Lou, gently shaking her head. "You look good. Content."

Julia smiled, then asked, "Hey, Lou, is DJ around?"

"Oh, no, honey. He's gone."

"Gone?" she questioned.

"Sure," Lou continued. "He left a couple days ago with Abigail."

"Abigail?"

"Yes," Lou spoke matter of factly. "They went to New York to catch the ship to France."

"France?"

Lou scowled. "I know you've been gone but surely news traveled all the way out to Blanche's farm."

"Yes...but I must have missed this tid bit."

"Humph!" replied Lou. "France, Julia, Paris France. Billy's there already and working. Max got him an apprenticeship with a designer he knows. Billy left over five months ago!"

Julia's brow furrowed. Then, she remembered – "Yes, yes! Oh, of course! I remember hearing that."

A loud bang echoed in the hallway as the front door slammed shut. Lou looked over Julia's shoulder and waited expectantly.

"We're home!" Will's voice erupted.

Lou began to push past Julia, then paused. She dug into the front pocket of her apron and pulled out a small envelope with Julia's name written on the front. "Here, this is for you. Almost forgot I had it," Lou apologized. Then, anxious to welcome the newest family member, she hurried out of the kitchen leaving Julia alone.

Julia stared at the envelope gripped in her hands. She could hear the happy voices out in the hall and decided to open it in her room. Quietly she headed upstairs, almost afraid to breath. A note from DJ. What could he possibly say?

Carefully, Julia tugged at the flap until the glue gave way. Then, with trembling fingers she pulled out the note card.

The hand painted flowers on the cover betrayed the artist. Slowly, she opened it up and began to read:

"Dear Julia...going to Paris...your friend, Billy," she murmured. Julia crunched the note in her fist and threw it to the floor. She ran from her room and back down the stairs. By now everyone was gathered in the livingroom so she was able to slip out the back door unnoticed. She immediately headed to her one place of solace. The barn.

When she got to the big, heavy door, Julia grabbed the handle and pulled it open. The sweet scent of hay and manure was released and Julia took a deep breath, then walked inside. For a moment, Julia could only make out the large, shadowy shapes of the cows. She felt their musky heat and heard their feet shuffling against the barn floor. As her eyes began to adjust, she spotted Bea.

"Hey, you," she crooned, and walked over to scratch the now grown cow's head.

Large brown eyes looked up at her and Bea nodded her head as though she understood. Julia began to bite her lip, trying to fight off tears that were threatening to spill.

"Oh, Bea!" she whispered, hoarsely. "I waited too long!"

"I should have known you'd come to see this cow first."

Julia jumped with a start, then spun around. "DJ?" she cried.

"Welcome home!"

"Why are you here?"

DJ paused, his brow furrowed. "You're crying."

Julia turned away and swiped at her eyes. She felt DJ place his hands on her shoulders and gently begin to turn her toward him. She didn't dare look up – this wasn't at all how she'd planned it.

"Where did you think I'd be?" he asked.

"I didn't know," Julia began. "Not until Lou told me."

"Oh," he answered. "Yeah, I just got back from taking Abby to the ship. But why the tears?"

"I thought you were going with her? Are you planning to join her later?" she asked.

"Join who? Where?"

"Abigail! In Paris."

A grin spread across DJ's face. "No," he answered, "I don't think Billy would appreciate me moving in on his wife."

"What?" asked Julia, completely confused.

"Julia, Billy and Abigail have been a couple for years now. They eloped just before he left. He went first to get everything ready. A few weeks ago he sent her a ticket so she could join him."

Julia felt a rush of heat spread over her cheeks. She closed her eyes and searched desperately for something to say, but, there was nothing. She could feel DJ move a little closer. He leaned in and asked again, softly, "So why are you crying?"

It felt like a weight was crushing Julia's chest and when she tried to answer, she could only choke out, "Because I thought you had left for good. I thought I'd waited too long to tell you."

DJ let out a chuckle and then leaned in further, gently kissing her lips. When they parted, he whispered, "I love you, too! And," he continued, slowly lifting her chin, "I think I could love you for the rest of my life. Is that something like what you wanted to tell me?"

Julia nodded, her eyes wide and beginning to tear again.

"What did I do?" he asked, hoarsely.

"What did you do?" Julia reached up and touched DJ's cheek. "You have always made me weak in the knees. You have pushed me away and then pulled me in. You have made me crazy with desire. And you…You have always loved me." Then, Julia pulled his face down toward hers and whispered, "And I have always loved you, too!" Then, she closed her eyes and with slightly parted lips, began to kiss him.

15

Toot! Toot! Julia's eyes flew open.

"Oh, my goodness!" she exclaimed, "I didn't think I was that tired." It took a moment for her to realize she was in the North Pasture. She'd arrived home after dark the night before, then woken up early so she could watch the sun rise over the ridge of the mountains.

She found it hard to believe it had been one year since she'd been home. One year since that day in the barn when she'd confessed her love to DJ. And one year since they'd begun planning their life together. She had gone to Keene to earn her teaching certificate and he had gone to Canada to help Peter renovate the lodge. There had been so many letters and some phone calls, but now it was time for them to be together – finally together!

Julia pushed a stray curl out of her eyes and sat up. She began to pick loose stalks of straw from her curls.

Toot! Toot! The whistle echoed off the mountains announcing the approach of the express train from Ontario. Julia gazed off across the ridge searching for the wispy threads of smoke that always followed the locomotive.

"There," she said, under her breath, and strained further until she spotted flashes of color flitting through breaks in the sea of deep green pines. Julia felt her pulse quicken and began to stand.

"Here, let me help you," a deep voice offered from behind. Julia smiled. "Phil? What are you doing here?"

"I'm here for the wedding, of course," he grinned.

Julia held out her hand and allowed Phil to help her up. She took a moment to brush off her slacks and then paused. She looked up into Phil's calm gray eyes. It was hard to believe this was the same man who'd confronted her that day in the barn. The man whose hurt and anger had driven him out into a blizzard leaving her and her unborn child alone. But that day in the storm was when his transformation had begun.

After slamming out of the barn, Phil felt a pang in his heart. He didn't know why, but he couldn't abandon Julia. So, without wasting a moment, Phil bravely fought his way through the snow to bring Blanche back in time to deliver the baby. And since that day, it was decided to have Phil become part of their family. It was also Blanche's idea, and Will had agreed, to have Phil stay on at her estate and under the direction of DJ, learn to run the place. At first it was hard for Phil to let go of the pain that had tormented him for so long. But with a lot of patience and kindness, Phil began to trust and heal. He and DJ even become good friends!

"I didn't realize how jealous I was," he confessed at one point and even admitted to causing damage at the farm whenever Julia came home. He even revealed he was the one who took Abigail from the woods after mistaking her for Julia.

"How are the crops coming along?" Julia asked, easily.

"So far, it's been a good start to the season," Phil answered, as they began to make their way down through the pasture towards the house.

Julia paused for a moment. Her hand gripped Phil's arm. "Do you hear that?" she asked.

The steady whirr of a truck engine faintly hummed in the distance.

Phil broke into a grin and began to chuckle. "Only you could hear that," he said, "But not one single word I've said since we started walking."

Julia grimaced. "Sorry, Phil, I'm a little preoccupied."

"I can see that," Phil teased, "You know, some people think it's bad luck to see each other the day of the wedding,"

Julia scowled, and refocused her eyes on the end of the driveway. After being apart for the past twelve months, she wasn't about to let some silly superstition keep her from welcoming DJ home.

Off in the distance the rumble of Will's truck grew louder. A light cloud of dust billowed toward the end of the driveway announcing their approach. Julia began to squeeze Phil's arm tighter until finally, he yelled in protest.

"Hey, leave a fella a little circulation!"

"Sorry!" she cried absently, the truck was just turning in.

Will turned into the well worn circle and pulled up to the front of the house. Even before the engine could sputter to a stop, the passenger door had been flung open and DJ was running to meet Julia. Within seconds she felt his arms embrace her and his kiss on her lips.

"Okay, you two," Dad joked. "You'll have plenty of time for that later. Right now we have to get this fella cleaned up and presentable enough to marry my daughter."

They all began to laugh and reluctantly, DJ and Julia parted. Then, with his arm around her shoulder, DJ leaned in and whispered in Julia's ear, "Can we go someplace quiet? I have news. And it can't wait."

Julia nodded and allowed DJ to steer her toward the frog pond. "Let's take a short walk?" he suggested.

Julia could feel the muscles in her stomach tighten. By his tone, she could tell it was not good.

When they'd finally reached the far side of the pond, DJ stopped. He looked across the water, watching as small heads disappeared beneath the surface leaving only rings.

"Izzy's gone."

The words hung thick in the air.

"What?" Julia stammered. "What did you say?" She struggled to breath. Tried to take in the words.

"Her father's responsible."

"Gone?" Julia managed to cry out. "But where?" DJ simply shrugged, helpless. Julia felt a weight descend on her chest. She shook her head and murmured, "But we have plans. She can't be. We have plans." Then, lifting her eyes she looked up at DJ and asked, "What happened?"

" We thought he'd given up. We really believed he had accepted her decision to be with Peter." DJ shook his head, sadly. "He had her kidnapped. She was on her way to the station to join Peter. All the plans. All the documents and stock certificates were in her satchel. As she was waiting on the platform two men grabbed her and threw her into a waiting car."

Julia couldn't say a word. She simply stared at DJ with fresh tears running down her cheeks.

DJ continued, "He never abandoned his dream of forging a European business alliance. So he had Izzy taken to a remote chalet in the White Mountains. Her "fiancé" was waiting. It was a matter of hours, married and taken to the wedding chamber – all within a matter of hours."

"But Bitsy said...her mother promised..." Julia argued.

"It was the only way the kid was gonna get his Dad's money."

"But Izzy never would have allowed it," Julia protested. "She would have fought."

"She was drugged," DJ swiped at his eyes and then, taking out a kerchief, quietly blew into it. He continued, " The bastard was deranged. Sick and evil."

"Was?" Julia questioned. "You said was"?

"Yes. He hurt her, but when she started to come out of it, she did fight. That's when she was able to escape."

"Escape?" Julia whispered, hopefully. "So she's safe?"

"Yes and no," DJ replied. "She fought him. Hard. But in the end she only got away after pushing him down a steep granite staircase."

Julia stood in shock. Her face wet with tears and head continuing to reel.

"His body was found crumpled on the floor in a pool of blood," DJ continued. "His neck was broken."

"So where is she?"

"Noone knows."

"But Peter," Julia suddenly remembered Peter. "Does he know? About Izz? Oh, poor Peter, does he know?"

DJ simply nodded. Peter knew.

DJ and Julia stayed by the pond for hours. Talking. Comforting. Consoling and praying. When they finally walked back toward the house, it was to tell everyone that their wedding was postponed.

16

Julia watched the shadows gather as the sun sank into the trees. The final burst of yellow gold sent rays across her walls and then just as suddenly, they disappeared.

Julia rose and went to her dresser. She ran her fingers across the delicate lace until they found the edge of a small box. She picked it up and gently pushed on one end. A small drawer slid out and she fished inside for a wooden match. Deftly holding the box at an angle, she struck the match against its side and watched as it produced a bright blue flame. Carefully, Julia leaned over and applied the flame to the fat wick of her kerosene lamp. After it took, she gently blew it out and slid the glass globe onto the top and adjusted the height. She knew she could have simply flicked a switch, but somehow tonight, she longed for the soothing glow of the lamp.

Julia stood at the dresser watching her reflection in the mirror flicker in and out with the rise and fall of the flame. She had one last thing to do. She reached for the small velvet pouch and untied the ribbons. Julia slid her fingers inside and forced open its mouth. When she tipped it on its side a pair of crystal teardrops fell into her palm. Julia had waited till now to put on her earrings. Not just any earrings but the ones Izzy had lent her the night of their first party. Carefully, she screwed them onto her ear lobes remembering how they dangled and made her feel special. "My something borrowed," Julia mused and watched as her reflection faded and she felt herself drawn back to the days after Izzy's disappearance.

∽

Julia sat on the edge of the sofa, her fingers twitching as she watched DJ rip open a small yellowed envelope. Carefully, he slipped the thin telegram out and began to read.

Julia-
VanDorn detectives found her. In bad shape, long recovery expected.
More to come.
-Bitsy

Julia released the breath she'd been holding for the past few weeks. She looked up at DJ and asked, "What now?"

"Well," DJ paused, "There's nothing more we can do for Izz until we hear more from her mother." He stared through the paper in his hand and absently ran his fingers along the edge. "I should meet up with Peter," he continued, "I've already been gone too long and we can't afford to stop working. But you and I...we don't have to wait....we could still get married..."

Julia's brow furrowed. "When? How?" she asked.

"Tonight," he answered, slowly.

"But, DJ???"

"I can arrange everything,"

"I don't know. This isn't how we planned it."

DJ took Julia's hand and gently kissed it. "I know it's not. But I have to go. For at least a few months." He lifted his chin and his eyes met hers, "This waiting is making me crazy!" And suddenly, he was ravaging her hand, quickly moving up her arm, and attacking her neck.

"Okay, okay," Julia laughed. "You win."

DJ sat back and grinned broadly. "Tonight, eight o'clock I'll meet you at the truck." He rose to leave but then, paused, "And don't bother with a suitcase, you won't need it."

Julia aimed the book she'd been reading, ready to throw it at the back of DJ's head, but he ducked through the hall doorway and disappeared. She leaned back into the soft sofa cushions and bit her bottom lip. Izzy was found! And tonight she was getting married! It took everything in her to keep from giggling.

Later that evening, Julia slipped out the kitchen door. She knew Blanche was upstairs getting Lizzie to sleep and Will was in Alfred's room reading bedtime stories. Stealthly she crept around to the front of the house and down to the end of the driveway. The truck was already idling and as soon as she'd slid inside, DJ turned out onto the narrow dirt road. He drove a few hundred yards past their property before flipping on the headlamps and then applied pressure to the gas pedal. They jostled down the old, country road until finally coming to the main thoroughfare. Turning onto it, DJ and Julia began heading south towards the next township. It took about 45 minutes and they barely spoke until they reached the outskirts of Claremont, There, on a small dead end street lived a minister and his wife.

DJ slowed the truck and parked in front of a stone cottage with its outside lights on. He jumped out and ran around to Julia's door. With a slight flourish, he opened her door and extended his hand. Julia took it and slipped out of the truck.

"Nervous?" he asked.

"A little," she confessed.

"About me?" he asked, concerned.

"No!" she responded, quickly. "It's just, ... well, I know we'll be married. And I know what you expect."

"Expect?" he questioned, a slight grin lingering at the corners of his mouth.

Julia blushed. "You know what I mean!"

DJ pulled her in close. He leaned in and whispered, "Oh, yes, I will be expecting 'that', but I promise, I will take care of you." And with that, he kissed her long and hard. Then, taking Julia's hand, he led her up to the front door.

Brring! Brring! The door bell chimed.

The door creaked open and a tiny woman with silver hair pinned back in a bun answered. "Come in," she welcomed, "Come in, please." She moved aside and allowed DJ and Julia to step into her home. "Arthur," she called.

A moment later a slightly chubby man chugged down the hallway, smiling and welcoming. He wore a shabby brown sweater over a black shirt with a white clergical collar. "Please, in here," he directed, pointing toward a cozy livingroom. He followed them in and went to a small rolltop desk. Reaching inside, he pulled out a sheaf of papers and began to flip through. "Here it is, the marriage license." The minister turned to his wife and directed, "Alice, honey, can you please help these kids fill this out and I'll get set up."

Alice took the papers from her husband and began to ask DJ and Julia questions. Meanwhile, Arthur lay a delicate lace cloth on a side table. Then, he set down his bible and lit two white candles. "Rings?" he asked.

Julia's face fell. She hadn't thought of that.

"Here, sir, I have them," answered DJ, and he reached into his pants pocket and pulled out a clean, cotton kerchief. He walked over to the table and set it down. The minister opened the folds and placed the contents into his palm. There sat two shining bands of silver.

Julia gasped, "They're lovely!"

DJ smiled.

Soon, they were standing together in front of Arthur and his wife. Holding hands, DJ and Julia pledged to love one another according to God's holy word for the rest of their lives. The rings were offered as a symbol of this promise and placed on their fingers. And then finally, Arthur prayed and spoke a blessing over their marriage.

DJ looked down at Julia and gently kissed her lips. He turned and thanked the couple for performing the ceremony and they in turn, offered congratulations and best wishes.

Returning to the truck, they got in and began to drive off. Julia snuggled in close to DJ, resting her hand on his thigh. As he navigated the way on the dark windy roads, she kept wondering, where would they go from here.

The ride back to the farm seemed to fly and before she knew it, Julia was strolling up the driveway with DJ's arm around her.

As they drew closer to the darkened house, Julia began to hesitate, but DJ said nothing. He continued walking, never taking his arm from around her waist.

"Where are we going?" she asked, curiously.

"A place you'll remember well." DJ answered, with a sparkle in his eye.

Carefully, he guided her down the dark hillside and past the frog pond. The sky was lit with hundreds of tiny lights and a chorus accompanied them as they made their way to the small opening in the woods.

"Watch your step," DJ warned, and held her hand tightly while he led the way.

Soon, they were at the clearing. But it looked different than before. Julia stared in amazement! The simple structure that had formerly housed the still had been transformed into a romantic hide away. There were mason jars with candles already lit, a soft bed of straw covered with quilts, and a clear Mason jar accompanied by 2 glasses. One of the wooden crates had been turned on its side and draped with a cloth. Placed in the center was a large plate covered with a ginham checked napkin and Julia could tell from the yummy smells it was roasted chicken and fresh baked bisquits.

She turned to DJ and asked, "When did you find time to do this?"

DJ grinned, "I had some help. While we were gone, I had the fellas set it up. Is it okay? I wanted to make it romantic."

Julia turned back toward the shelter and nodded, "It's lovely."

Then, slowly from behind her, DJ wrapped his arms around Julia's waist. He leaned in and began to softly kiss the back of her neck. A sigh escaped Julia's lips and she could feel her stomach tighten.

Julia's hands reached down to DJ's. She lifted them off her waist and slid them up to the underside of her breasts, straining against her bodice.

Carefully, DJ began to loosen the buttons on Julia's blouse. He pulled its shirt tails out of her skirt and slipping it off her shoulders, allowed it to fall to the ground. Then, he lifted her camisole over her head and gently turned her to face him.

Julia's breasts stood firm in the dim candlelight and DJ looked questioningly at her. Julia nodded her head slightly. She felt his fingers release the button at her waist and felt her skirt slide slowly down. She stepped out from its folds and with only a moment of hesitation, began to help DJ undress. When DJ began to explore her body with his hands and lips, it seemed natural. And she felt completely at ease running her hands over his muscular frame, feeling his strength. When they finally lay down on the bed of straw, it didn't take long for their lovemaking to be complete.

"Are you okay?" DJ asked, huskily as he lay spent in Julia's arms.

"I can't remember ever feeling this peaceful and safe," she replied.

"That's all?" he exclaimed, "Safe??"

Julia laughed. "Yes," she teased, "Safe. And extremely fulfilled."

"That's a bit better," he replied. "But I was hoping for something like – 'Oh, DJ,' he mocked in a falsetto voice, 'You are such a great lover. No other man could ever compare to you!'"

"Well, seeing as I don't want to fan that ego of yours …" she giggled.

Suddenly, DJ rolled on top of her and began to kiss her lips. At first softly and then with growing passion. Julia eagerly responded and hoarsely breathed in his ear, "DJ, you are such a great lover and no man could ever compare to you!"

ᢙ᠗

When the first songbirds began to announce the approach of dawn, DJ and Julia began to redress.

"I love you," DJ told her warmly.

"I love you, too!" Julia responded.

"And I promise, I won't be gone more than a few months."

"Go, do what you need to and when you come home, we can have a real wedding!"

With that, DJ kissed Julia lingeringly. Then, taking her hand, they left the clearing.

17

There was a sudden rap on the door. Julia took one last glance at her reflection. A smile played at the corners of her mouth. "I guess it's time." She gave a final tug at her skirt, smoothed out its folds and whispered, "Here we go." Julia's hands fell protectively to the barely perceptible bulge at her abdomen and stepped back from the mirror. She turned and walked slowly to the door, careful not to step on her hem.

Rap! Rap! Rap! "Get a move on!" chastised a voice from the other side of the door. "You don't want to be late for your own wedding!"

"Coming, Izz," Julia responded.

When she opened the door, there stood Izzy, grinning.

"Hey, Izz," greeted Julia.

"Thought you'd never open that door," Izzy teased.

"Thought you'd never stop rapping that cane," Julia teased back.

Izzy had been found unconscious in a neglected caretakers cottage on the outskirts of the chalet's property. She had been beaten severely and dehydration had left her feverish and near death. Fortunately, the detectives discovered her in time and were able to get her to a nearby hospital. Once admitted, a team of doctors attended to her injuries. Most of her wounds were superficial and would heal with time, but the use of her left leg would never return. Through it all, Izzy had the support of her friends. And she had Peter, who rarely left her side. Both DJ and Julia knew Izzy's recovery could take months, but they both agreed they couldn't have their "real" wedding until she was able to be there as Julia's maid of honor.

Julia reached out and and pushed an errant strand back in place. "I like the short bob." she commented.

"Thanks! My hair grew out over that 'small gash', and this is the perfect style to even things up. Plus," Izzy grinned, "It horrifies my mother."

Julia laughed. "How is your mother."

"Better now that my father's left for Europe," stated Izzy.

"I'm so sorry!" Julia consoled.

"Are you kidding? He's lucky she didn't have him thrown in jail for having me kidnapped."

Julia frowned for a moment and asked, "What about you, Izz? Did any charges get filed against you for that fiends death?"

"No," Izzy stated, "It was decided that I acted in self defense. And who was I to argue?" She grinned and bent her arm into a small muscle. "Clearly once the drugs wore off, he didn't stand a chance against me."

The girls laughed until Izzy became serious.

"You look lovely, Julia." She complimented. And then, as if from thin air, she produced a small posy. "Here," she extended, "Your something blue."

Julia took the delicate bouquet and smiled warmly. "Thanks, Izz, they're perfect."

"Now let's see…"Izzy mused, "Your veil is your something old, you borrowed my earrings and I just gave you something blue. So now you just need something new."

Julia smiled slightly and placing Izzy's hand on her abdomen stated simply, "I've got it covered, Izz."

"Oh, Julia," Izzy gushed, "Does he know?"

"Not yet. I'll tell him tonight when we're alone."

Izzy smiled and squeezed Julia's hand Then, the girls linked arms and headed toward the stairs.

"Is Peter here?" Julia asked.

"Standing right outside," Izzy answered. "Right next to DJ."

When they reached the bottom step, Julia saw Dad waiting in the foyer, tall and handsome. His hair was still thick but highlighted with strands of gray. And the wrinkles at the corners of his eyes and mouth seemed to make him more distinguished.

Will walked up to them and leaned over to gently kiss Izzy's cheek. "We're so glad you're here!" he said, warmly.

Izzy smiled back, "Me too!" She turned to Julia and said, "See you up front," and with a twirl of her cane, left to go outside.

Will held out his arm so Julia could take it. They hung for a moment, a father and his daughter on one of the most important days of her life. Will leaned over and whispered, hoarsely. "You remind me of your Mum, so beautiful!"

Julia blushed and gave Will's arm a squeeze.

Will paused a moment more, then asked, "Julia, you know how much we care for DJ and respect the work he's done both here, and for Blanche."

Julia nodded, not sure where he was going.

"I just want to make sure this is what you want to do. That DJ is the man you want to spend your life with."

Julia was stunned. "Don't you like him?" she asked.

"It's not that," Will responded quickly. "I just know that Jonathan was from a very different world, but he hurt you. I want to make sure you're marrying for love and not because DJ feels familiar."

"No, Dad!"

"Okay, my girl, I had to ask. Because we, Blanche and myself, think the world of DJ and his parents and wouldn't want any of you to get hurt."

Julia relaxed and smiling up at Will assured, "Don't worry, Dad, I love him. I think I've loved him from the moment we met."

"Okay," Will grinned, "Let's get you married!"

Will and Julia walked out the front door. As she entered their yard, her mouth fell open in awe! It looked like the night sky had draped itself across the lawn and trees. Twinkling stars lit the bows of the old maples and glowing mason jars shone a path all the way to the alter where DJ waited.

Off to the side Julia saw a young woman standing in the shadows. She had a bundle in her arms and was slowly rocking back and forth.

Julia paused, then looked up at Will. "I'll be right back."

Will nodded.

The grass rustled softly as Julia walked over. "Abigail, I'm so glad you came!"

Abigail allowed a hesitant smile to grace her lips.

"Is this little William?"

"Yes," Abigail replied, in a half whisper.

"May I?" asked Julia, and reaching out she pushed aside the edge of his blanket and gazed down at the sleeping babe. "Oh, Abigail," she exclaimed. "He's perfect!"

Abigail's eyes grew misty and her smile broadened. "He's a good baby!"

Julia replaced the covering. "I heard you returned a few months ago. Are you at your parents?"

"No," replied Abigail, quickly. "I tried but their shame was unbearable."

"I'm sorry," remarked Julia, sadly.

"It's okay, though," continued Abigail. "I've remarried."

Julia was stunned!

"But I thought after Billy died...I thought after Paris...?"

Abigail grew quiet again.

"It's not what you think. Billy was the love of my life and if he hadn't become ill..." Abigail's voice began to quiver, " If he hadn't become ill we would have stayed in Paris. Forever. But.."

"But?" prompted Julia.

Abigail took a breath. "But he did. And I have his son to take care of. Protect."

Julia waited.

"Phil came to me."

"Phil?"

"Yes," Abigail explained "He knows I will never love him the way I did Billy. But still, he wanted to offer me a life. Me and William."

The baby began to stir and Abigail gently patted his bottom and crooned until he fell back into a contented sleep. She looked up from her sons face, pensive, waiting for Julia to react.

"He's a good man."

"Yes," Abigail agreed. "And a good friend."

Julia reached over and touched Abigail's shoulder, "I'm happy for you!"

"Thank you," replied Abigail. "We're living over on Blanche's farm." She hesitated, then added, "Your father's been quite generous."

"Sounds like Dad," Julia commented. Then, as an afterthought she added, "The painting, thank you for bringing it to me!"

"You inspired him. He was never happier than when he had a brush in his hand."

Julia glanced back at Will. "I guess I better get back."

"Yes," Abigail agreed. "He's waited long enough for you!"

Julia turned and walked back toward her Dad.

"All set?" he asked.

"All set," she replied, took his arm and they resumed walking. As they approached the path to the altar, Julia saw the small gathering. Just a couple rows of chairs filled with their closest friends. Esther had come up from Boston. And of course, Davy, Jimmy, and Bobby were there. Lou and Don sat up front next to Blanche with little Lizzie on her lap.

Will and Julia continued down the aisle until they stood before a hand carved archway decorated with pine boughs and silver ribbons.

Arthur smiled. The kindly minister had agreed to perform their ceremony, again.

Julia turned to Will and lowered her head slightly. Will reached over, his hands trembling almost imperceptibly. Gingerly he lifted the veil over Julia's head, gently kissed her cheek and stepped back to take his seat next to Blanche.

Julia turned to DJ and was stunned to see him blinking away a tear. She mouthed, "Are you okay?"

"You're just so beautiful!" he whispered back.

"Ahem!" interrupted Arthur.

Julia and DJ chuckled, then gave him their full attention. The ceremony was simple and sweet and the same as before. Yet, when they repeated their vows, they felt like they'd never been said. And when Arthur prayed, it was as if God was blessing their union anew.

It was early October of 1929. DJ and Julia were leaving the farm and the mountains in the morning. Leaving for Canada and the new life awaiting them.

Later that night, as DJ lay sleeping next to her, Julia pushed aside the heavy quilt and walked out from under the shelter's overhang. She gazed up at the twinkling canopy and said, half outloud, "Whereever I see you, I know that I'm home."

The End

Made in United States
North Haven, CT
17 March 2022

17212572R00163